I0777855

Luke Clifford

PRIVATE LAKE

A Wind Song

WORKBOOK PRESS LLC
187 E Warm Springs Rd,
Suite B285 Las Vegas NV 89119 USA

Website: https://workbookpress.com/
Hotline: 1-888-818-4856
Email: admin@workbookpress.com

Ordering Information:

Quantity sales. Special discounts are available on quantity purchases by corporations, associations, and others. For details, contact the publisher at the address above.

Library of Congress Control Number:

ISBN-13:   978-1-965732-43-4   Paperback Version

REV. DATE: 03/12/2025

Luke Clifford

PRIVATE LAKE

A Wind Song

PREFACE

Acknowledgement of gratitude for God providing me the opportunity, my wife's support, and for my children.

THE BEST THINGS...

To the best things in my Life...
My God - my Children - and my Wife!

These are the ones who revive my soul...
They restore my heart, and make me whole.

Without these things to sustain that I exist...
I am left without significance, I'm just a shadow in the mist.

These are those who can validate my worth
and explain how it all began...
My Wife as my lover, - and My God as my friend.

I Embrace that - to which endures forever,
I Cling to the perfection that never fails...
I Hold to the love that never ends, and
I Keep to what preserves me from being frail.

With God's infinite wisdom, He trumped all of my flaws,
and opened my eyes to see...

It's His power and His might that allows me to prosper,
and ONLY in Him will I succeed.

The secret to happiness is finding, "Joy in the Lord!"
by seeking Godly wisdom from Him.
Follow His ways to the path of freedom...
and away from the bondage of sin.

My heart is made whole and my soul is revived
While I delight in the Lord for the blessing of my Wife...
I give all praise...all honor... and all glory to Him
For HIS mercy to sustain my "Breath of Life."

With HIM, I've discovered the true desires of my heart...
And blessed - with "The Best things in Life..."
My merciful God - My blessed Children - and the miracle - of my beautiful Bride.

My best friend and I were participating at the High Jump pit during the 'State Finals' track meet. We each had cleared the height of our first attempt before returning to sit at our make-shift camp nearby. It was our normal practice to "scope" on girls from the other schools when we weren't competing to pass the time. On this occasion, however, my friend was diligently working on an assignment on the computer while waiting to be called for his next attempt.

"Hey man, what are you doing?" I inquired playfully. "Are you on your computer to appeal to your intellectual side of attracting women? Wearing nerdy glasses wasn't working good enough to get attention from the opposite sex so you decided to break out your computer to look studious, huh? I could use your expertise as a 'Wingman' if you don't mind. There's a lot of cute girls out here I'd like to meet."

"Because I soar over a flight of hurdles… I'm your 'Wingman,' huh? Pun intended." he retorted in a likewise playful manner. "Give me a minute…I'll help you out soon." He reassured me. "I'm trying to finish up my English project so that I can concentrate on my race."

"What is so important that you have to do it now?"

"I just got some good thoughts about the direction I want to go with this project and don't want to forget."

"I hadn't noticed till just now that you close your eyes while you type out your thoughts." I observed.

"Yeah, I must visualize what it is that I intend to write about. Running hurdles will only get me so far in life…" he reasoned. "I'm really hoping to get that Creative Writing Intern Scholarship."

"Well tell me about what, 'out of the box' creativity you're planning to explore that will separate your work from the other candidates and that will effectively, 'WOW' the judges?"

"I'm going to introduce an idea dealing with 'Cooperative Contrast' terms – I'm going to coin a new English language concept and call it 'Microview.' A 'Microview' explains how opposite things are actually the same."

"That sounded kind of complicated. Are you referring to something like, 'Oxymorons?'"

"No, not really." He explained. "Oxymorons aren't necessarily opposites. Their purpose is to creatively describe a specific situation. Although when people use an Oxymoron, the impression is that the two don't belong together because the perception is that each word represents polar ends."

"Okay, teach me…" I surrendered.

"Oxymoron…" he began to clarify as he continued to type what he spoke. "Military intelligence, sweet sorrow. The word Military and intelligence and like sweet to sorrow are not opposites but the play on words give the perception of being so. These are either jokes or something that popular belief accepts as opposites. They should not go together or refer to one idea.

'Microviews,' on the other hand, such as, Love and Hate, Day and Night, Pain and Pleasure, Light and Dark, Good and Evil for instance, good does not need evil but evil needs good to exist to be understood as evil. Each of these are two individual opposites for each concept, yet each of the two words in fact coexist and are dependent on each other. With these terms I'll be explaining how a single word of each dual cannot exist without the other. Therefore, each of them is bound together as one thing for each category."

"How do you plan on managing to accomplish making the argument that *two* obvious differences are instead, 'one thing' when they are… as I mentioned, in fact two different things?" I interrupted. "Who do you think you are, Houdini? Do you plan to use misdirection and make something out of what isn't by making something that is clearly visible to become invisible?"

"First off let me congratulate you… you just used a "Microview" when you said 'visible and invisible' without realizing that you had done so. Secondly, allow me to demonstrate. Would you agree that 'heads and tails' are opposites?

"Yes, that's how you tell one *completely* different from another." I said defensively, supporting my logical conclusion.

Well, you're right, they are two *different* things which is the first qualification of a Microview, being perceived as contrasting ideas. However, *together* they are what make up *one* coin. They truly are polar ends, but only together do they exist as one thing… a single coin." He flawlessly simplified his rationale.

"And… 'Ta-a, Da-a!'" I pretended to announce that he had just successfully performed introducing a magic act of making something appear out of thin air. I continued acknowledging the success of his example by playfully inquiring about the name of his new concept, "…And now -- ladies and gentlemen, I introduce you to… 'Houdini' who for his next act will provide the explanation of his newly coined word… 'Microviews.'"

"I'm glad that you appreciate the reasoning." he said proudly. I call them 'Microviews' because when the lower-case letter 'e' is viewed through a microscope, it demonstrates how the view when observing things through a microscope is not just upside down but also reversed. My concept of taking opposite things and then joining them to be the exact same thing is at first upside-down being opposites and then the reverse concept making them the same. So, 'Micro', for microscope; and then add 'view' for how they appear."

"Well, I admit, you do have skills. I don't know what the judges may think… but I am impressed."

At that moment a hail from the intercom, informed participants to report in for their pending running events. "First call Men's 110-meter-high hurdles…second call…women's 100-meter hurdles… third call men's 100-meter dash."

"Well, my friend… to be continued..." He announced as he set his computer aside and got up to report to the starting line "…duty calls". "If you'd like to help, you're welcome to read what I started so far to see what you think. I could use a novice's opinion on whether how and what I say make sense."

"I think I can do that for you." I said retrieving his computer. "I'll also "check you out" of the high jump rotation."

"Okay, thanks. If the screen locks out… you know my code, right?" he inquired as he continued to walk toward the starting line."

"Yeah, I got you…go break a leg."

"Ahh, Y - Yeah… I don't think you say that to a hurdler… that could foreshadow bad things to happen. That quote is only meant for acting and drama."

"Yeah, I know. It's their way of saying, 'Good Luck.' I don't get it, but it's supposed to work." I acknowledged. I figured that since you're a writer that it may still work for you."

"Luck is when preparation meets opportunity…" he replied, confident of his abilities. "I've prepared and now finally my opportunity is at hand. I got this. I have my dime in my left shoe that represents each hurdle. Prepin' time is gone, running time is here. It's time to kick butts and make my name a legacy. And as one of my favorite cartoon characters might say, 'I am the quick one out of the blocks. I am the terror of the 110 high hurdles. I am the State Hurdle Champ…Let's – get - dangerous!'"

"Okay, I like confidence. Go do 'you.' I'll read and then meet you at the finish line with your sweats."

"Thanks. See you in about 13 flat." He stated, referring

to the time he was aiming to run with inevitability, a time that would finally set the state record he had been chasing all season while raising the index finger as a number one symbolizing the place he expected to be at the conclusion of the race. As he turned around, I began reading his English thesis listening to each P.A. announcement to ensure not to miss any of what promised to be an epic race. His report began:

'The following quote is a thought to marvel about: "What factor causes one to pursue a dream?" Take thought to wonder about the part of humanity that encourages us to seek the companionship of others to make our lives content. Be lost in thought contemplating the idea behind what enables us to exhibit the jubilation of life, rather than to humbly accept the mediocracy of simply surviving.

Then be left to wonder and inquire about what attribute is responsible for the enlightenment of the human spirit. What characteristic leads to the illumination of cognitive reasoning. What wisdom connects the realization that true living is not limited to the modesty of coveting and possessing desirable things, rather it's finding a worthy cause to fight for. Then after having discovered that noble purpose, summoning the heroic resolve to willingly sacrifice everything you possess for that purpose.

As we search to enrich our existence, usually with the company of another, basic life experiences make it increasingly difficult to be trusting. The eventual outcome of experiencing 'life' leads rather to the disparaging alternative from enrichment, causing us instead to grow increasingly cynical with each exposure. The inevitable conclusion gives way to this unfortunate reality; the belief, that a dream… any dream, becomes only a fleeting and elusive illusion. And so, our entitlement to carefree childlike romanticism diminishes into the shadows of nostalgia. Ponder these insights of a poet's reflection on dreams:

With contempt for the passage of Time

I compelled our lives' paths to cross.

Daring audaciously against hope to dream my dream,

While I endeavored to embrace your soul.

In a cruel twist; destiny whisked your heart away.

Leaving me to ponder… 'Just what went wrong?'

Now

Yielding only to what's true -

My thoughts are restrained to dark silence

As I'm forced to bow, to His Majesty, Time,

To plead for mercy to end the eternal isolation from you.

At last, I surrender - realizing this inevitable fate;

"Those wonderful delusions –

…taking form in my dreams, are Subjects to Time

And therefore, are brief – and fleeting

To touch you – regrettably, I concede - is too late."

Here is the hope that you will find in this story the value of life and the purpose of dreams; here is the hope that you will find the resolve to fight against the struggles of the world and discover that no matter how elusive – 'dreams… are attainable.'

The robotic sounding voice hailing over the intercom announcing Malachi's race interrupted my reading, "Third and final call… Men's 110-meter-high hurdles. Ladies and gentlemen," the man announced. "You may wish to turn your focus to the starting line as the caliber of the participants who are competing in this event today may very well enable us to witness a new record."

It seemed like the backdrop of his announcement was a perfect stopping point to capture the mood of the day. My friend would be racing for his attainable dream that was now only one hundred ten meters and a mere thirteen seconds away. I locked his computer, set it aside and stood looking in the direction of the starting line. By this time all of the runners were in their blocks and the gun was already up. The silence was deafening in this anxious minute I stood motionless, focused with anticipation of the start.

I noticed a very subtle cross wind just as the Starter's second arm was theatrically raised as if to heighten the drama that was about to unfold. The runners slowly lifted their backsides, and that frozen moment suspended time. The runners were static like statues. They anxiously anticipated the signal from the Starter who also stood like a sculpture as he meticulously surveyed each runner for any premature forward movement before firing the gun. It was as if in that instant the earth stopped spinning to observe the unveiling of this event. I could hear the wind in my ear and felt the pounding of my heart increase with intensity as I stared at the gun with anticipation.

Finally, I see the smoke rising from the gun and an instant later, I hear the pop echo starting the race. It is through that simplistic action that not only seems to resume time as the clock runs sending the runners toward the flight of hurdles. They looked like racehorses as they all cleared the first hurdle with no visible leader.

Next, they ran past the second and then the third. Only then does it become noticeable that the outside runners begin to faintly drop away from the leaders. Clearing the fourth and fifth hurdles my friend begins to pull into a slender lead, it looks as though a possible record is well in hand. The sixth hurdle he effortlessly covers as if there is no obstacle. He had been running at a Nationwide record speed as he cleared the seventh hurdle.

As he attempted to skim over, the eighth tragedy struck

as quickly as lightning causing a flurry of action. I watched as he loudly struck the eight-hurdle causing him to stumble into a summersault motion before coming to rest on his side writhing in pain.

"Medic! Medic! We need someone now!" the opposing coach demanded as he ran to attend to my friend's injuries. "Get that ambulance down here…now!" he insisted with passionate intensity.

It was easy to see even from a distance that my friend was groaning in seething agony. I ran from the High jump pit from where I had been observing the race toward the finish line to assist in aiding for his care. His trail leg knee had hit that eight-hurdle causing him to get caught up in the crossbar. He attempted to regain his form, but his momentum hurled him viciously into a thunderous tumble that entwined him into crashing and breaking the ninth hurdle as he pugnaciously smacked the ground. He finally came to a rest five yards from the tenth hurdle.

It was a horrific scene as it was apparent from the unnatural wailing he had bellowed out. That cry was sufficient to express how terribly excruciating the pain was, but the extent of his injury would not be immediately realized by me.

As I approached it was evident that the coach was already tending to apply first aid --- my first glimpse was surveying his upper torso. I was unable to see what that coach was doing to his leg because my view was blocked as I approached from the coach's back. At first all I could see was that his arms had scrapes and minor bleeding. I noticed that my friend's face was bleeding and swollen and a bruise was already forming around his eyes, so I focused on tending to those injuries.

I noticed that several other participants coming from the opposite direction gasped and paused, a few of them even covered their collective gaped mouths with their hands as they were stunned by what they were witnessing.

At first, I ignored their reactions, having not yet realized the extent of his injury. Instead, I focused on tending to his head injuries. I was surprised to notice that my friend appeared to be incoherently wallowing in pain in a state of apoplexy. It wasn't until after I kneeled by his face and applied a towel to stop the bleeding from his forehead that I finally looked down at his leg and noticed that the femur protruded through his skin. All at once… it all fit. The coach's decisive critical reaction to immediately request for the ambulance, the impetuous look on the bystander's faces, and the mental state of my semi-conscious friend. The injury was much worse than I had anticipated…it was life threatening.

As he slipped in and out of consciousness, he would gasp for air like he came to the surface of the water and then the swum of the pain would sink him back underneath the waves, to unconsciousness.

The ambulance arrived and stabilized his condition, strapped him to a gurney and then quickly whisked him away. His parents, who had been watching from the stands, made their way to him, it was quickly decided that his mother would travel with him in the ambulance and that his father would follow in their SUV.

I gathered up our gear and tagged along with his dad. While waiting at the hospital for news during his surgery I thought it would be prudent to take the opportunity to document the events that led up to this moment. I figured that if the events were written as a story, it would give him something tangible to work on when he awakened. If his mind was employed with something constructive, I reasoned, it would improve his spirit and by proxy would improve his physical health. The journey had started out non - eventfully. Here is our story…

It was a Sunday morning in late May. The cool grass sparkled as the spring dew began to evaporate in the early morning sun. Having returned from college two days before, I was preparing to go to the exclusive "Topflight Hurdle

Camp." The camp was scheduled to run from May to June. The top forty hurdlers, twenty male and twenty females from around the country were invited to attend a two month all-expense paid intense training session designed to springboard the best athletes to the best employment opportunities through notoriety and endorsements.

I was given the privilege to attend the prestigious event as the final entry, because the number seven hurdler was obligated to cancel for personal reasons. I would be joining my best friend, Malachi, who had recently attended his grandfather's funeral and would be arriving to camp late; exactly when I didn't know.

The site where the camp was being held was called Camp Muskingum, located in Ohio about two hours from my home. The brochure the directors of the camp had sent described the camp site as being secluded from civilization - way out in the countryside. The nearest "town" was paved with dirt, graveled paths that serve as roads.

The only business consisting of a time warp, "last stop for gas" filling station that doubles as a General Store complete with a payphone and vintage bottled Coke machine. The convenience of proximity being about a fifteen-minute walk from the camp, and I would later discover that this so-called town would become a welcomed distraction and destination meeting spot for the campers to hang out after a long day of rigorous training.

The placement of this camp by the directors was a deliberate effort to isolate us to minimize distractions during our training. As invited participants we also agreed to surrender our electronic communication devices to further regulate and to reduce possible outside distractions. I can recall the excitement of the morning I left for camp as I contemplated the possible bright future Malachi, and I could envision by being exposed to this tremendous opportunity.

"Do you have everything you need, Zaylen?" my mother inquired.

"Yes, I should," I replied, addressing her while double checking what was packed in the car. "I didn't unpack very much when I came home from school so I should have everything."

"Already then?" my brother asked while sitting in the driver's seat.

"Yep, it looks like it." I said closing the trunk. Then I walked around to the passenger side where my mom was standing waiting to say goodbye.

"Okay," she said as I kissed her on the cheek, "God Bless, and be sure to write to let us know how you're doing."

"I will," I told her as I opened the door and began to sit down. I then pulled my feet into the car. Once my whole body was in the car I reached for the door with my right hand as my mother began closing it gently.

"Now Matthew," she said, "you drive carefully."

"Yes, ma'am I will."

"Yeah, I'll make sure of that." I said jokingly as he began to pull away from the curb. "Bye."

After a few stops at traffic lights, we were on the highway and cruising steadily. I had the state map out on my lap constantly monitoring the signs acting as the navigator. Before we were to reach the camp, we would have to make a turn off the main interstate onto a state road. Then finally onto a country road which was not on the map but was in the directions of the brochure. So, if we were lucky, I would not get us lost. Fortune seemed to be on our side as we had gotten to the county road without too much trouble. Now that my job was done, I was able to put the map away and relax.

"Gee," Matt said in amazement, "You guys are for sure going to be a long way from anything; aren't you?"

"Yeah," I answered while looking out at the miles of country scenery, "I didn't realize that it was going to be this far out." "They said that they wanted us to be isolated so that we could concentrate on our training with minimal distractions… I guess they were serious."

"I'm glad I'm not coming out here to stay. I don't know about all this isolation. I think I'd get stir crazy." He responded.

"Nah, it'll be all right, believe it or not I'm looking forward to the seclusion, as being able to experience something different. Besides, at least when Malachi comes, I'll know someone."

"Well, that's true," he said, "by the way, when is he coming?"

"I'm not sure, check – in starts at 4:30 but he was given permission to report late. The camp directors are aware of the circumstances, so he might be in at any time." As I was talking a sign came into view.

"Finally," Matt said while reading the sign aloud, "Camp Muskingum 5 miles."

Within a few minutes the camp was in sight. Matt pulled up behind the cars of the other campers and turned the car off as I jumped out.

"Wait here, I'll go find out where to take my stuff."

I got out of the car and quickly ran into the log cabin. On the doors were signs posted, "Check – In." As I entered, I saw two tables, one on the left and the other in front of me. The building consisted of one large room with a large stone fireplace behind the table in front. Behind the table on the left was a sign that read "Women's Check – In." There was a guy at that table trying to check in. I overheard one of the lady workers tell him that the men's check in table was in front of the fireplace as she pointed in that direction.

"Your name please," one of the four guys at the table

said to me. Upon approaching the table I noticed the name tag he was wearing. His name was Peter.

"Camble," I said, answering him, "Zaylen Camble."

"Ok, Zaylen," he said while looking at the list, "… you're in cabin 2C. Just go outside and straight --- you'll see a trail leading to the right down the hill; it'll take you right to It." he continued, "Here is your key, and there will be a meeting here at six o'clock."

"Thanks," I said to him walking away.'

"No problem, welcome to 'Top - Flight.'"

I walked back to the car to get Matt so that we could see where I'd be staying for the next couple of weeks before we unpacked the car.

"Here it is," I said approaching the cabin. "2C."

There were several cabins connected four to a pod and shaded lightly by newly budding leaves.

"It sure looks peaceful. It's almost surreal how quiet it is; just a few birds chirping." Matt said as I unlocked the door and began to step inside. He walked past me as I took the key out of the lock, "Wow," he continued as he expressed his impression of the setup, "this is nice; do you get this all to yourself?"

The cabin had one room furnished with two beds in opposite corners. Someone had already taken the liberty to place their gear on one of the beds. There were two dressers, a walk – in closet, four electric plugs and a fireplace like the one in the cafeteria but smaller. A single door led to a bathroom. Although it was one room the cabin was fairly large.

"I assume the other bed must belong to my roommate, I'll tell you one thing, this is more than I expected."

"Well, come on," he said. "Let's get you unpacked so that I can get going."

After several back-and-forth trips we had finished

unpacking the car. I said my farewell to Matt, and then he left. I put up a few posters, put my clothes away and made my bed. Fifteen minutes before we were to be at the meeting a counselor knocked on the doors to remind us to attend the meeting that was scheduled for orientation. Soon I began walking towards the cafeteria at the same time as three other campers. We introduced ourselves to each other and walked together.

When I walked into the cafeteria, I noticed a significant change. There were five round tables covered with nice tablecloths that seated eight people per table with a fourth large rectangular table in front of them and perpendicular. The tables had been formally placed with plates and utensils and complete with name plates.

After looking at a few name plates, I found my own – at the same time realizing that they had the seating arrangements so that a girl would be sitting between two guys. There was already a girl sitting next to my place by the time I arrived. She had dark hair fixed in a ponytail and wore silver wire rim glasses to help focus her salient hazel eyes. As I began to sit down, she looked in my direction and smiled. I smiled back and after sitting down extended my hand to introduce myself.

"Hi, I'm Zaylen Camble."

"Hello," she replied taking my hand and continuing as we shook hands," I'm Ruth Zephaniah,"

"What school are you from?"

"USC." She replied.

"You certainly are a long way from home, aren't you?"

"Why? Where are you from?" she asked.

"Oh, I'm from W.L.S.C, a small school two hours south of here."

"Well, I suppose coming to this camp must have been convenient for you." She complained. "It took me more than

10 hours to get here including my actual flight time, flight delays, waiting for transportation to drive me to the camp, and then being driven from the Columbus airport to here. It seemed even longer than that because I had to sit by some sweaty fat guy that was snoring." she explained.

"Well, I guess you're right… compared to your ordeal my trek was pretty convenient, you should have told my brother about your ordeal he was complaining about how far out here we are."

As we continued with small talk, more people began showing up trying to find their place. A tall, large, athletic framed man stepped to the podium and began to speak.

"Excuse me." He said politely as he looked around the room. "If you will all please take your places we'll begin."

Most of the shuffling stopped as more people found their places. I noticed that there were two empty seats after everyone in the room sat down. I knew one belonged to Malachi; the other I reasoned must be a girl because the empty chair was between two guys. The gentleman at the podium looked around then back at some papers he had in front of him as he mumbled.

"Humm… we seem to be missing someone."

At that moment one side of the double doors swung open, everyone in the room turned and looked on with baited curiosity in that direction while everything in the room paused at the subtle disturbance caused by the late arrival of the mystery character as the missing person had just emerged in an ostentatious fashion.

Standing in the doorway for a few moments she grinned with a mischievous glimmer that encompassed her face. A saintly aura adorned her flirtatious country-like persona and was enhanced by the backdrop of the golden light that was cast down by the evening sun.

This sunlight also contributed to illuminating the translucent, hovering, fine mist that was suspended in the atmosphere. With a stature measuring five feet two inches tall; heightened by cowgirl boots and a firm healthy physique of nearly 120 pounds, her body sensually accentuated the reason that jeans were created. She wore jean shorts that were tantalizingly cut off merely several inches below her hips, thereby enabling her to generously expose the solid definition and the softening bend contours of her lustrous feminine athletic legs.

The outfit was accented with a fitted powder blue, printed short sleeve "tee" that displayed an image of an American flag rippling in the wind and covered a white laced cami. The fringe of the cami clung tightly to her sensual hips which enunciated a mesmerizing shift. Her walk emulated more of a proud prance as she sauntered across the room. Her presentation displayed a sensual confident swagger in her sashay step. Surrounding her sleek soft medium tone skin was long, curled, naturally golden blonde hair that bounced and swayed gently in the air as she sauntered across the room.

Lucid sapphire eyes adorned the depth and shade of a cloudless sky while their glimmer manufactured the warmth and peace of a burning fire on a winter's night. Pouty, radiant, soft pink lips exhibited a silky shimmer that taunted the imagination - inviting one to surrender cognitive thought and to rather fixate on their soft, sensual texture and to marvel over her taste. A boy's imagination could run rampant thinking about the discovery of the flavor of the gloss that adorned her lips.

When her lips lengthened into a smile, a pearl of white teeth was revealed that caused pronounced small childlike dimples to appear on her slender cheeks. Her smirk depicted an intoxicating smile that captured the kind of moment that would linger on your mind long after being deprived of her presence.

In this flawless performance of producing the superb façade; the sun, in its role, was typecast as the perfect supporting character to act as a radiant heavenly accent to compliment her aura. Upon at last approaching her seat, she took her place as the speaker resumed.

"Dinner will be served in a few moments, so I just want to take this time to introduce myself. My name is Coach Doug Tenzos. I'm the director of the camp and the head coach for the male hurdlers. First of all, I'd like to welcome you all to "Top - Flight Hurdle Camp." It's an honor for you to have been invited to this camp, and I want to encourage all of you to take full advantage of the opportunity." He was interrupted by the cooks bringing the food out, "Well it looks as though the food is ready, so I'll finish after dinner… enjoy."

During dinner I met the other girl on the other side of me, her name was Jane. A little while later the coach wrapped up the evening by explaining how camp would be run. He introduced the other coaches, explained how we would be divided into groups of eight, and laid down the ground rules for bed checks. We were given between 6p.m. through 10 p.m. to hang out with friends which as it would turn out would give us plenty of time to explore the landscape outside the camp and the limited facilities the town had to offer. Finally, he explained the reason that we were seated in this manner of alternating the sexes.

He continued, "Now I'm sure some of you are wondering why you are seated in the manner that the opposite sex is seated on either side of you. For the first few meals there will be a name place to direct each athlete on where to sit. It will not be the same place each time, but you will be seated in between the opposite sex. We do this for the simple reason of helping to encourage all of you to interact so that you will get to know each other.

Since we usually separate the sexes during drills and training it gives the perception that there are two different groups here. We are all going to be here for two months, this camp provides a good opportunity for you to start honing your networking skills. We're a family now, so get used to it. You're going to be working hard while you're here, knowing the people you're living with may make things easier and more enjoyable."

After his explanation he then provided us with the agenda for the next day, "Just a few more quick things…tomorrow you'll meet with your primary tactical team. The teams will be posted on the bulletin board by morning. There will be no morning workout involved – just introductions. The coach of your first group will be asking you for a call name such as in the movie 'Top Gun'. The name you give will be used by everyone in the camp.

In addition, we will routinely provide entertaining activities during the down times in the evenings to help develop cohesiveness between the teams, so everyone is expected to attend unless you are working with a trainer at those times. Tomorrow night there will be a dance, as I mentioned, everyone is expected to attend, but dancing is up to you. Are there any questions?" He paused and looked around. "Okay, see you bright and early in the morning."

As he dismissed us, we all began standing and talking among ourselves as a few of the coaches joined us. I was talking with the three guys I walked over with; Seth, Tyler, and Colby, two girls who also joined our conversation Rae and Leanne. As we were talking, I noticed that the blonde who walked in late didn't have trouble getting attention.

About fifteen minutes later I heard someone outside talking about a car coming up the road. I quickly excused myself from the group to go greet Malachi. I knew it would have to be him because anyone out this far would have to be here on purpose. By the time I got outside the headlights were in view. Within a few moments the car began slowing. Malachi was in the back seat, his mother on the passenger side and his brother was driving. As the car stopped, I began opening the door for his mother.

"Hello Mrs. Benson," I greeted.

"Hi Zaylen," she replied, "How are you doing?"

"Just fine," I answered. By that time Malachi was just getting out of the car. He was a towering 6-foot 2 solid athletic frame. I hadn't seen him for a few months, but it was evident that he had been working outside as he had a glowing darkening tan. - The care and strength of his upper body was well documented by me because he and I would often compete with one another regarding our training.

Being country boys, we would help each other's family around the farm most often with bailing hay in the hot summer months which helped to condition our entire bodies. His broad shoulders mimicked the strength of an ox as I witnessed the height to which he could pitch a bale of hay. Our school friends would playfully refer to the two of us as a dynamic duo Rock and Ox.

Working on the farm produced extremely firm physiques. Thunderous muscular powerful thighs were bulging through his tight boot cut jeans. These commanding legs supported an athletic hour-glass torso frame. His arms rivaled large tree limbs and his short sleeve hugged tightly around his defined biceps. The black breathable workout shirt highlighted his tan and was form fitting to his muscular frame. Boot cut jeans were adorned to compliment his brown cowboy boots as his ensemble was completed by a signature cowboy hat.

The two of us would often jest about each other's physic; in reference to our ribbed firm abdomen area, he'd refer to mine as "2PAC" instead of a six pack and I'd refer to his as wash- "broad" eluding that he was soft like a lady in lieu of an illustrative washboard. His tall dark statute made him popular among girls that he hadn't yet met - while his low key, evenly tempered, charismatic personality kept him a popular choice with those girls with whom he was familiar. I approached him throwing a fake punch at his stomach as I greeted him, "Hey Malachi, what's up?" His typically confident persona was understandably somewhat reserved.

"Not much," he responded as we put our arms around each other, "What's been going on around here? You're going to have to fill me in."

"I will, but first, you better get checked in so that you can get your room assignment."

He got a cabin that was across the trail and diagonal from mine. With the four of us, his mom, dad, Malachi, and I working to unpack his gear it didn't take too long. After we finished and his parents left then I filled Malachi in on what was going on.

"I wish I could have been here earlier so that I would know what to expect and so I could have met people."

"Don't worry about that," I told him, "There's plenty of time for that." ---

By that time, it was late, so we all turned in with anxious anticipation of the first day of training. I heard little animal sounds coming from the surrounding woods and saw unfamiliar creepy shadows dance across my room that had been cast from the moonlit sky. My covers acted as a perfect warm remedy to soothe me into a slumber on that cool night.

Although I slept soundly, I was awakened early by a subtle recital of birds tweeting as the sun began creeping above the horizon. I felt well rested while I lay in bed savoring a few more moments resting under the warm covers. It wasn't long before I heard the voices of people outside my room talking about breakfast. I decided to get out of bed and see if Malachi was ready. Once I was out of bed I began dressing. I put on a pair of cotton sweat bottoms and a sweatshirt. Then I slipped on my Converse running shoes and, on my way out the door, put on a baseball hat.

I stepped out the door and as I looked around the camp – the surprise of seeing patches of dense fog caused me to pause in astonishment. Recognizing that the sun would soon burn off the fog and that the day would soon be too busy with training exercises for me to be able to enjoy the scenery; I decided to steal a few solitude moments and walked behind my cabin so that I could look across the lake.

The stunning view revealed white patches of dense fog the size of ships slowly drifting across the lake. I observed the sun rising from in front me, it would glitter on the lake for a few seconds only to then disappear as the dense patches of fog rolled past completely blocking its light causing this scene to emulate a calm stillness.

The serene mood seemed to have a silent melody all its own, as if there was a whisper hidden within the mist as the dampness brushed against my face. I found it to be a most tranquil communication with the creator. There was a reassuring Word in my mind, "Be still and know that I am God." The enjoyment of this moment was interrupted when I heard Malachi knocking at my door.

"Zaylen," he called out, "…are you going to eat?"

"I'm around back," I called out.

"What are you doing back there?" he questioned as he came around to join me. Walking fast at first, I heard his footsteps slowing as he turned the corner. It appeared that the surreal scene had the same effect on him as it had on me. "Wow!" he whispered in amazement, "This is beautiful."

"If you think that's something," I advised, "…take a moment and just listen."

He put his hands behind his back and looked from side to

side as he listened. Then for a few seconds he closed his eyes and took a deep breath. After a few seconds he opened his eyes and breathed out. Then he shook his head and looked at me.

"You gotta love life's simple pleasures…," he paused, smiling, "…huh..." he contemplated, "seeing stuff like this takes the guesswork out of believing in God, doesn't it?"

I nodded slowly agreeing, "If we're in tune, life's simple pleasures are all we really need."

We stood silently enjoying the scenery for a few more minutes before finally heading for breakfast. When we approached the cafeteria, Seth and Terry were outside on the balcony talking. When we climbed the stairs to the balcony, they greeted us.

"Morning," Terry said as we slapped hands in a manner of welcome.

"What's up fellas?" I replied.

"Unfortunately, I am," Seth complained as we greeted each other in the same manner. "So, who's this?" he inquired of Malachi.

"Aye, I'd like you to meet my best friend, Malachi. We grew up together." I introduced Terry and Seth then continued as I presented him to another guy that walked out named Colin, "this is my friend Malachi. We're from the same town. Then looking at Malachi I turned and presented each of them to him.

"How you doin'?" Malachi greeted, extending his hand.

"Well, it's nice to finally meet the 'Mystery Man.'" Seth answered, "So, you two are best friends huh? What do they feed you guys back home that enables both of you to be so good that you both qualify to be here?"

"I don't think we've ever put much thought to it. We've always competed against each other; I guess it was just an asset to have each other to train and encourage one another." I responded as I reflected on his insight.

We remained standing on the balcony talking and joking. A few moments later a group of girls began coming up the trail. We all turned noticeably in their direction.

"That's the girl I'm hoping to ask to dance with me tonight," Seth said.

"Which one?" I asked.

"That one, there on the left," he said as he pointed in the direction of the girls.

"Hey, don't point you idiot," I said excitedly while grabbing his arm and pulling it down. "You don't want them to know that we're talking about them! Just describe to us what she's wearing." Terry and Malachi glared at Seth shaking their heads and smiling as they chuckled.

"Okay, it's the girl in the white jacket with blue strings and maroon sweatpants."

"Sweatpants?" I teased as Terry and Malachi laughed along. "Who calls them pants? Don't you mean sweat bottoms? Where did you say you were from again?"

"I'm from West Virginia, what difference does it make? You know what I mean."

"Okay, okay, I was just kidding. Don't get excited. Well, you said you were going to ask her to dance; that's a pretty bold move for having just met. I mean… that is assuming that you have indeed met the girl. She at least knows that you exist because you two have met… right?"

"Well…" he began unconvincingly.

"Come on Seth…" I tried being hopeful. "Do you at least even know her name?"

"Yes, as a matter of fact I do, it's Rae, Rae Merryman. I talked to her last night." Just then Malachi interrupted as he leaned towards me – grabbing at my arm.

"Hey, who is that?" he asked astounded, "The blonde with the light blue cutoff sweats and white shirt?"

"Hey, I don't know everyone in the camp yet?" I conceded.

"Is he talking about the one who came in late last night?" Terry inquired.

"Yeah, I think that's the one he's talking about." Seth Chimed in.

"She's one of the girls I was sitting by last night at dinner, her name is Cammie Cannon. She seemed pretty nice."

Suddenly we cut off our conversation because the girls got in range of our voices. Soon they began climbing the stairs to the balcony. We all waited to see if Seth would ask Rae, maybe if he were successful the rest of us might be needed for the other girls as wingmen. "Seth," Malachi coxed, "…this is your chance. Let's see what you've got."

"Good morning boys," one of the girls called out flirtingly, it could have been anyone of them as they were all smiling and giggling.

"Good morning, ladies," Seth replied in the same manner. The girls passed by between us one by one to enter the cafeteria door. It appeared that he was trying to summon the courage to stop Rae but the intimidation of being shot down in front of all of us became the overwhelming factor.

Instead, Malachi surprisingly turned out to be the one to speak up vying for some feminine attention. As Cammie walked by, Malachi watched her and noticeably cleared his throat trying to get her attention – then he attempted to make eye contact, but she didn't take notice of his subtle advance so quickly he spoke to her.

"Hi," Malachi shyly called out as he strained again to make eye contact.

Her eyes met his as she slowed her pace. She then smiled and waved, whirling her fingers playfully in his direction to acknowledge that she specifically noticed him. Without a word she continued to gaze out of the corners of her eyes at him until she passed through the door.

"Where do I know her from?" he inquired, speaking to himself out loud as he searched his memory.

"You don't know her," I responded unprompted, "-you just wish that you did."

"No, really," Malachi insisted, "I'm sure that I know that girl from somewhere."

"Come on you guys," Seth said leading, "let's go eat. I'm starving."

We all went inside and took our places at the table. The girl that Seth wanted to ask to dance had been seated between Malachi and me. We gestured to Seth throughout the breakfast hour; teasing him as if we were going to talk to her on his behalf just to watch him squirm. We would get her to look in his direction by asking her about things that were close around him as we pointed at the items to make him think that we were pointing him out.

After breakfast, we had a half hour to let the food settle before we broke into the first training groups. Between the groups, meals, and meetings our schedules were packed with a strict scheduled regiment. After the five o'clock hour there would be some kind of activity or lecture to keep us busy with light entertainment, which also gave us a chance to get to know each other. Of course, on this night it was the dance that had been scheduled.

The dance had been going on for about forty minutes, everyone was having a good time. In our group the four to five of us guys were hanging out together. We had been teasing Seth because he had not yet asked Rae to dance. A song came on that we all liked so we headed to claim our spot on the dance floor. I wasn't aware if Cammie was present as I didn't see her all night until she seemingly appeared from nowhere.

Because she was looking back over her left shoulder, as she walked in our direction, she failed to see our group coming toward her. Likewise, Malachi was preoccupied talking to the guys about hurdling. So, as fate would have it…instead of the two passing like ships in the night, these two proverbial ships would collide on the dance floor.

Her lighter body mass bounced back after Malachi bumped into her. The impact caused her to stumble back as Malachi reached out and grabbed her to prevent her from falling. Surprised by each other's presence they both stood motionless. It was humorous to watch her eyes follow up the length of his body to his eyes as her head tilted back as if she were looking at a tall building.

They soon ended up gazing at each other with bewilderment trying to figure out how the other had just appeared from thin air to now occupy the same space… she is looking up, and he is looking down. She looked fragilely petite that close to his statuesque solid six foot two – two hundred-and five-pound broad shoulder frame. Startled, she quickly regained her composure and began to pardon herself.

"Excuse me," she begged politely as her blue eyes shimmered from capturing the illumination of the intermittent dance lights. Then innocently fixated on Malachi who appeared to tower she accepted the over her she elaborated. "I should watch where I'm going."

"No, the pleasure is mine…" Malachi replied clumsily as he instantaneously realized the transparency of his response. He paused then quickly shook off his stare as he continued stumbling over his words, "I mean… it's my fault. Sorry." She smiled flirtingly; pleasantly surprised by his unguarded moment then turned and began to walk away. Malachi called out to her before she got too far. "Excuse me! Do I know you from somewhere?"

"I don't know from where," she replied.

Malachi closed his lips into a half smile, blinking his eyes then said, "Sorry, again."

After the dance some of the guys returned to the rooms, changed, and then met back up where the trail divides. A few girls joined us, and it just so happened that Cammie was one of them. We all decided to explore a little and walked down the road to the General store.

It was then we discovered a pleasant secret that had been hidden by the faded sign that the country store also served ice cream in Flossy Mae's old fashioned Soda Shop. We relaxed a while talking about where we come from and telling stories. It wasn't long before Malachi and Cammie were carrying on a conversation of their own. I heard Malachi begin to excuse himself again about the event earlier at the dance.

"I'm sorry about earlier tonight," he said.

"That's okay, I don't mind," she said as she paused and looked down at the ground, and then continued as she inquired, "So… it was your *pleasure*, huh?"

Malachi looked at her out of the corners of his eyes avoiding direct eye contact as he pulled in his bottom lip biting down as if he pondered how best to reply. "Well…" he hesitated, then he became resolute and boldly owned his statement by proclaiming, "Yes… yes, it was. As a matter of fact, it still is."

"That's good," she replied approvingly. Just at that time Jane, Cammie's roommate, came from behind them interrupting their conversation.

"Cammie, I've been looking all over for you. Are you still going to braid my hair for tomorrow?"

"Oh, I'm sorry Jane, I forgot." Then she stood addressing Malachi. "Well, I better go; tomorrow is going to be a long day. I'll talk to you tomorrow if you want to."

"Of course," he insisted, "it'll be my pleasure."

She looked down at him as he remained seated and grinned pleasingly, "Ok, then, I'll see you tomorrow." He watched her as she jogged with Jane down the road back to the camp. It wasn't till she was out of sight that he noticed me glaring at him while shaking my head.

"What?" he exclaimed with a guilty look. "Come on now Zaylen, it doesn't hurt to have friends."

At first, I made no comment, I just kept shaking my head in disbelief. "Come on man, we better be going to bed too. Like she said, it's going to be a long day."

We got up and walked down the road. The sun was beginning to set behind the hill side as the full moon became exposed in the east. When I arrived at my cabin, I found it impossible not to take the liberty to taunt Malachi, "It's my pleasure to say, 'Good night.'"

He glared back, not nearly as amused as I, replying, "Yeah, whatever… see you tomorrow." Then he continued down the trail to his room.

Days passed by uneventfully as Malachi and Cammie spent more time together. I didn't pay too much attention as it didn't seem as though anything was out of the ordinary, they were just hanging out; keeping company with each other while other people were around.

However, that occasional stare that became so common between those two wouldn't let me dismiss from my mind that something was bringing them together. I realized that I wasn't the only one who noticed this as I heard a few people inquiring about the same thing. Eventually I decided to ask Malachi if anything was going on.

My group finished later than the other groups because our last training station was endurance. When I got back to my cabin, I took a long, hot shower to soothe my aching muscles. After I got out of the shower I got dressed and went over and knocked on Malachi's cabin door.

"Come on in," he called out. "The door is open."

I tried opening the door, but the handle wouldn't move. I called back while twisting at the knob back and forth, "The door is locked." Promptly he came and opened it. I entered and began closing the door as I greeted, "Hey, man what's happening?"

"Oh, nothing… just thinking," he said as he started to sit.

"I know," I answered with an omnipotent smirk; "Cammie is pretty, isn't she?"

His eyes shifted in my direction looking somewhat relieved that I knew what he was thinking so that he could talk freely. "You know, it's more than that." He said leaning his head to rest on his fingers in a thinking manner as he shook his head searching for a way to explain the scope of the situation. "I think she's perfect!" He paused for a moment then continued. "Do you remember the first morning we were here – behind the cabin? That morning when we saw the fog rolling past on the lake; do you remember how perfectly unassuming the beauty caught your eye while something else subtlety caught your attention in an almost spell-bounding attraction - keeping you from wanting to leave?

"I kind of got the sensation as if something profound was whispering from the silence?"

"Yeah, exactly…" he reasoned as if he had experienced enlightenment by recalling his experience while mumbling the words to himself again, "as if something was whispering. Yeah, that's a good way of describing how she came into my life. 'Profoundly whispering' subtle yet significant. It is so that now the days mean nothing without the hope of seeing her. When she isn't around, I am consumed with craving her presence while hoping that she's just as obsessed with thinking about me. And just a look from her makes it feel as if she is predisposed to understanding my thoughts… my needs.

I find myself in a calm "oxymoron state" he explained,

"I'm vulnerable when I'm with her yet, being in her presence seems to give me strength as if I'm invincible. My fear is that I'll never have the chance to show her what she means to me. In every way she, to me, is beautiful. She is pleasing to the eye, and I am so calmed by her charm. But … I hear – no, I feel a cold whisper warning me. I don't know how to explain that I am able to feel a whisper; but I know that's what it is."

He appeared somewhat detached from reality in his attempt to make sense of the perplexity from the thoughts that swirled around him. He looked as though he might cry at any moment, but then actually seemed angry rather than sad; angry perhaps at how life permits one to covet objects of entitlement while denying the enjoyment of possessing such warm pleasantries.

He spoke as though he knew what he wanted but was unable or unwilling to pursue possessing it. I could empathize the gravity of the situation he now found himself; disillusionment and sadness are two of the most helpless situations a person could be without someone to lend a hand in figuring out what card to play next because one could suffer a lifetime of regret because of what was … or was not done.

"So, are you going to tell her how you feel?"

"I don't know," he exhaled exasperated, "if nothing is going to come out of it, I figure, what's the use?"

"Let me ask you another question," I hesitated, "…if this is none of my business just say so… but, what about Jenny?"

"That's a hard question. I've been considering what to do about this. What I know is that I've never been this happy… what I know is that Cammie makes me want to be better."

"So, what does that mean?"

"It means that I plan to enjoy as much time with Cammie as I can, with full knowledge that in a week she'll be out of my life forever. And now that I realize how I feel; rather than worrying about hurting Jenny, I've got to do what's right. I'm going to have to tell her it's over between us.

"Are you sure about this Malachi?" I said in disbelief, raising my eyebrows.

"I told you; I've thought about this a lot. I am not taking lightly what I have decided to do. But I believe that I must do it. I never wanted to be with anyone like I wanted to be with Cammie. To stay with Jenny even after I knew how I felt about Cammie would be wrong. It's too difficult to live a lie."

"If you're really that serious," I cautioned "then it's my observation that you have no choice but to tell Cammie and let her make her own decision of whether it is worth it."

"Maybe you're right," he conceded. "...perhaps I should entertain taking a chance."

"By the way, what nickname did you bestow on her? I know you had to assign her one by now."

"Of course, I've given her a nickname" he explained "- as you know it's customary to assign important people with their own name; I nicknamed her, "Sommer-Reighn" because I have a feeling that her hugs are warm and comforting like summer, and I've fallen for her like the rain. I changed the spelling to reflect her uniqueness."

"Hey," I responded encouragingly, "I kinda like it; simple yet smooth. The only problem is…" I interjected jokingly, "to prove the validity of her newly minted name - someone will have to give her arms a test ride. And… since you, technically, are already spoken for…" I concluded in a pretentious tone as I pretended to head for the door, "I just guess I'll have to sacrifice myself in the interest of science and find out."

"Don't you dare..." he responded emphatically, pulling on my arm to halt my forward movement. "If anyone is going to do any kind of experimentation it's going to be me." He conceded playfully as if he were performing an essential chore for the survival of humanity. "You know of course… all in the interest of science."

"Yeah…" I replied glaring at him to demonstrate that I purposely prompted him to show his true feelings. "That's *just* what I figured."

Just then there was a knock as a voice came through the door.

"Hello… Malachi. Are you there?"

"Sommer's here early this year!" I teased as I approached the door to let her in.

"Oh, hi Zaylen is Malachi here?" she questioned as I opened the door.

"Funny though," I continued my banter ignoring her question, "it still feels like spring to me, and the Reighn is not falling."

"Huh?" she responded confused.

"I'm right here," Malachi said, approaching her, "just ignore him."

"I'll excuse myself," I said as I began weaving my way past the door.

"No, don't bother," Cammie said, "It's such a nice day I was hoping Malachi might take me for a walk."

"Of course, I will, that sounds like a terrific idea. We'll see you later, Zaylen."

After they left, I sat down and listened to the radio until it was time for dinner. I watched for Cammie and Malachi to show throughout the dinner hour and based on our earlier discussion the longer time elapsed that I didn't see them made me increasingly intrigued to know what they were talking about.

I lingered around the cafeteria waiting to see if they would ever show up for dinner, but they never did. I walked out onto the balcony and stood for a while admiring the simplistic beauty of the country landscape.

Evening slowly became night as the golden light of the sun began to disappear behind the soaring trees on the distant hillside, leaving darker shades of blue drifting behind to the eastern skies.

Soaking up the shadows of the night the fresh green tint of the newly budded leaves dissolved into murky grey against the backdrop of the vibrantly white illuminated sunset. The limbs creaked in as they gently swayed in a calm breeze appearing as though they stretched to touch the heavens. A single star flickered brilliantly as its reflection danced across the waves on the lake. Again, that uncommon quietness dominated, interrupted only by that gentle chilling wind that whistled around my ear and face.

Pulling my arms close to my body, I raised my shoulders to maintain warmth as I inhaled deeply and shivered slightly. When I breathed out, a white cloud formed then quickly dissipated. As I continued to gaze across the valley, I had an epiphany of an analogy that explained what it was that Malachi had envisioned when he attempted to articulate the situation regarding Cammie. Just as the cold wind at my ear was a subtle warning that the lake was still wintry lethal; similarly, attractive situations, especially one that was perfectly awesome - something about the situation still was devastatingly cold.

It wasn't much longer that I stood there when I heard the noise of rustling leaves underneath where I was standing. I looked down and saw Cammie walking by herself.

"Hey, Cammie!" I shouted out to her while rushing down the stairs to meet her.

"Oh, hi Zaylen," she said cheerfully as she paused her walking for a few seconds to allow me to catch up.

"Where's Malachi?" I inquired.

She looked at me in a mischievous manner and smirked as she answered, "I gave him something to think about."

Her lips stretched as she smiled. It was then that I noticed the absence of the glossy shine that I had been accustomed to seeing on them. Then at further inspection I observed what I thought was a discoloration on the right side of her neck. Since it was twilight I was unable to conclude for certain if there was a mark on her neck or if it were just a shadow so I moved closer attempting inconspicuously to get a better look. She, however, looked at me strangely as I intensified my observation - then quickly she discreetly raised the collar of her jacket.

"My," she said, providing a plausible excuse for her action, "it sure is getting chilly, isn't it? I better get back to the room. When you see Malachi, tell him I'll see him later." She instructed while trotting down the path.

"Hey, wait, where is he?" I called out.

"He should be coming any minute." She shouted as she trotted backwards.

She turned back and continued running away. I wondered what she meant by 'giving him something to think about.' I was anxious to know and as it turned out, I didn't have long to wait. Within a few minutes I saw Malachi emerging from the shadows of the trees. My first impulse was to immediately ask him what the mystery was, but I managed to keep my composure and be patient.

"Hey Zaylen, what's up?" he said, approaching me.

"Whatever is not down." I replied playfully to downplay my anxious curiosity.

"Anything going on?"

"No, nothing... I was just admiring the beautiful evening... *a-lone*." I stressed, hinting.

"Yes, it has been one terrific day."

He didn't take notice that I was attempting to let him know that I knew something. He, apparently being in his own world, wasn't paying attention to what I was saying so I used a sure-fire way to get his attention.

"I talked to Cammie a few minutes ago." I responded tauntingly as I turned to walk away in a nonchalant manner. "She told me to tell you that she'll see you later."

"Is that all she said?" he questioned; following me.

Now that I had his attention, I had the perfect opportunity to spring into action. "No!" I exclaimed. "She came walking along flaunting a demeanor like a kid in a candy store. Do you want to know what her response was when I asked her where you were?" I inquired of him rhetorically, 'I gave him something to think about.' That's what she said. At that moment I stopped, turned, and looked at him with glaring eyes and questioned, "So, Malachi, what are you thinking about?"

He looked at the ground with the same mischievous smile that Cammie had displayed as he began to explain, "Well… something happened."

I intensified my stare as I stressed my voice. "Yeah, I kno-o-ow that much! Try telling me exactly what that 'something' is that you two are referring…"

"Alright! I'll try to give you a "Cliff Notes" version of a long, wonderful story." he said smiling as he began his narration. "First, we just went walking through the woods… admiring the scenery. Of course, you may know I was admiring her."

"Of course," I replied playfully, showing interest in his colorful narration.

"We made small talk at first just talking about our favorite things. I told her about looking at the stars on clear dark nights during the spring when everything comes to life. That conversation eventually directed us toward discussing how we feel about each other."

"Now we're getting somewhere." I spoke with anticipation to encourage him. "Go on, I'm interested."

"We asked each other questions like… 'Where would we like to be? What our favorite place is? What makes us happy as well as the things that make us sad.' I told her about my dad and showed her a picture of him; she observed that I looked just like him, commenting that I have my dad's same ornery smile.

It was a cool moment when we were testing each other to share personal things that don't usually get talked about. The kind of things that get shared to show special interest in someone. While we were talking, at some point she took out her lip gloss and put some on her lips. I thought it might be an incidental humorous gesture to mock her, so I took the bottle from her to tease her."

Malachi began to detail their conversation:

"Now what are you going to do with that?" she inquired as she released the gloss into my hand.

"Nothing," I replied in a dismissive manner as I began to extend the stem of the gloss bottle to squeeze some onto my lips.

"No!" she exclaimed, grabbing my hand to pull it away from my lips. "You can't put it on that way!"

I just assumed that it was a hygiene concern that she didn't want my lips on the gloss dispenser, or I figured that I was attempting to apply it wrong and that she was taking it from me to instruct me on the correct manner to adorn the gloss. She wrestled the bottle from my hands; but was unaware that the struggle caused a little gloss to spill from the bottle onto my fingers. As she started to put the bottle away, I reasoned that I wouldn't waste what was on my fingers.

"Okay," I announced, conceding to her order and then in a dismissive manner began to put my glossy fingers to my lips.

She looked back towards me as she questioned, "Hey, what are you doing?" Then she quickly snatched my hand from my face before I could touch my lips, effectively denying my new strategy. She persistently reiterated, "No Malachi, you can't put it on that way either!" For a few moments I struggled with her indomitably to put my gloss-soaked fingers to my lips, but she, using her body weight, was persistent with preventing me from doing so. "No," she spoke in a soothing whisper, "you can't put it on that way."

As she wiped my hands clean, I became acutely aware of the warmth and softness of her hands holding mine. All at once a sensation traveled through my body making me feel as if I were basking in the sun on an autumn evening. Even after my hands were free from the gloss, she continued to rub her hand gently over mine, she looked away from our hands and gazed profoundly into my eyes; then with an innocent and sincere whisper she convincingly coaxed, "You can't put it on that way."

Finally, I comprehended her intentions. I became intensely aware that her lips were generously covered in what I have been desperately attempting to put onto mine; at last, I reasoned that if I were going to put the gloss on my lips; 'only one option remained.'

I became mesmerized by her sensually glossy covered lips. Fixated, I carefully examined her responses to my subtle advances. I stared in her eyes for a few seconds – wavering anxiously in anticipation that the gaze of her pellucid azure eyes was boldly encouraging me to touch her.

It was in that moment that it became apparent that we each became the object of the other's desire. As her warm, petite, feminine hands soothed me - I became acutely aware of the passion swirling around us. My heart raced with eagerness as I cautiously began leaning forward slowly closing my eyes. As I drew closer still – I felt the warmth radiating from her lips - I hesitated momentarily, opening my eyes, still in disbelief that my conceived dream was about to be born into reality.

I reclosed my eyes and leaned further toward the final approach; touching her; softly pressing my lips to hers. She responded willingly and leaned into me reaching her arms around my neck pulling me into her embrace.

Under the influence of the moment, I became intoxicated by the sweet taste of the gloss that had been smeared onto my lips. Our tongues meshed lovingly and sensually triggering an intimate stimulation. After a few moments she gingerly pulled away, leaving her arms around my neck. Then, as if to see as if both she - and the moment were real, I lightly stroked my right hand on her flushed cheek and gently slid her hair back while lowering my hand to the back of her neck.

We continued to gaze into each other's eyes as I slid my hand across the back of her supple neck; pressing gently with my fingers, in a massaging manner. She purred with pleasure and her eyes rolled as she closed them, raising her chin in that same instance so that her neck was generously exposed.

Again, I leaned towards her, slowly – this time kissing her neck with a noticeable sucking motion and gentle nibble with my teeth to send a surge of sensation to course through her nervous system. She put her hand on my head and pulled me closer as she leaned forward spontaneously exhaling hot air on my neck with a satisfying feminine moan of ecstasy. We cradled each other for what I would describe as a new yet cozy, familiar embrace. Enjoying the company of each other we hadn't realized how much time had gone by until we noticed that the sun was setting, it was then we decided that we had better get back."

Nodding my head, I began speaking, "So, indeed she did give you something to think about."

"Yes, but she doesn't realize just how much."

"Well Malachi, I have two questions for you… did she validate the worthiness of her nickname and if so, what are you going to do now? Are you going to tell Cammie about Jenny?"

"This is where things start getting complicated," he said with thoughtful consideration, "to answer your first question, yes, her arms are every bit as inviting as I could ever dream; and even though I previously decided that there wasn't a reason to tell Cammie anything because nothing had happened.

I now have to reconsider my first assessment after what happened between the two of us this evening… that situation became a "game changer." I believe now that I have no choice but to tell her something; what I'm unsure about is how she'll react. The big question is will she understand my reasoning for not being straightforward with her from the beginning?"

"The problem with that question" I observed, "is that, until you tell her, you won't know that answer."

"Ok Zaylen, I need your opinion…" he said as he looked at me while pacing, "do you think I should tell her right away so that she'll know that I had nothing but good intentions or wait and see how things play out?"

"The way I figure it is that if you tell her now, she will probably realize that your intentions were genuine because you told her so soon after you two kissed. Even so, she still may choose to "bail out" of the situation. Since you really care about this girl – then I suggest that you wait.

Give her a chance to experience your affection towards her rather than you telling her how you feel. Give her the opportunity to react more to who you are and by what you do. That way when the time comes for her response perhaps it will be her heart that weighs in on her decision, rather than a shotgun reaction from her mind. I have a feeling that the battle between her heart and her mind is one you won't lose."

"I've got to admit, that sounds logical; but do you think that I may be inviting more trouble by procrastinating the inevitable?"

"That is certainly a possibility; but I don't believe it to be a probability. Obviously, nothing is full – proof at this point or we wouldn't be having this discussion - if it were anyone else who was in this situation, I would advise them to tell her now. Here's my reasoning for suggesting for you to wait. I've observed that the more people get to know you, and the more you open up to them, they have a propensity to like you.

I consider myself your best friend, and as many years as I have known you, I have never witnessed you being more honest and open with your feelings than you have been about Cammie. It is apparent that she has touched your heart in a very positive way. As I see it, you have nothing to lose if you choose to wait, but what you must gain is time spent with her."

In appreciation of my logic, he looked at me and smiled as he spoke, "You know… you're right. Comparing all that I have to gain versus what I potentially have to lose in this situation favors me waiting."

Our conversation continued for several more minutes waiting for the "Treasures of The Mind Night" to start. Guest writers were invited to the camp to read and tell stories. Before long a few people began walking down the path to the event. So, we walked in the building with them.

A few moments after we walked into the building Cammie came in with Jane and they made their way to where Malachi and I were sitting. Coach Tenzos got up and introduced the four people who would be telling the stories. My favorite was a story about some intriguing creepy invisible follower called the "Hidebehind."

After we were dismissed, I saw Cammie and Malachi talking alone. Later that evening when we were about to retire to our cabins for the night, he informed me that he was feeling guilty about keeping a secret from her and in an attempt to clear his consciousness he tried to tell her everything.

The only thing he was successful in communicating, however, was that he had something pressing on his mind that he needed to tell her. I reasoned that it was probably a good move on his part for him to use the opportunity to soften the blow. Effectively minimizing the shock of when he does finally tell her.

When I went to bed lying under the covers, I prayed that I had told him the right thing to do, and more importantly that everything would work out in his favor. It was quite a while before I fell asleep wondering how it was going to be when Malachi finally told her. I concluded that no matter what he did, that the situation wouldn't play out as we had anticipated. I concluded however that she could never let him go once she knew him, or perhaps it was just what I wanted to believe.

The next morning was Sunday so there was no practice all day. We got up and went to church services and then the rest of the day was left for us campers to spend how we wished. Malachi of course spent the day talking with Cammie while I was hanging out on the docks with Jane. I had been walking in the woods alone when she saw me and asked me to go down and sit on the banks of the lake. I was intrigued with the invitation and decided to accompany her.

As we approached the water, we spotted a dock extending out onto the lake and decided to make that our destination. When we stepped onto the dock our "land lover legs" buckled slightly, throwing off our balance as the random shift in direction of the dock caused us to clumsily bump into each other as it continued to bounce and sway while floating on the waves of the water. We eventually staggered like a couple of drunks to the end while learning to counter our balance as we gingerly sat.

Once safely seated on the dock Jane proceeded to kick off her shoes without untying them and then removed her socks. I looked at her with a sharp stare as if she were crazy; she glanced back at me with a jovial smirk and a suggestive nod encouraging me to do the same. Not to be out done I shrugged my shoulders and followed her lead by taking off both my socks and shoes.

Once my feet were bare, I began to reconsider what it was I was about to do. I thought to myself as I rolled up my jeans up to my knees, 'You really don't want to do this.' However, against my own better judgment I slowly submerged my feet into the chilling water up to the shin. I made an "O" shape with my lips as I let out a quiet bellow, "Wh-o-o-o, that's brisk!" I admitted. Both of my legs tingled like ant bites that was caused by my warm legs responding to the quick cooling of the frigid water. Finally, I closed my eyes and let out a sigh as I waited to get used to the coldness. Jane, who playfully sloshed her feet around in the water, was now laughing at my reaction. After a few moments my feet became accustomed to the water, and I leaned back to bask in the warm sun.

"Wow!" Jane exclaimed as she gazed looking up at the breath-taking scenery provided by the green trees on the high Ohio hills. "It's beautiful out here, isn't it?"

Looking down at the small ripples on the lake I replied, "Yes, it certainly is. It's refreshing to take time out and soak up some of life's pleasantries."

"That's an interesting way of looking at it," she said smiling. "Do you think you would be able to live out here? I mean… it's nice and all, but it seems like it could get pretty lonely. I do love it out here though, but I wonder if I lived out here if whether I'd appreciate it as much as I do now. I'm not even gone yet but I'm thinking that after I am gone that I would like to come back sometime."

Yeah, I'd love to live out here, one thing you can't renovate is scenery. Peace and quiet extends beyond the walls of your home. My dad always said, 'Buy the perfect house in the wrong location and you'll regret it.'"

"Yeah, I guess you're right. A Godly scenery is a luxury and quality of life that cannot be overrated, and it is pretty relaxing," she said while looking up at the sky. Then looking at me she continued. "It would be a lot nicer to have someone you'd like to share serene moments with while you were out here. Just wondering… do you have a girlfriend? If you do, how would she feel about you hanging out with me?"

"No, I haven't been involved with anyone for a while."

"Me neither." She quickly clarified her statement, "I mean … I don't have a boyfriend. It's been a while since I've met anyone I really like." She explained the reasoning for her choice to be independent. Then without provocation the dialog shifted with an unexpected inquiry, "What about your friend Malachi? Is he going out with anyone?"

I looked at her with a stunned surprise at the quick change of the conversation. My silence left a revealing and uneasy lull to the conversation… I didn't want to lie to her, but I didn't feel comfortable with telling her the truth; and worse I was running out of time to give a reasonable rationale for not providing a decisive answer. As a result Jane continued to press for an answer. "Hum, interesting." She purred aloud, pondering about my delayed response. "Silence speaks volumes, Zaylen. Well… are you going to answer? Is he seeing someone?"

I provided what I believed would be a satisfactory response. "Well, that's not for me to say," I said confidently at first but then quickly realized that my response would not suffice to relieve me from further interrogation.

"Soo… he does have a girlfriend?" she shifted her body assertively in my direction studying my uneasy body language with her judgmental eyes. I figuratively felt her turning the pages as she seemingly read my reactions like a book.

"I didn't say that" I responded defensively. "All I said is that it isn't for me to say, which by the way… it isn't right for me to divulge his personal life. But why do you ask?" I attempted to divert the line of questioning.

"I was just wondering because he's been spending a lot of time with Cammie."

"Well, there's nothing wrong with that?"

"Well, if he has a girlfriend then there's a lot wrong with that because Cammie likes him." She expounded.

It appeared that Jane knew how to push my buttons. I didn't want to say anything else, but she had backed me into a corner with the clever use of her bold line interrogation tactic. I didn't want to end the conversation with the possibility of Malachi having a bad image. Frustrated with my poor performance thus far, I pulled my feet from the cool water and put my arms around my knees as I remained seated. I carefully contemplated the choice of words that I would use next.

The heat from the sun warmed my feet and was a welcome relief as I watched the beads of water roll down my leg and off my feet. I used these incidental distractions to steal a much-needed solitude moment to collect my thoughts.

Hesitant to continue the conversation, I glanced over at Jane to survey the intensity of her interest. Finding that her focus was unflinching as she patiently waited for a reply to her question. I immediately turned away and looked back down towards the water in an effort to deflect the passion of her stare. Instead of looking her in the face I decided to watch her response from her image that floated on the rippling reflection of the lake as I continued our dialogue.

"Look," I began to explain, "…all I can tell you - is that he likes Cammie too - a lot. He is very concerned about the progression of their relationship and is planning to deal with things in the right time. He is taking my recommendation that he make careful consideration before taking any definitive action. He doesn't intentionally mess with people's minds; he's too nice to play games with people's feelings."

"Well, if he's so nice then why doesn't he socialize more with people in the camp? I mean he seems to portray a stand – off-ish attitude."

I looked at her somberly as I answered her, "This just hasn't been a good time for him."

She looked back at me in a confused manner, "Is it Cammie?"

"No, well… not entirely," I explained cautiously. "Before I tell you, you have to promise me that you won't tell anyone."

"Ok, I promise."

"I'm serious. This is personal. You can't tell anyone."

"Ok," she said as her sincere bold, hazel eyes looked directly into mine. "I won't tell anyone."

I looked back toward the lake at her reflection and began to explain. "The reason he's having a tough time is because his grandfather died last week."

"Oh, I'm so sorry, were they really close?" she questioned with sincerity.

"No, they weren't all that close, but I became privileged through a conversation with him about just how much this is affecting him with the memory of his dad who died three years ago this July. He has only talked to me once about his dad's death, and that wasn't until a few months ago. I'll never forget it – he told me that he never realized how permanent forever is - until you want to tell a person how much you care about them…but they're not there anymore.

He talked about thinking of all of the missed opportunities to express the affection and appreciation that were never taken advantage of. He further explained his observation about experiencing the empty hopelessness that remains due to the absence of a loved one.

The pain of losing a loved one heightens the troublesome philosophical insight that the most terrible things happen only to the good people while those that are evil emerge unscathed. It wasn't until that moment that I gained clarity on how much he had been effected. For the past three years, he hadn't mentioned anything like that lonely observation; he seemed to be managing the loss of his dad with no residual affect; but for those few moments he let his guard down and openly shared his thoughts.

For the first time I saw that there was a lot of pent-up, unresolved, underlying emotion he was managing waiting to erupt. Somehow, he's been able to keep it under control. He always seemed to know how to assist other people through their issues but in his sorrow, he is unable to help himself. So, you see; if he seems a little distant, it's only because he has a lot on his mind."

"I'm sorry," she acknowledged candidly; "I really didn't mean to pry. I was just happy for Cammie and was trying to find out if Malachi feels the same because she really does like him. She can't stop talking about him. I just thought that I might be able to help move things along for them."

"It's okay, don't worry about it; you couldn't have known. I'm just trying to be protective over him as he processes through his feelings."

Finally, I looked away from her reflection and back directly at her and smiled to mitigate the tension and she smiled returning the sentiment. I then turned around and began putting my feet back into the water; at that moment four people came down to the dock. Jared called out my name while waving his hand above his head.

"Hey, Zaylen, do you know where Malachi is? I found his ticket holder."

"No, I don't know where he is, but if you bring it here, I can give it to him."

He walked over to me while the other people remained on shore waiting for him to return. His shifting weight caused him to emulate the same, 'drunk walk' that we two had encountered. The dock bounced prominently as he knelt down to me smiling mischievously as he began handing me the item.

"What's wrong with you?" I said looking at him. "Why are you looking at me like that?"

"Oh, nothing," he replied, "I was just wondering who the girl was in here… is it his girlfriend?" I quickly cut my eyes at him without answering. "Well, I had to look in it to see who it belonged to… didn't I?" I remained silent - glaring at him while bending the corners of my mouth. "OK, I get the point." He stood up and raised his hand to signal that he was leaving. I nodded back and he turned around. I could feel Jane examining my reaction as if to say, 'I knew it.' I gave her the same look that I gave Jared as she satisfyingly retorted.

"Looks like the secret is out," she mumbled.

I put my head down shaking it, "Just don't tell her," I pleaded. "He likes her and plans to tell her soon. He would have actually told her by now if it weren't for my advice. I'm the one who encouraged him to wait. It won't go well for either of them if Cammie finds out from someone other than him." I reasoned.

"Don't worry. Unless someone is in imminent danger, I never meddle with other people's relationships. Especially serious situations. That's just not right." She acknowledged. "I've learned a long time ago that most things work out better when they're allowed to play themselves out naturally."

Her answer got me thinking and wondering about her opinions. "I'm curious…" I questioned starting a dialog. "What exactly is your view and expectations about relationships?"

"As you can tell, I'm just down to earth. If someone is honest with me, courteous, and shows me respect, we'll get along just fine because that's what people can expect from me. I want to know that I'm their priority. I don't want to be with someone who puts other things before me. Dignity and respect go a long way."

"That's logical." I acknowledged as I probed further to explore the meaning of her intentions. "Like what for instance?"

"It seems too simple to declare the obvious," she

observed. "…that men and women *are* physiologically different. Forcing a false narrative that the sexes are one in the same is ridiculous. We're different... and have different roles," she expounded. "That reasoning doesn't make me weak or any less than a man. We're equal…just different…" she concluded. "…and we just need to acknowledge that fact."

"So, to be clear, you don't like some women's efforts of besting a man."

No, I don't," she reiterated. "Our efforts should focus on embracing our natural variation and stop being afraid of being who we are and to draw on our individual strengths. I don't have patience listening to a blame game between the genders."

"Yes," I agreed with enthusiasm. "That sentiment is refreshing to hear." I emphatically praised as she continued to particularize.

"I really don't like it when I hear women put the blame on men for the reason why they are failing. When I hear some woman declaring that 'I can do anything as good as any man...' I reply, 'Well, you just lowered your standard.' Competing *against* each other and tearing each other down is counterproductive," she condemned. We all are supposed to aim at trying to be like Christ - not try to elevate our position."

I was impressed with her no - nonsense revelation and offered my own antidote about relationships as we bantered back and forth with our preferences. "I love women who are confident with being women and I appreciate not being challenged and condemned for being a man."

"I'm not wasting my time on reassuring a metrosexual about his masculinity." She declared. "A man better be able to hold his own and keep up with me."

"And I prefer a lady who enjoys being treated special like a lady." I interjected. "She should enjoy being treated in a special way. I prefer to be appreciated for being a caring gentleman.

In a more relaxed atmosphere, the conversation turned back from dating philosophy to learning about each other.

"Well, so…Zaylen?" She questioned. "That's a different name. How exactly do you spell it and where did your parents get that from?"

"Z-A-Y-L-E-N" I answered as she interrupted me from being able to completely answer her question as she sought to confirm what it was that she was hearing.

"Z -Y…"

"No," I corrected, "Z-A-Y…"

"Oh, I see Z-A- then Y."

"Yes, now you got it. It's Jewish origin and it means 'God is gracious.' My mom named me after my father John, which has the same meaning and sometimes members of my family adoringly call me John because the names' meanings are one in the same."

"I'm really kinda likin' that," She acknowledged approvingly. It's refreshing to find a guy who has more than just good looks, talent and intelligence." She complimented. "You have a lot of mysterious dimensions. I'm impressed and that's not easily accomplished."

"Well, thank you ma'am. It's nice to be appreciated."

After talking a little while longer we noticed it was getting late and since it was about dinner time, we decided to go.

"Well… Zaylen, it was nice getting to know you." She began talking while taking her feet out of the water. "I can't think of a better way I could have spent my day."

"Thank you, I found you to be quite a stimulating audience." I replied playfully in a proper voice. " Really, I did enjoy spending the day with you."

"If I don't see you at dinner then I'll save you a seat at 'Activity Night' later on, okay?" Jane suggested.

"Sounds good, I'll see you later then."

I went back to my cabin to clean up for dinner. Malachi and I joined up and walked to dinner together. I didn't want to cause him to worry any more than he needed to, so I didn't disclose to him what had transpired earlier. I did however ask him how his day was, and he told me that he'd tell me when he had more time.

After dinner he talked to Cammie for a few minutes then she left. Soon after, he made his way back to where I was.

"What do we do now?" he asked.

"You have time now to tell me what happened today. So, I guess you could start talking."

"The big news is that I was very close to telling her today."

"Wait a minute," I interrupted realizing that we needed a little more privacy to keep from being interrupted. "…follow me." Once outside I led him down the stairs away from everyone. We slowed our pace as we neared the trail, "Okay, you can continue now." I instructed.

"Okay, well we just went to what has become our favorite tree to spend some quality time together. At first, we just spent the time hanging out and holding hands. Everything seemed perfectly pleasant. I leaned against the tree, and she sat on the hill across from me. We didn't talk about anything for a while until she noticed me looking at her occasionally in a peculiar way. She could tell something was on my mind.

"What?" she questioned, interrupting the silence.

"What do you mean, 'what'?" I responded, putting on my ignorant act.

"Why are you looking at me that way?" she inquired.

"What way?" I replied innocently.

"You-u know," she said clairvoyantly as she got up, approaching me to grab my hand.

"Okay," I defiantly confronted her, "what if I say that I really don't want to talk about it?"

"Well, you have to anyway," she ordered.

"That's where you're wrong," I retorted playfully.

"Okay," she warned, "maybe not now – but you will."

"Anything else… maybe, but this is my own private thought. I don't have to reveal my personal thoughts, yet."

"Okay," she spoke again warningly as she sat back on the hillside, "…remember this."

My conscience started to get the better of me and I thought again about telling Cammie as I began to pace. She caught me just looking at her as my smile slowly dissolved. I wondered if this was the time to tell her about Jenny. I looked at her trying to force it out once and for all but instead I fretted about the consequences when I finally would tell her. I cowered back and looked away from her and back down towards the ground.

She stood up and stopped me from pacing and cupped her hand around my chin to keep my head focused on her direction so that she could ascertain my sincerity by looking into my eyes. Since I was restrained from looking elsewhere, I attempted to avoid direct eye contact by darting my eyes from side to side. She insisted on my undivided attention. She asked in such a sweet and reassuring manner about what I found so troubling that she almost coaxed me into divulging it right then and there.

"Hey, you. Look at me," she asserted softly.

I looked gazed into her soothing eyes and found myself drowning in a sea of blue admiration emanating from them. With a simple look she enamored my thoughts to acquiesce her unspoken request for me to share my innermost secrets and I instantly longed to satisfy her.

I sought to gain courage by finding reassurance in her eyes to do what I should but instead my confidence waned, and

I quickly looked away from her again. I desperately wanted to put this behind me and I kept trying to prompt myself into thinking, ' It'll be okay, just do it,' but I was so afraid of the consequences of possibly losing her.

"Come on," she continued to encourage, "you've already said it a hundred times in your mind, so just say it."

I slowly backed away from her and looked back at the ground. I reasoned that she was right – I have said it many times in my head. The problem was that there were so many different ways for me to tell her, but none seemed right. My mind was in total chaos. Finally, my mouth opened, and words started coming out.

"I have something to tell you," I confessed, attempting to soften the blow while steadying my resolve. I kept encouraging myself to just get it out.

"Do you not like me?" she asked as if she prepared for the answer to be no.

"Of course, I do," I smiled assuringly as I stepped towards her.

"Well, what is it then?" she asked, relieved, "you can tell me."

"I wish I could, but it's just so hard."

"Do you not want to tell me or are you afraid that I can't take it?"

"Let's say it's a little of both," I said, trying to prepare her as I once again extended the distance between us.

"I won't press you to tell me," she said graciously as she looked at me trustingly. "You can tell me when you feel ready. Just make sure that you do."

"I will," I assured her. "Believe me, this is one thing I plan to do."

"Since I'm letting you off the hook with this," she coaxed,

"– you have to tell me why you were looking at me strangely."

"Ahh, come on," I begged looking at her with a pitiful face as I continued, "Please don't make me tell you."

"You have to tell me one or the other." She shrewdly bargained. "It's not nice to keep secrets from me. Who's in charge of this relationship anyway?"

"You are," I submitted.

"That's right," she commanded, "…and I say that you have to tell me."

"Okay," I said as I began to pace. "I pictured you in the future in three different ways." I paused while looking at her. She was watching my every move. I thought about what it was I was about to tell and all at once I felt as if I were exposed, because I was uncertain about how she might respond. I decided that it may be best to rescind my agreement, "No, I can't tell you." I declared while pacing nervously. I was hoping that she would give me a reprieve from my agonizing predicament. I was counting on her to rely on her judgement to trust me; that her awareness of knowing that I do like her would be adequate grounds to suffice at this point. I miscalculated her curiosity as she challenged my commitment of honoring a reasonable request.

With a soothing tone, she made her appeal irresistible, "Malachi, I'm not asking for much. I only want to know what it was you were thinking about me. Please tell me."

Her petition was innocent and sincere and I discovered at that moment that if our relationship does progress further, whenever she uses that tone, I will be incapable to resist or deny what she wants. "All right," I conceded, "I'll tell you but first I want you to know that I didn't mean any harm." I began to explain my reasoning for wanting to keep my thoughts discrete. "I was only daydreaming. So please don't take offense to it. These thoughts were intended in the sweetest of ways."

"I understand." She acknowledged reassuringly. "I can take it."

"So, I told her." Malachi paused from sharing his narrative and looked at me as if he were finished describing the events, but my curiosity was heightened as I began shaking my head.

"Well, what did you have to tell her," I insisted, "…and what did she say?"

"It was tough enough telling her" he justified while insisting to an agreement before he disclosed further details. "So if I tell you, you have to promise not to laugh."

"I promise." I acknowledge his requirement so that he would continue.

"All right," he hesitantly reengaged telling his story, "I pictured how she might look in the future. I thought of how she might look like as my bride on our wedding day. Then how cute she would look as my pregnant wife, and finally how she might look as the mother of our children. So, you can see why I didn't want to tell her. It's kind of soon to be thinking along those lines but honestly that was what I was thinking. I didn't anticipate her ability to coerce my own private thoughts out of me.

I was grateful for her tenacity to make me disclose my thoughts because when I finally told her she reacted positively. She just grabbed my pinky finger and said, 'I don't have a problem with the way you look at me.'

"It sounds as though things are going smoothly. At least now she knows something needs to be discussed so when you're able to tell her it won't be a total shock."

"Yeah, but I'm still afraid."

"If you would like I could break it to her."

"No, as much as I'm dreading the thought of telling her, I don't think she would appreciate finding out from someone else at this point. I'm fully aware that it's what I alone have to do. I care about her a lot… I just need to find the right time and the right words."

I nodded my head acknowledging him, "I truly hope that everything works out. In deserving the best that life has to offer, you two deserve each other."

"Thanks, that's reassuring to hear."

Later that evening we attended 'Activity Night' with the other campers. Everyone as usual was having a good time, as there were all sorts of things to do; board games, playing cards, shooting pool or as I was doing, bowling. It wasn't long, however, that things got really interesting.

Malachi had been bowling on my team, when our game finished, he and Cammie sat a close distance from everyone enjoying a solitude moment talking to each other. They were alone for only a few moments when a girl named Rachel approached them blurting out the inevitable question to Malachi.

"Is that picture that Jared saw in your billfold your girlfriend?" she asked in a not-so discreet manner. When I heard her asking that "nuclear bomb" question, I turned around looking in their direction in startled dismay. Malachi exhibited an obvious stunned look, as he was temporarily impaired from responding to her with words.

His eyes were fixed and unblinking as if he were in a deep trance as he desperately searched for a way to get control of this unforgiving moment. It was necessary for him to move forward cautiously to guard every movement with meticulous care because everything he did from this point would be scrutinized.

His mouth opened slightly as he paused in a manner consistent with reconsidering what he was about to say as his attention remained keenly focused. Rachel, having observed the pause and delay in his response, she correctly interpreted the lack of a reply as his inability to process a quick and reasonable explanation.

Using this information presented the opportunity for her to continue to pounce. That moment of indecision to answer quickly and decisively by Malachi provided Rachel with an opportunity to modify her tactic and enhance her exchange to an interrogation. She refused to allow him the one moment of grace that he so desperately needed and instead questioned him more persistently, as she obstinately pressed for an answer, "Well, is it?" she demanded.

At that moment it appeared that some of his cognitive reasoning returned to his control as he turned to assess Cammie's response. She, who was understandably visibly upset, displayed a look of complete bewilderment. But surprisingly, somehow, she remained stoic. She reacted as if she was not surprised by this revelation and rather reacted as though she had been aware all along. I wondered what must be going through Malachi's mind and I wanted so urgently to assist him out of this dismal unforgiving instance, but I wasn't sure how. Finally, Malachi spoke for what seemed at the moment to be a viable escape from the calamitous situation.

"Will you excuse us please?" he said politely addressing Rachel. The plausible escape, however, was short lived as Rachel remained undaunted.

"Oh, come on, just tell me," She insisted in a flippant manner causing the tension to intensify.

"Please!" he insisted more sternly, losing his patience as Rachel remained standing in front of the two awaiting an answer. Malachi then looked down at Cammie searching for some support and assistance with dismissing his nemesis; Cammie obliged with a welcoming nodding of her head in Malachi's direction before turning to address Rachel.

"Please excuse us," Cammie spoke with a dreadful emotionless, toneless voice, "I need to talk to Malachi alone."

Without further comment Rachel left as Malachi and Cammie walked around the corner exiting through the open doors that lead to the patio where they were reasonably isolated from everyone. It was a peculiar site to witness this solemn atmosphere looming over them. It was surreal to watch the two of them being so quickly immersed in such a somber ambiance.

I considered how I reasoned that what transpired was just as I had predicted. Despite the best laid plan designed to control when and how he would tell her; the scenario would not play out the way he expected. Ready or not… the time had now come for him to face the consequences. I strategically positioned myself by the open door so that I could listen in on their discussion.

"Well," Malachi began to explain in a quiet shameful voice, "this is what I was trying to tell you earlier. I was trying to wait for the right time… and to find the right words, but I found it difficult to do so. I was afraid that you would think that I purposely kept a vital secret from you but that couldn't be further from the truth. I wanted to tell you, but I was afraid that you wouldn't give me a chance to explain how I feel about you. I wanted to be able to show you that I truly meant everything I've said to you and done with you.

You've become the center of my world as it has become increasingly difficult for me to be without your presence. I soon realized that my addiction to you couldn't be satisfied - the more of you I got… the more I wanted…" he hesitated and redirected his emotional thoughts as he clarified, "…no that's wrong… the more of you I needed." I figured that the best way for me to show you the amount of importance that you have in my life was to let you get to know me. By giving you time to get to know me, I reasoned that it would be unnecessary for me to have to convince you by *conveying* to you that my feelings for you are sincere, rather you would already know in your heart for my love to be true."

"I understand why you didn't tell me, "She spoke, still remarkably calm and supportive. "I know that you tried to tell me, but … what do you want (from me)?" she inquired with a somber heart, "What about your girlfriend?"

He looked away from her as he sidestepped to his left then confidently, he reestablished eye contact with her as he boldly proclaimed, "What I want - is you."

"But are you sure?" she asked earnestly, searching for some validation.

"If I wasn't sure, I wouldn't be here now." He sincerely declared. "This has not been easy for me, and I know I must be hurting you. If I wasn't sure about how I feel, please believe me… I wouldn't have put us through this." *1 (Second Chance – 38 Special)

A soft, steady rain began descending from the sky as if on cue to echo this dismal mood as she leaned back against the pillar of stone that was behind her. Gazing up at him with her lucid eyes full of tears, she at last, physically surrendered to her emotions. There was an obvious internal struggle amid the pain of her wounded heart opposing her strong mind as she slowly lost the ability to maintain the appearance of cognitive tranquility.

The somber sentiment she had managed to prevent revealing; began to gradually surface and was exposed on her face as her lips quivered ever so slightly. In desperation she closed her eyes, holding them shut for an instant. This fraught attempt was a last-ditch effort from her to prevent the aching of her heart from seeping into the windows of her soul.

Her resolve to conceal her raw emotions, alas, was in vain as the heart-wrenching passion percolated out of her eyes in the form of streaming tears that symbolically, just like her, were falling hopelessly for him. The tears rolled uninhibited down her glimmering cheeks.

When she finally opened her eyes, they displayed a

portrait of anguish – the whites of her solemn blue eyes were now painted the somber color of 'crimson sorrow' and depicted a lustrous glimmer as more tears continued to stream from them… trickling down her face. Her eyes had a look of such desperation that they would have softened the most rigid of hearts.

Without saying a word her eyes seemingly begged him to caress her in his arms for comfort; and he gazed long into her eyes as if to reciprocate the sentiment; it seemed, however, to be a silent mutual agreement that it was not yet time for an embrace. For a while the two of them remained motionless in a lovingly tense standoff, only staring sincerely, as each assessed the next appropriate move to make.

"I'm sorry," Cammie whimpered, breaking the silence, "I wasn't supposed to cry." She declared still clinging to what little strength she had left.

"It's okay;" he reassured lovingly as he accepted responsibility for the problem that now threatened to consume their relationship, "…it's me who should apologize for putting you through this. The last thing I want to do is hurt you," he proclaimed as he addressed her directly. "Cammie, there are no reasons for me to feel as strongly about you as I do – except that those feelings are so natural when I'm with you and being with you makes me enjoy my life more abundantly. The memory of your touch is something that even time could never erase – but even so, I still crave for more of your presence.

My reasoning is that with each second that I'm kept away from you, simply put, - becomes time that is wasted." He explained, then his voice became unequivocally solemn as he declared, "If there is anything that I'm sure about … it's the undeniable, unquenchable and unsuppressed yearning I have of wanting to be with you. Look in my eyes," he boldly invited "…and you'll see the sincerity of what I'm feeling… you'll realize that what my actions desperately seek to convey is that … I love you."

Her eyes which were once fixed on the ground slowly raised until she was looking directly into his. It was apparent that the tone in which his words were delivered stirred a rejuvenated passion within Cammie's heart as her tears noticeably quickened, rolling down her cheeks uncontrollably.

Her eyes sparkled; shimmering as she shifted them slightly from side to side as she closely examined his demeanor and scrutinized the windows of his soul. Malachi gazed long and unflinching into her eyes allowing her to observe his innermost thoughts through his compassionate eyes. It was clear that the two of them shared equally with the fear of uncertainty that swirled around them in that indiscreet moment.

It looked as though any second, he also might submit to the moment as his eyes glossed over with the appearance of tears, but it was then that he closed his eyes and somehow… remarkably summoned the strength to remain steadfast. She reached out with her right hand and gently touched his cheek with the tips of her fingers. Then, her voice softly sneaked past her lips in a strong whisper as she returned the earnest sentiment of the moment.

"If I didn't love you…" Cammie courageously declared, "…I wouldn't tell you that I'd still be here (regardless of what you decide)." Then, in a sacrificial gesture she offered, "I just want you to make sure you do what's right for you."

He opened his mouth to speak, pausing for a breath he then replied to her with resolve, affirming his commitment in a remedial manner, "You are what's right for me - don't you realize that I'm crazy for you?"

His eyes sparkled but remained still as her emotional gesture appeared to strengthen his resolve. In a very subtle and nurturing manner he put his left hand on her shoulder and with the fingers of his right hand he lightly stroked her hair back past her ears. Then slowly and without warning he leaned forward, then keeping his head high he kissed her gently on the forehead. As he pulled his lips away, he began putting his arms around her. She leaned forward into him resting her head on his chest while sliding her hands up his back, eventually, grabbing his shoulders. They remained clinging motionless to each other for several moments.

I wondered to myself whether this might be the defining moment of their relationship. Somewhat poised, Cammie finally looked up at Malachi only to momentarily lose her battle of maintaining composure once again as tears still streamed down her cheeks compelling her to lean her forehead back on his chest as she struggled to speak. Finally, she was able muster some fortitude and once again raised her chin - this time managing to verbalize her thoughts as she began talking with her voice slightly cracking.

"I'm going to go to my room …okay?"

"Yes, of course," he acknowledged quickly.

She stepped back away from him slowly with her eyes fixed staring directly into his; their bodies separated but their hands were still clamped at the fingertips as she bid him goodnight. "I'll see you tomorrow," she whimpered.

He nodded his head slowly as each of them released one hand and she was about to let go of the other as she turned to walk away, but Malachi, instead of releasing the second beckoned her attention by grasping her hand firmly; causing her to hesitate and turn back towards him.

He glanced at her longing for a sense of reassurance; and she responded with a carefree smile as she closed her eyes in a nurturing manner to reaffirm that not only, she but also, 'they' were okay for the moment. Without a word he nodded his head then finally released her hand and she walked down the stairs and was soon out of sight. A few minutes after she left, I walked outside to see if Malachi wanted to talk. When he saw me, he smiled, and I knew without asking that he wanted to be left alone. Even so I offered him my support.

"If you need anyone to talk to," I said while resting my hand on his shoulder, "I'm here any time of the night."

He acknowledged with a nod as he put his head down. I patted him on the shoulder and without another word walked away. I strolled back to my cabin wondering what was going to happen next. When I got to bed that night, I looked out the window towards Malachi's cabin. He was sitting on his porch alone no doubt thinking about what had happened and where it may lead.

There was a cold chill in the wind; I could feel it coming into my room through the cracks around the window. I shivered and pulled the covers around my neck. The chill however seemed to have little effect on Malachi. He just remained sitting on the porch. I tried to sleep but it was useless. I kept wondering and worrying about Malachi as he sat out in the cold. I drifted to sleep a few times but stirred awake frequently. Each time I would look at my watch; then look out the window. Every time I would see Malachi still sitting in the same spot motionless.

Finally, around three o'clock I heard a noise, and I looked out the window with my eyes widened. Malachi was up and walking around with a stick in his hands dragging it along the ground. A few times he pretended to golf using a rock for a ball and a stick for a club. I remained watching him for a few minutes wondering what was going through his mind and hoping that soon he would be able to get some sleep.

Maybe he was thinking the same thing because at that moment he threw the stick high into the air towards his cabin. I heard it land on the roof as it slid with a grinding sound. Malachi kept his head leaned back, looking towards the sky for just a few seconds as he spread his hands out palms up as if to make the statement that I've heard him say many times referring to God's will, 'As always, it's in your hands.'

His head lowered quickly, looking toward the ground as

he walked in his cabin. At last, he was inside from the cold. Morning would soon be coming and by no means was their situation considered to be remotely resolved. The best thing he could do to prepare himself for what was to come was to be well rested for whatever it may bring.

All the next day, stories reverberated around camp about Malachi's display in the morning practice. He had clocked his worst time since he had been running hurdles and at one point, he ran through a hurdle shattering it. Needless to say, he was not able to concentrate. He was excused from practice for the day because the coaches assumed that he might be thinking of his grandfather. I finally caught up to him at dinner time, that's when I got the firsthand account of what transpired earlier that day.

"I hear that you were a mad man today." I said jokingly.

"Let's just say that I was a man with… 'Something to think about.'" He creatively referenced what Cammie said days earlier.

"You know, your day may have gone much better had you gone to bed at a decent hour."

"I'm sorry did I keep you up last night?"

"No, of course not, I was just worried about you. So, what did happen today anyway?"

"Well, the first time I ran an embarrassingly slow time," he narrated. "Determined, I declared that when the gun sounds, I will erase any memories of what had happened. I concentrated on staying low to the hurdle to ride over it – but I obviously got too low, putting my foot right through the crossbar. The coach could see that I had my mind on other things, so he told me to take the day off before I hurt myself, or any more hurdles."

"So, how did it feel breaking through the hurdle?"

He looked at me as he closed his lips tightly trying to hold in his grin then he muttered barely opening his mouth,

"It felt pretty good. I don't know why but breaking things is therapeutic to the psyche."

"Yeah, they say it can be useful for relieving stress as well as working out frustration," I agreed with his assessment as we entered the doors to eat dinner. Malachi's appetite was noticeably nominal. He didn't eat much of his dinner; a bite or two of his salad and a few sips of orange juice to wash it down was all he managed to stomach. At times he would look at Cammie to see what she was up to.

I noticed that her appetite was not her focus either as she scarcely ate much from her plate; she would also be the first to leave the cafeteria and worse yet she left without so much as to acknowledge Malachi. This gave Malachi cause for concern and to feel even more uneasy as he leaned across the table whispering in distress expressing his discontentment for her lack of attention.

"Did you see that?" he winced. "She wouldn't even look at me."

"Maybe she's waiting to talk to you alone," I whispered assuringly, "I bet she'll stop over at your cabin later as she always does."

"I don't know. She seemed pretty determined to avoid me," he said, dejected. "I guess we'll see…" he reasoned out loud. "I'm ready to go when you're done."

I could tell that he felt uncomfortable remaining in the cafeteria with everyone else observing the drama, so I snatched up the remainder of my sandwich and drink and expressed that I was prepared to exit with him, "Okay, I'm ready." Soon after we got up from the table and as we walked out the door, we immediately encountered Cammie who had been waiting for Malachi on the balcony.

"I need to talk to you," she addressed him in a direct and determined manner.

"I need to talk to you too," he replied as he extended his hand offering her to lead the way, "…after you."

Just as they began walking down the stairs Jane and a few other girls came out.

"I'll catch up to you guys later," she said to the other girls as she approached me. "Well… hey Zaylen, what's going on?" she asked while grasping onto my arm as she playfully bumped me with her shoulder and hip.

"As if you didn't know what's going on," I said rhetorically, smiling.

As Malachi and Cammie walked into the woods and out of sight, she turned and gazed at me with that signature devious smirk of hers; then suggested we participate in an act of espionage on them.

"Let's follow them," she stated in a coy tone.

"Let's do…w-what?" I questioned in a chastising manner.

"Come on," she encouraged, repeating in a more suggestive fashion while pulling me into walking in the direction of the woods, "…let's follow them."

"Are you suggesting that we eavesdrop on them?" I asked condescendingly as I began to pull away in the opposite direction.

"No, I'm suggesting that we act like private eyes and investigate." She justified rhetorically tugging me back to go her way.

"It's called eavesdropping Jane, and it's wrong." I instructed sternly as I increased my resistance.

"You call it 'eavesdropping;' I choose to call it something a little more creative, so come on now before we lose them." She braced relentlessly and yanked at my arm in an effort to encourage me to give in.

"No, I can't do that." I declared. "I'm not going to violate their privacy to satisfy our curiosity to know what is happening between the two of them."

"Ahh, come on winey-baby," she teased.

"No, I can't do that. Have you forgotten that Malachi is my friend?"

"Yes, and Cammie is my friend," she justified. "We're not doing anything that's going to hurt them and it's not like Malachi isn't going to tell you what's going on eventually anyway…so you're not doing anything wrong; and besides, this way - it'll be fun…cause you'll be with me," she enticed. "Now, hurry before we lose them!" I continued to resist slightly as she pulled my arm in the direction they had gone - but then at last I reasoned that Jane would probably go without me if she had to; so I followed her as I resumed to protest.

"You know this isn't right," I barked. "We shouldn't be doing this."

"Oh, quit whining, we're not hurting anyone." She snapped defiantly. "And do you really want to risk the possibility of me knowing more than you about your friend's relationship?" She threatened.

True to her observation I reasoned that she made a very good point. In retrospect I replied, "No, no I don't think I'd like that one bit," I conceded, while announcing a 'Rules of Engagement' to terminate our surveillance in for my willing participation in this covert mission, "…but let's agree that if things get too personal between them, that we leave." I insisted as I proceeded to tag along with her.

"Shh, there they are," Jane whispered without responding to my ultimatum.

We were able to make out movement ahead of us through the dense trees that concealed us from view. They were walking next to each other on the path in the direction of the dock. Malachi had his hands behind his back, Cammie with hers in her pockets. I was thinking that if their destination was to go out on the dock, that our mission would be cut prematurely because there was no way for us to get close enough to hear their conversation without being seen. It was about that time that it became evident to Jane that her 'surveillance plan' was in jeopardy.

"Shoot!" she exclaimed. "I hope they're not going out to the dock. If they do, we're sunk."

We soon learned that the dock was not their destination as they passed it by. We were still in business for the moment. We followed the two down a long trail that looked as though it was not frequently used. The path itself was barely visible but in order to make it passable branches and vines had to be moved or simply avoided completely. That coupled with the fact that we were attempting to quietly be in stealth mode made the trek more difficult to maneuver undetected.

At one point Jane had mistakenly released a branch that swung back before I could get a hold of it, and it smacked against my forehead. The force of the impact abruptly stopped me in my tracks and the instinctive response to the pain immediately dropped me to my knees. Realizing what she had done, Jane came to my aid.

"Oh, Zaylen, I'm sorry," she apologized as she kneeled on one knee to render me aid. I had put my hands over my forehead in an attempt to dampen the pain and she was now trying to move my hands so that she could evaluate the welt on my head. "Are you okay?" she questioned as she pried my hands from my head, "Move your hand and let me see."

"Yeah, I think I'm okay," I squawked, laughing bravely.

"Why are you laughing?" she asked as she surveyed my wound, "You have a big red mark across your head. Doesn't it hurt?" she inquired, pushing in on my forehead with her index finger.

"Ouch!" I shrieked, while still laughing. "Yeah, of course

it hurts. I just can't believe that you let that branch go. You couldn't have hit the target better if you had aimed at it."

"I'm sorry," she expressed compassionately as she leaned forward with a sensual gesture by pressing her lips to my forehead. This act immediately swept me into a surreal atmosphere in which I became acutely aware of the slightest contact. The distinct contours of her soft feminine lips were pronounced and generous as was the warmth radiating from them. I found myself instantly closing my eyes and inhaling a breath of the sweet-smelling fragrance she was wearing from the nape of her neck.

Remarkably, this surprising moment felt comfortably familiar. Then as she leaned back, her lips clung to my skin for a moment making a slight sound once they detached. When I opened my eyes, I realized that my face was still close enough to her body that I could see small goose bumps raised, and I also noticed the subtle vibration of her silky skin that was caused by the pulse of the blood surging past the nape of her neck.

This imprint moment became intoxicatingly exuberating as I discovered myself being swooned by the sweet ambiance that was created by both her scent and actions. I hesitated for a moment while an insatiable urge to kiss her on her neck surged through my thoughts but subconsciously reasoned to restrain my impulse, 'Don't you dare.' I thought as I raised my eyes slowly following her neckline to the small dimple in her chin. Eventually glancing directly into her hazel eyes, I then responded pleasingly as I expressed approval of her sensual gesture.

"Well…now… that feels better." I cooed. Then I arose to my feet aided by her pulling up on my arm. My head was still swirling with the recent yearning thoughts of Jane. She, rather than being enamored in the moment like me – was instead preoccupied with the "spy" mission by realizing that Malachi and Cammie's voices hadn't faded in the time we were delayed.

"They must have stopped," she whispered. "We've got to be careful now."

We walked meticulously toward their voices both slowly and quietly. To our perception the slightest noise created by our movement seemed to be amplified. A twig snapped under my foot causing Jane to react in a negative manner, like a mother about to scorn a child, showing her displeasure by turning back toward me with her left hand on her hip as she sighed, breathing noticeably through her nostrils urging me to be careful. I turned the palms of my hand toward the sky and shrugged my shoulders while whispering.

"Well, what am I supposed to do? We are in the woods you know!"

She put her right hand over her eyes momentarily in a disapproving manner as she shook her head. "Ahh, come on…" she ordered. "and try to be more careful." She insisted.

We continued down the trail being extra careful not to be seen or heard. Finally, we came to a huge opening in the canopy of the trees. The clearing opened wide enough to house a skyscraper. Trees stood tall, like pillars and the sky resembled a dome. Directly in front of us was a wide, flat-topped hill and protruding out of the hill was a huge building sized boulder that emerged skyward from the ground.

The boulder diverted the direction of the path from continuing straight instead altering to the trail to the left which acted to keep us completely conceal our approach. We stood at the base on the backside of the boulder for a few seconds listening to them. The huge boulder not only concealed our presence from them, but it also doubled as an obstacle that impeded our ability from hearing their conversation.

"I can't make out what they're saying… can you?" Jane asked.

"No, I can't either. So, what now 'Sarge'?" I questioned sarcastically expecting for sound reason to set in and for us to turn and head back. I was puzzled at first when she smiled at me and then gazed up the side of the boulder; I followed to where her eyes guided, then quietly exclaimed in disbelief. "You've gotta be kidding me! You want to scale the boulder?"

"Come on! Buck up soldier!" She coaxed, "You've managed to come this far."

I peered up at the boulder again, carefully surveying the landscape of the rock, assessing the crevasse for climbing ability and then rolling my eyes, sighing as I resolved myself to surrender, "Humph…Might as well."

Pleased with her ability to convince me to capitulate with her escapades yet again, she rewarded me with a kiss on the cheek, "Good boy… now give me a boost."

Just as she began climbing, her foot slipped suddenly sliding her body back into me, I quickly reinforced her with the palm of my hand as she used my support for a brace to get a better grip; we paused frozen motionless and listened to be sure that our scuffling wasn't heard. Confident that we were still undetected, we reengaged with our climb. I whispered back, "Be careful."

We managed to successfully negotiate climbing past the first difficult bulge on the boulder, then we were able to shimmy easily to the top. It was evident that we must have been directly over them as we could clearly hear everything. We smiled at each other gloating over our accomplishment of getting this far without being caught. Then we rolled over on our backs and relaxed as we listened.

"You seemed kind of upset when you told me that you had to talk to me," Malachi said.

"No, I wasn't upset." Cammie expounded. "It's just that I needed to talk to you; and I wanted you to know. It wasn't my intention to sound angry. My purpose was to sound determined."

"Well," Malachi offered, "I guess I'll ask you first; what is it that you are wanting to discuss?"

"I just want to find out what you're planning to do." Cammie said directly.

"What is it that you want me to do?" he inquired.

"I want you to do whatever it is that you want to do." she fired back.

"I choose to be where I am; here with you."

"Well, what about Jenny? I have a problem with that." She retorted. "You know this is going to hurt her something terribly."

"I have a problem with that too." He insisted agreeing, as he acknowledge, "I've made a mistake that is not easily remedied; I've committed myself to someone only to later betray that confidence – then to compound the error I've made the unilateral decision to end the relationship without giving her so much as the opportunity to consult about the decision - for that alone sooner or later I'm certain to face some consequences for that transgression. I've done wrong and there is no right way to correct my indiscretion. I didn't plan on liking you – but the reality is that I do."

"Well, that makes me feel a little better;" she exhaled somewhat relieved, "but I don't want you to 'break up' with her for me."

"Cammie, I understand that this is something that I must do for me, and I take responsibility for what I must do. Ever since I started liking you… actually even before I thought that you might respond favorably to me, I've had a problem with how I decided to deal with Jenny. I first reasoned with myself that it be "unfair to Jenny" if I stayed with her; I attempted to justify my decision to break up with her as some noble gesture in an effort to deflect the responsibility of my actions – but after further consideration I have come to realize that the reality of the matter is that this situation was caused as a direct result of my own selfish desires - and as a result I became a willing participant by making a decision that will hurt her.

I wasn't sure if I was prepared to accept the consequences of what I've done; but I believe that I'm willing to submit to the high cost I am willing to pay - I am committing myself to my decision and to you. It was my opinion at first that you didn't even really notice me – but still I felt strongly, even then, that I would have to break up with Jenny. I know that it's not going to be an easy thing to do, but more importantly, I know it's something that I must do.

I know you would never ask me to hurt anyone; for any reason, especially just for your benefit nor would it be fair for me to misplace the blame of Jenny's pain of being hurt by the breakup of our relationship onto you. That's one of the things that make it so wonderful to be with you… your willingness of self-sacrifice. So, this one thing I'm doing for myself. After this, everything I do will be done with the purpose of pleasing you."

His words and the sincere tone in his voice were impressive, and strong. I heard crackling vegetation by continuous footsteps as if one of them were pacing back and forth. The sound stopped abruptly, interrupted by Cammie's voice.

"I'm glad we're having this talk," she expressed her delight regarding the content of the conversation; "I'm feeling a little better."

"Does that mean that you understand what I'm saying?"

"Yes, I do; and it makes me happy."

"That's good, all I want to do - is to make you happy."

"Well, you said that you had to talk to me too." She stated, transitioning the focus on his needs. "So, what do you want to talk about?" she inquired.

"I was just wondering where this leaves us." He questioned.

"You mean…do we have a relationship?" she questioned as her tone changed.

"Well, you know how I feel, and I'm pretty sure of how you feel about me, but I just wanted to get everything out into the open."

"I want to have a relationship with you…" she explained "…but I'm kind of afraid because I'm used to seeing how my brothers operate."

"What do you mean?" he asked, perplexed.

"Well, my brothers have 'so called' steady girlfriends," she expounds, "and then they also have girls in different towns; and I have a problem with that." She expressed, displeased.

"I think you know that I'm not like that." He assured.

"Yes, I'm pretty sure that you're not. I'm fairly confident that you've had misgivings about how we got together - I know how hard all of this has been on you, but I mean… you fell for me when you have a girlfriend, and I don't want that to happen to us. I have concerns about getting in over my head to only later lose you to someone better.

"I don't want you to go in over your head right away. That would be too easy. When you finally decide to go in over your head, I want it to be because I've earned your trust, and because you feel comfortable. Rest assured; I understand the importance of making provisions to safeguard my heart to be faithful only to you.

I can see on your face that when you look in my eyes you're still wondering if what I'm expressing are my true feelings. It isn't enough for me to simply *tell* you that it is. I need to be able to prove myself to you through my actions and I know that in time I will. My question is… are *we* going to have that chance?"

"I don't understand exactly what you mean by, 'are we going to have that chance?'" she inquired puzzled.

I heard the same steps pacing again. I was sure that it was Malachi pacing because it was a familiar technique he used to clear his mind.

"Okay," he explained using a metaphor as an analogy. "Let's pretend that we have an imaginary lake. Neither of us is comfortable with risking going in over their head prematurely; but what I'm asking is; - do you plan on at least testing the water?" He further illustrated as he pressed for a definitive answer. "You can't stand on the outside afraid to come in and wonder if the water is all right, and no one else can gauge if the water is too turbulent for you because only you can determine for yourself whether the water is fine. It may seem scary at first - and once you get in, you might bump into some cold spots. But if you take my hand, I promise that the waves will be gentle and the water soothing. For now, I need to know if you're going to take the chance and at least come into the water."

"I have already been testing the water," she insisted. "But how deep do you need for me to come in?"

"Just enough, so that you feel comfortable," He requested.

"I'm sure I can manage that." She concluded. "Now what else did you want to ask?"

Again, there was silence. He would begin to say something only to hesitate, it was apparent that he was attempting to ensure saying what he was trying to communicate in the correct manner. This happened several times as he feverishly sought for the right words but was having a difficult time trying to find the right way to express his feelings.

"I'm afraid to say this because I'm afraid of what the answer might be." He cautioned.

"You've already said it a hundred times in your head…" she encouraged. "…so just say it."

"Okay, let's see how I can put this," he sighed a final time in order to calm his nerves, as he braced himself for the possible undesirable response to his inquiry, "I was just wondering if other people were going to be allowed as invited guests into our lake or whether we are going to have a private lake?"

"Why?" she questioned with a concerned and confused tone, "Do you want to go out with other people?"

"No, I'm pleased with where I am. I don't care to be with anyone but you. The only reason I asked is because I don't want you to feel like I'm smothering you."

"I don't see that as a problem." She stated defiantly, "I don't like anyone else."

"Then does that mean that we have a private lake?"

"Yes," she declared definitively, "I don't want to share how you make me feel with anyone."

"Now that makes me feel good. I like the way you said that - that was really cool. I can't take the credit for the good things that I do… it's you that brings out the best in me. For the record…I don't want to share you with anyone else either."

"I was hoping you'd say that."

After that statement it was quiet for a while, and I assumed that they were being intimate. I rolled onto my side and whispered into Jane's ear. "It's getting personal; we agreed that at this point it would be time to leave."

"Stop whispering in my ear," She pushed back playfully, "your voice is giving me goosebumps." She then nodded her head agreeing and whispered back, "Okay, let's go."

Carefully I started leading the way to climbing down off the rock – as we scaled down the back of the boulder. We made sure to be extra quiet to keep from disturbing them as we tiptoed away from the rock. After about twenty-five yards we felt it was safe enough to begin to walk normally.

"Well, what do you think?" she inquired of my opinion.

"You know… I think they may actually have something pretty rare. I'm relieved for Malachi that things worked out the way that it did for them. I was very concerned last night. The outcome could have been much different. Malachi had anticipated and made a controlled plan for an idea of how he had hoped things would pan out, but I tried to caution him to prepare for his plan to go awry.

It seems almost as if the observation is when things don't work out the way they're planned to - that they instead somehow work out better. By getting through this tough situation, I think that their relationship will be stronger because of what they already had to go through." I observed.

"Yeah, I know what you mean. It seems that the worst experiences that you must go through appear to have the residual benefit of making you stronger. – I'm glad things worked out for them; I think they look sweet together. But didn't it seem to you that it was hard for them to trust each other?" she inquired.

"Not really. Based on what they've been through I'd say that they processed through things smoothly. Last night there was a high potential for an irrational "knee-jerk" reaction that could have caused the whole thing to completely blow up to end their relationship last night.

I've learned that some women have the propensity to purposely sabotage a good relationship because of jealousy. Their personality prevents them from enjoying a good relationship, so they seek to make others as miserable as they are. In fact, that may have even been Rachael's plan. She may have purposely initiated an unpleasant situation so that she could witness their drama play out for her entertainment but to their detriment.

Thankfully, however, in the face of adversity their maturity prevailed instead. They obviously like each other a lot; it just seems to me that their fear of facing rejection from the other is still too much to risk. Despite the commitment they made to each other even today there still remains an atmosphere of apprehension that is created by the fear of rejection from the other that still looms over their new relationship due to the concern of revealing too much reliance too soon."

"Well, Dr. Freud. That was a very philological interpretation of beginning relationships. Thank you for that..." Jane retorted humorously. "And maybe you're right but still I wonder why they couldn't just say exactly how they feel and face the consequences one way to the other. That's the way I am."

"That may be true… that is to say that you are that way once you're in a relationship, but when you're in the infancy of a relationship it's probably best not to be perceived to be too pushy."

"True, very true; now that I think about it – I suppose perhaps you're right – I agree that a subtle attitude is the better approach." She conceded as she elbowed me drawing my attention. She had a strange look on her face as she peered at me at the corners of her eyes.

By that time in our conversation, we had reached the clearing where the cafeteria was housed. There was a group gathered talking so we went to join in on their conversation. As we approached one member from the group acknowledged our presence with a rhetorical greeting. "So-o, where have you two been?" Seth inquired in an accusatory manner as if he were a parent waiting for an explanation., "Comin' out of the woods together, huh?" he questioned with the obvious intent of catching us in a compromising moment. "That looks mighty suspicious."

"Oh, really? Does it now?" Jane unflinchingly retorted back with a direct assault effectively deflecting any attention away from our escapades. Then with her next statement she cleverly turned the table and put him on the defense. "Is it any more suspicious than you eyeballing Rae?"

"Ewoo-o" was the collective moan response from the other members of the group to Jane's statement as if to imply rhetorically, 'Oh no she did not go there.' It was a non-verbal acknowledgement that everyone was aware of Seth's attempt to hide his affection for Rae, but they had pretended not to notice him pining for her but instead remained silent.

Caught completely off guard by Jane's quick wit, he responded with an embarrassed flush manner, "Wa-what are you talking about?" he nervously responded in an attempt to downplay her observation. He had no idea of the minefield he had just walked into. It was as if he had attempted to take out the 'badest' dude in the prison yard to get respect and was about to fail miserably.

He had not experienced the full flavor of Jane's uncanny ability to manipulate the situation, but as the deer to a hunter's scope, he was now in the 'cross hairs' isolated and vulnerable and her talent was about to be unleashed on her victim. It was as if he had just volunteered to be the guinea pig for everyone else to witness that Jane was no one to be trifled with.

"Oh, come on man, everyone can tell that you like her." Jane began to relentlessly beat him down. "Are you ever going to ask her out? You only have one more day to do something about it… so what's your failproof plan." It was as if she looked into his very soul and exposed his most vulnerable attribute.

"Well, I don't know. I'll be honest… I do think that she's pretty but she's out of my league." He confessed.

"Ahh, that's darling," Jane continued her indirect psychological approach of manipulating him to submit unwittingly into following her suggestions, "…girls just love humility. That girl is going to eat you up when she finds out you like her." She encouraged running her fingers through his hair. "Hey, I'll even help you out with a plan." Then addressing the entire group, she continued, "How about you all take him up to the soda shop and I'll go get Rae and meet you there - then we'll all arrange it so that he can be alone with her so that he can ask her out."

Right then and there I got a vision of Jane being like a deceptively cute but dangerous tiger. If some poor unwitting soul placed themselves on her radar, due to some nefarious attempt at 'besting her' - they were doomed to find themselves in the unenvious situation to experience her unforgiving attack. With a no-nonsense disposition, once she is determined to sink her teeth into something, may the Lord have mercy on them because she won't.

All of a sudden, I found myself in dangerous territory. I was intimately intrigued and liked what I saw in Jane's personality. As I watched her in action I was turned on and scared at the same time. I wondered if I might be worthy of her company and whether I should dare to pursue having a romantic relationship with her. I began to consider if I perhaps had a good enough rapport with her to have earned mutual respect and thereby gained her interest as a viable romantic companion.

I concluded that our relationship was complimentary and felt special to be considered worthy to be her equal. I immediately devised an appropriate nickname that identified her personality and would colorfully describe the way she would strike and if need be...ruthlessly subdue any threat. The unsuspecting victim would discover that Jane's mind was a lethal sedative to anyone who would dare to oppose her. Her newly minted name aptly would be dubbed, 'Jugular Vein Jane.' and would serve as a warning to potential combatants... to beware.

Seth was no match for Jane's cunning mind, and I found it humorous watching Jane do to someone else what she always seems to do to me...employing her signature "quick wit" to control any conversation so that it fits her agenda. This time however, in her defense what she had proposed sounded like a pretty reasonable idea. I was so impressed with this plan that I got caught up in the moment and helped her to persuade him by volunteering my services to participate.

"Hey, that's a good idea; if you want, I'll be your wingman." I excitedly declared to Seth.

"Look at that," she urged. "Everybody's pullin' for you. You'll never get a better chance. Come on, you have nothing to lose," Jane chimed in as if she were a persistent salesman who was unwilling to let the consumer off the hook by dangling just the right bait, "I'll get you all set up so that you won't have to figure out how to approach her; I'll serve her right up to you, and she won't suspect a thing; and who knows…you-just-might 'get the girl.'"

"Okay, what the heck, let's do it." He declared justifying his decision. What's the worst she can say? No?… right?"

"At-ta boy." Jane praised his decision enthusiastically. "Now, remember to put all of your charisma together," she instructed, "be sweet and vulnerable but stay confident, she'll like that about you. Now you go with Zaylen" she instructed. "He'll take good care of you. You two find a comfortable place a short distance from everyone else and look natural; when I get there, I'll do the rest." Then she addressed the group like a movie director, "You all know your places people, now let's make it happen."

As we all started to move, I nudged Jane on the shoulder with my elbow and inquired, "Now just how'd you manage to do that?"

"Do what?" she smirked and winked. It was a cool moment that she was acknowledging that I knew what she had done and was impressed with being in her presence.

Seth and I joined the group as we all headed down the country road to the County store, Jane headed in the opposite direction toward the cabins to find Rae. The group situated themselves on the patio in front of the store while Seth and I arranged ourselves on park picnic benches in the grassy area under a tree. About fifteen minutes after we got to the store Jane arrived with Rae in tow. When they arrived, they walked over to our strategically semi-secluded position about 15 yards from the group under the large Pin Oak tree.

We all surrendered to act out our roles as puppets to the puppet master, that being Jane who was orchestrating her well-devised plan. Sure enough, as promised, she inconspicuously manipulated Rae into isolation with Seth. Her scheme began by tactically maneuvering the four of us into a conversation about dating experiences to help Seth gage Rae's dating preferences but more importantly it was a ploy to see if Rae spoke about a specific love interest or if she just spoke in generality so that we could ascertain indirectly about her possible dating availability.

Then, once we were confident that Rae had no liabilities of being in a relationship - the mission was a "go" and Jane set the plan in motion. First up, Jane needed to prepare the 'topic of discussion' so that Seth wouldn't have to struggle to get Rae to engage in the desired topic when the two were finally isolated. In order for Jane to accomplish guiding the conversation to the desired topic she tactically made the comment of the commonality that she observed between the two of them. This was done to ensure that the focus of the conversation would be on each other's interest. Psychologically, this tactic bridges a common subconscious attraction for the two to foster.

Then to give them the necessary privacy, Jane coordinated our discrete departure. My leave was staged when she gave the pretense of sending me to get her a Chocolate ice cream cone for her; then soon after I left to retrieve her bounty, she excused herself to the restroom. With that done, operation "Seclusion" was a success. The completion of the mission was now left for Seth.

"It's kind of crazy that camp is going to be over tomorrow.

I was just kind of getting to like the slow pace of the country." I heard Seth comment as Jane and I left.

"Yeah, this is a pretty cool experience. Now that you mention it, I wouldn't mind staying a little longer myself," Rae replied.

"Yeah, I remember what coach said the first night at orientation; he pointed out that although we all started out as strangers that eventually we'll get to be good friends, now with the thought of leaving tomorrow I'm kind of missing being around everyone already and I'm not even gone yet." Then he made his subtle but bold move, "I'll miss some more than others…like you." ---- "I'ya was ahh… kind a hoping that you might like to stay in touch with me."

"Oh," she replied startled, "are… you asking for my phone number?"

"Well…" he swallowed noticeably. It appeared that he was hesitant with the uncertainty of whether to make his response direct, but the momentum of the plan was already in full swing, and it quickly became evident that he realized that he'd gone too far to back out now. She was waiting for an answer and with everyone looking on he had nowhere to retreat. Therefore, he proceeded with his approach very cautiously. To minimize the risk of being denied the goal of getting her phone number he cleverly disguised his answer with a hint of comic relief, "…ahh…well, only if you're inclined to say, 'yes'."

"Well…ahh, I don't know how my boyfriend will feel about that?" she retorted with a serious look on her face.

For the second time in less than an hour Seth was stunned by the revelation of a girl's comments. In a startled and embarrassed manner he tried to back out of the conversation gracefully but instead he nervously stuttered into creating words that didn't belong in the English language, "Oh-wha… yeah,… I-ya didn't know you had a boyfriend."

As he answered I looked at Jane for guidance wondering

if there might be a way for us to help him out of this mess, since we were complicit with getting him into this jam. Instead, it became apparent quite quickly that he would have to take this one on the chin with everyone watching. Jane verbally announced her surprise which demonstrated that she too was caught off guard.

As she watched this "train wreck" of a moment unfold she blurted out, "Oh, snap! I didn't see that one coming!" she declared. Then she glanced over at me shaking her head with a confused look as she explained, "I was sure that she was single, but… sometimes... you just don't know." She conceded.

We all looked on with bated breath to see what would happen. It was then that Rae disclosed another surprising admission, "Yeah… ah, he probably wouldn't say anything, because… I don't have a boyfriend" she declared teasingly "…not yet anyway." She hinted.

Seth's cognitive reasoning had not yet been reestablished because he was still reeling mentally about the "boyfriend thing." He failed to realize that Rae had been jesting with him about having a boyfriend; and therefore, he mistakenly misinterpreted how to process and respond to the new information that was just divulged by her about the fact that she did *not* have a boyfriend… so Seth, not yet realizing that it had just been a joke, continued to flounder.

"You what? Ahh, why not?" He fumbled trying to understand her statement.

"Oh …you, *WANT* me to have a boyfriend?" she questioned sarcastically. "I was under the impression that it would be good news for me *not* to have a boyfriend. Did you *not* want my number?" It was humorous to watch him as he continued to struggle to find the correct response.

"No…" he answered, still confused.

"No?" she inquired in a surprised tone repeating her question. "You don't want my number?"

"No… I mean yes… I mean no," he finally declared, "… what I mean is -no, I don't want for you to have a boyfriend and that is good news that you have no boyfriend and yes I do want your number." He was flustered but somehow plowed his way through.

"So, you're *sure* that you want my number?" she questioned playfully. "I wouldn't want to force you to take it."

"Yes, yes I do." He finally responded definitively.

At that point Jane addressed the group accepting the credit for the success of her plan, "And that …is how you do that." She declared victory.

"You weren't so sure about, 'how you do that' a few minutes ago." I pointed out.

"So, she got sneaky and made him squirm a little;" Jane justified. "It was a nicely played move by her to force him to play to his strengths…remember what I told him? '…be sweet and vulnerable yet with a touch of confidence.' The fact that she made him squirm a little only proves that she was a worthy catch, and it'll make him appreciate her even more."

Jane then took liberty to reiterate our responsibility as the group to see this operation through and directed us back to our positions. "Come on, and let's get back to them so that we can help to keep the burden off of him to carry on the conversation alone; nothing is worse than that awkward silence." So, upon her instruction we all exited the ice cream shop and as we returned to them Jane addressed them, "Well, it looks like you two are going to do okay."

"What do you know about this?" Rae asked.

"Who do you think organized all of this?" Jane explained – "Seth was so adorable with his cute, shy self - that he was too apprehensive to ask you out, so I had to make him think that I was serving *you* up to him in order to help him to feel confident – but realistically my plan was to serve *him* up to you." She explained her method of planning. "You know how guys need all the help and motivation they can get."

"Yeah, he seems to be the adorably defenseless type." Rae agreed. "I'll have to protect him."

"See," Jane confirmed with Seth, "didn't I tell you that she'd like your personality?"

"So, what exactly did you organize?" Rae inquired.

"All of this…" Jane responded proudly. "This whole atmosphere."

"You mean everyone here was in on the set up? I must admit that I'm impressed and flattered."

"Glad to see that you appreciate all of the hard work." Jane replied.

"Well… I hate to break all of this up." I interjected, "This has all been really exciting but I'm gonna need to get packing to leave tomorrow." At that, many of us finished eating our ice cream as we headed back to camp. Eventually I made it back to my cabin and began to pack. Malachi appeared at my door about a half hour later.

"Hey, where have you been? I stopped over to see you earlier." Malachi said in a jovial manner.

"I've been involved in Jane's escapades as she worked her magic - you should have seen how she set up Seth."

"What got Jane started on him?"

"Jane and I came walking out of the woods…" I explained, "… and Seth started to insinuate that we were up to something. So, Jane… being Jane, took the opportunity to turn the table on him by asking him about his infatuation with Rae in front of everyone. It was hilarious; she had the two of them dating by the end of the night."

"So, what exactly were you two doing in the woods alone together?"

"Well, if you must know… I was trying to manage Jane."

"Humph, manage Jane? Good luck with that." He muttered rhetorically. "I'm not sure how she manages herself. That girl is a wild cat."

"It's funny you'd say that she's a 'wild cat.' I just christened a nickname to describe her personality. She doesn't know it yet but after what I witnessed what she did to Seth tonight I'm gonna call her, 'Jugular Vein Jane.'"

"Well good ol' Jane has a nickname. I like it… it fits her perfectly." He approved as he redirected the conversation. "So, if you christened a nickname on her, she must have become something more tangible to you. What exactly were you two doing in the woods anyways? What were you trying to *manage* about her? What else was that girl up too?"

"No, it wasn't like that," I began to correct his insinuation. "Well, if you must know, she planned to follow you and Cammie." I answered abruptly.

"What? Following who? Me… and Cammie? What are you talking about?"

"Yes, you and Cammie." I declared unmistakenly. "As Jane figures it…she has a duty as Cammie's roommate to help protect her from unforeseen circumstances. Jane has a feminine responsibility to help protect Cammie's interests. Jane conned me into participating in a mission to follow you two by declaring that she was planning go with or without me when you two went into the woods." I explained to legitimize my reasoning for eavesdropping.

"Really, both you and Jane followed us?" he questioned as a statement. "Just how did you manage to do that?"

"After dinner Jane was already out on the balcony watching you two heading into the woods and when I came out, she suggested that we should follow you guys. I wasn't going to, but as I mentioned she insisted. She questioned if I would be okay with her knowing more than me about what's going on with you and Cammie. So I tagged along to keep an eye on her. You're not upset, are you?"

"No, I'm not upset. I'm just trying to remember what I was saying. How much did you hear?"

"Well, the truth, pretty much the whole conversation."

"Are you serious?" he sighed as he sat down covering his face with his hands and repeating, 'Jane too? Where were you? How could you be close enough to hear us without us seeing you?"

"We were on top of the rock."

"Up on top of the…" He paused as he processed my answer, "Oh… the rock! You scaled the huge boulder to spy on us?"

"That's exactly what I told Jane – that's what we were doing, was spying – but she reasoned that our act was just good investigation. I'm really sorry. Like I said, I tried to keep Jane from following you two but, as I said… knowing Jane, I figured that she was going to follow you with or without me, so I tagged along. I'm sorry. Are you sure you're not upset?"

"No, it's okay, you know I couldn't be angry with you about something like that. I mean, if I was in your place and I had a chance to follow you and Jane to see what's going on between the two of you I'm sure I'd find that prospect too alluring to pass up."

"Now what are you even talking about?" I questioned defiantly. "Jane and I are just friends." I argued dismissively.

"'Uh huh, yeah. Try to play that, 'We're just friends…' routine." he echoed as he mocked sarcastically. "Okay, you stick to your story! But must I remind you that you gave her a nickname? Giving someone a nickname puts them in a special category. Why give a nickname if you don't plan on having them around." He reasoned. "And it's funny how she continually seems to get just you two to hang out *alone* with the pretense of spying on me and Cammie. Either she must be getting under your skin or you're getting under hers…or both." He concluded.

"I told you that we're just friends." I repeated, defending my statement. "She's the kind of girl that isn't afraid to let her intentions be known. If she liked me she would have expressed it by now."

"Okay, 'you're friends'" he sarcastically repeated. "Maybe she's been dropping hints, and you just haven't been picking them up." He reasoned, "Let's see how you two, "as friends' say goodbye tomorrow."

I was about to continue to defend my position, but our conversation was disrupted when we heard Cammie pounding at Malachi's cabin door. "Malachi!" she called frantically, "Are you in there?"

"No! I'm over here at Zaylen's." He called out to her as he exited the door to meet her.

She scampered over toward my cabin and began to talk quickly as she approached him. "I'll be leaving tonight. My mom is coming to pick me up."

"What! Why, is something wrong?"

She broke eye contact with him and lowered her head shamefully muttering in a low voice as she began to explain the reason for her early departure, "I was so excited and happy about us that when I called my mom to find out what time she would be coming to pick me up tomorrow; I couldn't hide my excitement and couldn't help but to tell her about you. Instead of being happy for me she…" Cammie paused for a moment as she reestablished eye contact, I could see her eyes were filled with tears. Malachi grabbed her shoulders and encouraged her to continue.

"It's okay, go ahead…tell me."

"Well, my mom began scolding me and telling me how much of a disappointment I'll be to my family because…" embarrassed of the reason she deliberately paused once again unable to complete her sentence; instead, Malachi intuitively finished it for her.

"I think I know," he replied, dejected, "it's because I'm black. Isn't it?"

"Please don't think it's me." She pleaded. "I don't care; I just want to be with you. I just need a little time to straighten my family out. It may take a while but don't worry; I'm going to stay with you no matter what. Please understand that it's not me!"

"I do understand Cammie, don't worry, take all the time you need. As long as I know you love me, I'll be waiting. I've waited all of my life to find you; waiting a little while longer won't do much harm."

"I better go; I gotta be ready when she gets here. I promise - I'll make this up to you."

"That promise itself already makes it worth the wait."

"You're terrific." She said as she leaned forward to embrace him in one final passionate kiss. I turned away to give them some sense of privacy as they kissed farewell. "I'll always be your 'Sommer Rein.'" She declared, proudly reassuring Malachi.

As she left Malachi grunted, "M-m-m, well… if it isn't' one thing going wrong - it's another. I may as well go and pack too."

"I'm pretty much finished here. Do you need any help?"

"Yeah, sure… if you don't mind."

I accompanied Malachi back to his cabin and as we worked on packing up his things I inquired about Cammie's knowledge about her nickname in an effort to keep a positive mood. "I see that you told her what her name is, huh?"

"Yeah, I just did when we were at our rock; did you and Jane not hear that part of the conversation or did you two just do selective spying?"

"No, we didn't hear everything because I suggested that we leave when things get too intimate so we must have left before that part of your discussion – anyway it sounds like she was pleased with it."

"Yeah, she thought the comparison was cool. She calls me her 'Clifford' because everybody loves, 'The Big Red Dog' and she sleeps with him every night."

We were in the middle of arranging the furniture back to the way it was, it was then that we heard a light knock at his door.

"Just a minute," Malachi called out as he pushed the desk that was blocking the door out of the way, enabling him to get the door half-opened.

To my amazement standing at the door opening was not anyone from the camp. She proceeded to enter the room without an invitation. She was a short, small, overweight framed woman that stood before us. She was harshly aged long past her true years.

She was wearing a dated polyester flower print blouse, high-water brown slacks with black orthopedic shoes and oversized glasses on her small, wrinkled face. Her frail appearance did not match the overbearing and condescending manner with which she displayed toward others; it was apparent that she had perfected the technique of intimidation and flawlessly used that method to control a situation. Her deep unfeminine, cigarette smoke damaged voice sounded cold and ungracious.

"I'm Cammie's mother. Are you Malachi?" the woman snarled.

"Yes, I am." He responded calmly.

"I understand you have Cammie's class ring… I want it." she blurted out. He promptly took the ring off his finger and placed it in her hand. Without any cause to do so she examined it as if it had been stolen and assessed it for damage. Then she rudely returned his class ring to him in such a harsh manner that his hand lowered when she pressed it down into his hand. Then she continued, "Are you twenty-one?" the woman snarled.

"Yes."

"I'm disappointed in you. Cammie is only seventeen and has a promising life ahead of her. She doesn't know what she's doing; you should be ashamed of yourself for taking advantage of her," she scolded. "I'm taking her home," she continued her onslaught of emotionless single sentence monologue, "I don't want any attempt from you to contact her. Do you understand? I mean no contact whatsoever."

Malachi's face revealed an emotionless yet stunned dejection, and I was simply flabbergasted at the antipathy that she displayed toward him. Her intention to intimidate him was obvious as she blasted her animosity through the degrading, harsh tone in her unforgiving crotchety voice; and as a further means to inflict as much discomfort she employed another chosen weapon in her arsenal; the bitter dispassionate aura that was secreted from her menacing eyes.

I was not accustomed to seeing anyone exhibiting such contempt toward their fellow man. Having to witness this miserable demonstration directed toward my friend infuriated me; so in support of Malichi I noticeably glared back at her boldly hoping to draw her attention so that I may reciprocate her distasteful exhibition. I stood in support; behind Malachi, waiting for him to sternly retaliate. I was surprised instead to find that he had somehow remained calm, showing no evidence of escalating hostility toward this callously unpleasant woman. When he finally answered her, it was with a plain quiet declaration.

"Yes, I understand." He submissively answered.

His calmness seemed to irritate her and increased her agitation. She attempted to entice him into an oral confrontation; by using her continued relentless negative verbal barrage she attempted to lure him into saying something that she could find objectionable about him so that she could validate a confrontation with him.

"You should know better than that," she muttered in a condescending tone, as she spit out more loathsome discontent and intensified her sinister stare. Malachi remained standing as he was; firm and tall, barely moving a muscle. Then he repeated his answer, this time with a more rigid tone.

"Yes!" he replied as he closed his eyes for a brief moment, summoning more resolve of restraint before opening them with a bold look, "I understand."

She opened her mouth about to continue but it appeared all at once that she realized that her attempt to antagonize him was fruitless; her plan to incite him to argue had failed. Malachi intelligently prevented her from getting what she wanted, an argument that she could not lose. She just looked at him puzzled as he stood motionless and unflinching prepared to withstand more of her onslaught. It was obvious that she expected more of a combative dialog and evident that she wanted to say more as she opened her mouth prepared to provoke him more. Instead, dejected, and without another word she closed her mouth and quickly walked away. Only after she was out of sight did Malachi finally show any emotion as he put his head down in disgust.

"How could you put up with that?" I questioned, astounded at what had just unfolded. "I wanted to tell that woman something. I was itching to put her in her place."

"Yes, so was I," he admitted, "but even more, I didn't want to give her the satisfaction of seeing me upset. That's what she wanted. There was nothing I could have said to help the situation. She wasn't going to be receptive to anything I had to say; I can't change her mind. I only would have made things more difficult for Cammie to later defend my character, thereby making it worse for us. She was pressing for an argument that only I could lose."

"Didn't that hurt though… having her speak to you that way? She was so demeaning to you I don't think I would have been able to take it. I would have said something."

"She's Cammie's mother, and she deserved the respect of being her mom and nothing more;" he justified, "so that's all I gave her. I answered her directly, nothing rude but also nothing polite. She tried to get me to say something so that she would have a legitimate reason not to like me other than the fact that I'm of another race, and happen to be in love with her daughter, but I refused to provide her with that purpose." He reasoned.

"I understand now, but I tell you, it sure takes guts to stand in a war zone and remain calm."

"Only if you're on the outside looking in does it look impossible. When you're in the heart of the battle… you just do what's necessary to survive. People make the mistake of using desperate times for an excuse to employ desperate measures. But desperate times call for appropriate measures."

"Well, why don't we take a break and go get some milkshakes…that'll lift your spirits." I suggested, "There's no problem that a frosty black-cherry milkshake can't solve. Come on, I'm buying."

"I might as well," he agreed reluctantly, "the fresh air will do me good." So we headed down the country road to the store. I thought about the "ambiance of calm" - that a stroll down a country road brings to the spirit with the serenity of a simple symphony from livestock and wildlife sounds, and I contemplated the tranquility that the backdrop scenery of the landscape can offer the soul with its various vivid colors splashed on the countryside "painted" like a canvas.

Rather than the proverbial, "not enough time to do everything," that characterizes the hustle and bustle of city life. Time in the countryside passes by incidentally providing the opportunity for one to appreciate the simple joy of living. I remarked to Malachi how the best part of being out here is the perception of being cut off from the rest of the world and all of its complexities. The unique perspective derived from the experience of living in the country provides the clarity and a whole new appreciation as to why country living is considered the "easy" life.

"I think living in the country forces you to reflect on how you live because there is nothing else to do." He commented lightheartedly.

"Yeah, you have a point, sometimes the lack of more engaging activities leaves one to wonder how to make the best use of down time and life can become somewhat tedious but it's cool to have the time to reflect on one's awareness. The tradeoff for the quality of life is worth the price of 'tedi-ism.'"

We had reached our destination and ordered our delicious, frosty shakes. I was trying to keep the conversation light with positive things to keep his mind upbeat. "Ahh," I exhaled after swallowing my first slurp while savoring the sweet taste of my frosty beverage, "…that's good stuff. Nothing cures the soul like good ice cream."

"Yeah, I kind of understand better, now, what my parents mean by enjoying some things that make you feel like you're a kid. It's kind of cool to have comfort."

Our philosophical conversation was prematurely interrupted as Jane approached us calling out to us as she hurried toward the soda Shoppe.

"Hey guys, I've been looking all over for you. I got a message for Malachi." She explained her reasoning for her exhaustive search.

"How did you know where we were?" I inquired.

"I went over to your room to find you; that's when Seth told me that he saw you two heading this way." She recounted. "Oh, poor Malachi," she consoled as she ran up and hugged him, "I'm so sorry. I was there when her mom came - she acted so dreadfully. Cammie feels terrible that her mom is acting so stupidly." Leaning back she then cupped Malachi's chin in between her hands as if to steady his face, "You poor darling," she continued to comfort him as she began to prelude Cammie's instructions,

"She wanted to leave you with a sweet memory of her, so she came up with an idea..." Jane paused looking in my direction as if this explanation was directed to both me and Malachi. Then looking back at Malachi, she proceeded to elaborate. "Cammie asked me to do this for her... so don't get mad. Okay?" She expounded as she hesitated momentarily as she once again shifted her eyes in my direction as if to signal that the, 'don't get mad' comment was a dual message for me as well as Malachi. just before she pressed her lips onto his - kissing him enthusiastically. Stunned by her action, I momentary lapsed into a state of apoplexy; with an ever-increasing difficulty to suppress my jealous emotions.

My attention was so acutely submerged into envious thought that I found myself being deeply and intensely focused on interpreting the sensual manner in which she pressed her soft, moist, pouty lips onto his. My physical reaction was to remain incredulously silent; hopelessly mesmerized, while being intensely absorbed in my thoughts about how alluring her kiss appeared.

I jealously watched while trying to suppress my internal emotional reaction to this authentic stimulating display of affection between Malachi and Jane. When she drew back, I noticed their lips were slightly sticking together. Then as a last crushing blow to my ego Malachi licked his lips and responded with an intrinsic smile nodding his head.

"The taste of her lip gloss, huh?" - Nice touch!" He

expressed savoring the sweet taste with approval, still licking his lips. "Nice touch!"

"She put a lot of gloss on her lips and then smeared her lips onto mine to coat her signature gloss for you to taste. She wanted me to give you, *'her'* kiss," Jane explained, "you don't mind, do you? She said you wouldn't get mad."

"No, that was cool. I liked it." He answered favorably, still nodding his head pleased.

Although I was sincerely impressed by the creativity of this refreshing expression, of affection from Cammie to Malachi; I still felt an enormous sense of jealousy surging through my veins and found myself venting disapproval with a sarcastic statement by rhetorically mumbling aloud, "Now that's how you make love - out of nothing at all." She then peered over toward me as if to get a reading of my body language on how I responded to this intimate moment while relaying another verbal response prepared specifically for him as she solicited a visual confirmation from me. With an inquisitive glance and a wink she continued with her earlier style of communicating a covert dual message.

"Good, I'm glad that you're not upset." Then after making that comment, she then turned away from me and back to address him solely, "Cammie also asked me to give you her bottle of gloss and I am to remind you with her message that – 'You can't put it on that way.' whatever that means; and she also told me to give you this." She handed him a picture of Cammie – he then turned it over reading it to himself. He smiled as he shook the picture. It made a whipping sound as he grasped and flipped it between his thumb and index finger.

"This makes everything better." He announced proudly.

"Well, what does it say?" I inquired curiously.

He handed it to me and as I began to read it. Jane leaned on me - bracing her weight with her left hand on my back while she gently grabbed my arm with her right, so that she was able to peer curiously over my shoulder to see what it was that Malachi was referencing to reassure him. I then read it out loud, 'I'm so sorry – please call me tomorrow. I'll miss you, and Malachi, I really do love you. (614) 439-1902.' "Well, at least you know how she feels." I concluded encouragingly.

"She calls 'Love' the 'L' word," Malachi explained. "… she told me that she refuses to use the word because the word has been both over and misused. What makes it so special is that she made a promise to herself that she would not say it to me until she was certain that it was for real. This is the first time she told me, so, yes, I truly know how she feels and that means everything."

Malachi walked over to the bench and sat down. I remained where I was until Jane, who was still clinging to my shoulder, nudged me to move over to him. The soda shop closed at ten and we sat for a few more hours just killing time talking of how we felt about camp coming to an end.

The thing we all agreed on was similar to what Seth had cited earlier that night when he recalled the Coach's observation as being right; we had become like a family, and we were dreading the approaching end of camp. The outside world and its problems had all but disappeared for the few solitude weeks that we were at camp. And maybe this was our way of accepting the camp coming to an end; we took notice of the little time we have left and held on to the nostalgic moment as long as possible.

"You guys ready to go?" Jane finally asked as the evening slipped away into early morning.

"I guess so," Malachi sighed heavily, answering as we all stood up.

We escorted Jane back to her cabin and she bid her farewell to retire for the evening. She walked up to Malachi and patted him with a nurturing sentiment on the cheek, "Good night, Malachi, don't worry; everything will work out I promise." she reassured.

Then she turned and walked up to me and stood at arm's length. While staring me in the eyes she lightly grappled at my shirt a few times and bit down wetting her lips, "And good night, to you too… Zaylen." She purred in a drawn-out manner. I couldn't help but notice the flirtatious crackling change in her sensual feminine voice along with the deep gaze emulating through the soft glow in her exotic golden hazel eyes.

I found myself completely immersed and heavily intoxicated by the ambiance of the moment. It was then that Malachi excused himself in a noticeable fashion as he physically brushed past my shoulder, mumbling in my ear as he began to walk away.

"You still saying that 'you two are just friends'… huh?" he taunted sarcastically. "...yeah right! I think not."

"Uhh, yeah," I addressed Jane in an attempt to ignore Malachi's gesture. Fearing the consequences of mistakenly misreading Jane's intentions, I found myself trying to resist the urge to pursue her possible subtle advances. I made a decisively conscious decision to refrain from bending to Malachi's peer pressure by hastily acting intimately towards Jane prematurely. So instead, my actions remained cautiously reserved as I searched for a more assertive response from Jane's prompting to ensure an accurate and informed decision.

Although I desired more of her attention, I found myself cowering… paralyzed under the fear of rejection. She continued with a dramatic delay tactic to prolong her departure for the night by procrastinating her withdrawal. With an encouraging flirtatious glare, she responded to my inaction by smacking her lips in a disappointing manner and curling her hair with her fingers. Then she lifted her hair past her ears as a submissive invitation for me to advance.

It was then that I noticed myself speculating as to whether any gloss had been left on her lips - wanting most desperately to find out what she might taste like. At that moment, however, it became apparent that my chance was quickly waning as she repeated in a drawn out, sultry voice – "I-ya…yea, I guess I'll see you tomorrow." She expounded as she turned to withdraw to her cabin door.

I watched as she began to approach into the cabin door; her body language still enticing me to act, I however was momentarily lingering in denial – still wondering at that late moment why, all of a sudden, my mind was consumed with only the thought of her. I found myself desiring to enjoy her presence, just a little while longer – realizing, unfortunately too late, that I had failed to accurately assess the moment in a timely manner.

"Good night… Zaylen," she seemingly taunted in that prolonged crackling sensual whisper as she slowly closed the door. I was in a daze remaining frozen with uncertainty as Malachi called out to me amused.

"Come on, Zaylen," Malachi informed unsympathetically, "you missed your chance."

"What was that?' I questioned myself aloud.

"What was what?" He inquired.

"The way she said good night… did you hear that?"

"Hear what?" he smirked, "…Her saying goodnight? Of course, I heard that. She said good night to me too."

"You know what I'm talking about!" I insisted. "It was the way she said it!"

"Ahh, you're reading too much into it." he continued his act of dismissal, "Remember… 'you're just friends'… right? Or perhaps … maybe, she just gave you something to think about." He teased. "Sounds like it's going to be a long night for you as well."

"It's nice to see you enjoying yourself at my expense – I guess misery does love company."

"Yes," he continued joking at my expense, "…you're in misery – and she's the company you desire. You know it's a shame…" he continued his taunting rant, "I got action from your girl without even trying. Do you want me to describe what her kiss is like so that you know what you're missing out on? I gotta tell you, she wasn't bad, not bad at all. She had this perfect balance of soft, moist, warm…"

"Oh, stop it!" I retorted, interrupting him - pushing him off of the trail. "You just had to bring that up, didn't you?"

"My girl…sending a kiss to me, though your girl," he reminisced nostalgically "you gotta like that."

"No," I admitted defiantly. "While I appreciate the creativity, I didn't like watching it at all!"

"This hasn't been a good night for you, has it? First, you hear about your girl kissing another girl: then you watch your girl kiss another guy and then you stand idle as she says goodnight to you like that… and you do nothing about it…? He amusingly recounted at my expense – "shoot, everyone's getting action tonight…well… everyone, of course… except you. If I were in your situation, I'd be lying awake *all* night long wondering where things went wrong and contemplating just how I managed to blow a perfect opportunity."

By the time he finished with his lighthearted chastising we had arrived back at our cabins – it was then that we realized that in all of the commotion that we had forgotten to finish rearranging his room, so I helped him to get things in order before turning in for the night. As I climbed into bed the events of the day swirled in my mind. As Malachi so eloquently noted, I was left still wondering whether I should have or was expected to make an advance with Jane; eventually, I drifted off to sleep with the lingering thoughts of Jane slipping into my dreams.

After an extended morning "sleep-in" there was a lull of time as people wandered aimlessly waiting for their pickup. My parents weren't expected until around eleven which gave me plenty of time to make my rounds to say farewells to everyone. I had gone over to Malachi's cabin, but he was already up and about. I was talking to Tom when I noticed Malachi loitering behind Jane who was talking on the pay phone. I immediately said goodbye to Tom and went directly over to where they were.

"Have you called Cammie yet?" I asked.

"Yeah," he sounded dejected, "Jane is on the phone with her now."

"So, what's going on? Any good news yet?"

He shook his head sadly as he lowered it as a signaling a level of discontent as he explained the dismal predicament, "Cammie said that her whole family, not just her mother, is treating her really badly, and that for now at least she doesn't think that she can take the pressure that they're putting on her."

"You know that she wants to be with you though." I encouraged. "It isn't her preference to be away from you."

"Yeah, I - I know." He sighed. "But being away from her; still hurts."

I put my right hand on his shoulder as he dropped his head even lower. Jane had just hung up the phone and walked over to talk to Malachi. I dropped my hand from his shoulder letting it rest at my side as we both awaited the verdict. Jane remained nearby not speaking; she stood quietly waiting for Malachi to acknowledge that he was ready to hear Cammie's message. With his head in his hands, he prepared himself for the worst. Then in an instance, he raised his head as he breathed in deeply only to release a strong sigh.

"Okay… let's have it." he dictated to Jane.

"Well, her parents are giving her a real hard time." Jane explained. "The area where she's from in West Virginia is rural and no black people live there. – so by her seeing you; well…

she's become an outcast in her own family. Cammie mentioned that she may have expected something like this from her mom but it's the way her dad is treating her badly; that's what's getting to her.

She's real close to her dad and since he's turned against her, she doesn't know what to do. She needs time to get things straightened out. But more importantly she wanted to reassure you that you know that she really cares for you and promises that she'll see you as soon as she can."

"Did she say whether or not I can call her?" he inquired, searching for some evidence of solace. "How is she going to get a hold of me?"

"She mentioned that her parents are watching her real close and has even gone through her phone log. She thinks that for now it might be best for you two to keep in contact through me, but she insisted that I reassure you that she's not giving up and that she is determined to make this work. Then Jane offered the details of the plan. "Cammie has my number and address, so she'll get a hold of me, and I'll get in touch with you through Zaylen."

"Me?' I asked, surprised about my sudden involvement.

She looked at me plainly as she stated almost knowingly, "Now I know you weren't going to leave without giving me your number and address!" she retorted playfully. "That is of course, if you know what's good for you!"

"No, I'm sure that I don't want to upset you," I responded submissively.

"Do you have any idea when I'll see her again?" Malachi redirected, searching for any kind of hope.

"No, I don't know," Jane responded honestly, "I'm sorry that it won't be real soon, but it will happen. We'll help you two get through this. Cammie is determined to make this work and really wants to see you as badly as you want to see her." She positively reinforced.

Malachi shook his head acknowledging her efforts yet his body language still displayed a dejection as he turned and began to walk toward his cabin. Then, suddenly he stopped – and turned to face us.

"Please, forgive me Jane. I don't mean to seem ungrateful for what you're doing for us. It's just that I've lost a great deal lately. But I do appreciate all that you've done." he paused for a moment putting his hands in his pockets as he lowered his head with a labored smile. "Seriously, thanks for everything."

"Sure Malachi," she replied in a nurturing tone. "It's my pleasure. Just let me know if there's anything I can do," she offered caringly.

He nodded his head then turned and walked away without hesitation. Jane's new role surprised me; specifically, her seemingly endless compassion caught me off guard. Until this moment, she appeared to me to be someone who would be lost in the midst of a relationship, yet it was she who offered empathy and compassion, it was she who exhibited a proven remedy to comfort Malachi. Her no-nonsense direct intimidating approach was beautifully balanced by her to mask the sensitive refreshingly, refined femininity; from where she drew her inner strength.

"You surprise me." I addressed her, pleased with this newly unveiled discovery. "I must confess... I'm truly impressed to see this softer side of you."

"There are a lot of things you might find interesting about me – if you care to take the time. I'm a beautiful puzzle when I'm all put together, but you have to be willing to put in the time." She invited.

"That - I don't doubt." I stated emphatically.

"Well, are you going to give me your address like you promised?" she inquired, handing me a pen and paper.

I began to write my information using Jane's back as a

table, "Here's mine, and in case you need to get in touch with him directly I'm putting Malachi's with mine at the bottom."

I recognized the next car coming over the hill as being my parents. I quickly finished writing Malachi's address and began to stand up, handing Jane the paper.

"Hey, wait! Here's mine," she handed me a folded piece of paper, "and you'd better not make me wait to hear from you." She instructed.

"I will," I said taking it from her hand, "As a matter of fact, consider that there's a letter in the mail right now."

"You just make sure they keep coming." She ordered.

"I will, have a safe trip."

When I turned to walk away, she grabbed me by my arm and pulled me back. She caught me off guard and as a result I stumbled momentarily as she pulled me towards her. With her free hand she palmed the back of my head to caress me into position and then in this clumsy moment she haphazardly pressed her warm, sensual, lips firmly to mine and opened her mouth causing my lips to also instinctively separate.

Slipping her tongue across my lips she moistened mine before slowly and intentionally stiffening it into a curl as she drew it back into her mouth to accentuate her feminine appeal. She leaned back beginning to break off her kiss and released a pleasurable sigh as she purred, causing me to draw in the sweet breath of her kiss. As our lips detached a deliberate suction was created by her - which caused a slight tickling vacuum as she gently bit my bottom lip. I found myself mesmerized by the surge of emotion she was able to stir in me.

Remarkably, I subconsciously became accustomed to accepting the fact that this was just Jane's way; that is; for her to be predictably unpredictable, and I knew in an instant that I admired not only her daring style, but I also greatly enjoyed the taste of her femininity.

Although this much anticipated gesture was a simplistically brief exhibition of her affinity; I knew instantaneously that this was a defining life correction moment and undoubtedly would be etched into my memory forever. When I looked at her, I noticed that her eyes were wide and bold, yet in an almost shy manner she raised her right shoulder towards her ear as she smiled confidently saying, "That's just something that had to be done."

Pleased, I instinctively responded without thinking, "Wow...that was really nice. I wouldn't mind having a little more of that."

"Good... then you're right where I want you. Now I know that you'll be thinking of missing me too."

Still grinning she turned and dashed towards her cabin. I remained unmoving observing her until she was out of sight. Then I gathered my things and approached my parents, who were outside the car preparing to greet me.

"Who was that?" my mother asked.

"Oh, her?" I replied in a dismissive manner. "She's one of the friends Malachi and I met here. She's from Kansas U." I continued to try and downplay my familiarity with Jane by using cold facts and by volunteering nonessential information hoping my parents hadn't witnessed the two of us kissing.

"She must be a pretty close friend..." my mom smirked as she ran her hand through my hair. "... and cute too."

I didn't want to have that, 'relationship' discussion with my parents, especially my mother, she always made a big deal if she saw me kiss a girl. Fortunately, my father came to my rescue.

"Leave the boy alone, Krysta," he commanded as he winked at me. "If he says she's just a friend; then she's just a friend."

I looked at him without saying a word, and thanked him

with a smile, and then I used the opportunity to change the subject.

"Well, can someone 'pop' the hatch so that I can load my bags?" I suggested. As my dad and I retrieved the bags my mother pushed the button to open the latch and after loading the bags in the car we headed for home.

I had a surreal observation; upon returning home. I noticed that there is a need for a mental transition adjustment period from the "ever-fun, never a dull minute" experience of being able to hang out with your friends at college and camp, "twenty-four seven" only to then be faced back to the dull routine of home life.

I was kept in the loop of the developments of Malachi and Cammie's situation. It was sobering to observe the disintegration of their bond as the days and weeks soon turned into months. As hopes of Malachi and Cammie's relationship waned my relationship with Jane flourished.

Sadly, Cammie had been unable to convince her family to accept Malachi as being the 'love of her life' and additionally found herself incapable of withstanding her family's pressure to end the relationship. It was nearing a year when plans were finally made for them to see each other one more time.

They had planned to meet back at Camp Muskingum in late May. Jane decided to come along with Cammie while I accompanied Malachi. This managed to serve two purposes; they wouldn't have to travel alone, and it provided Jane and I with the opportunity to support them while we enjoy getting together again. Malachi was quiet for most of the trip. I figured that he was concentrating on what he wanted to say to Cammie. So instead of talking we listened to the radio. It didn't seem to take that long before we reached the camp. When we arrived it was a little before six o'clock and I rolled the car to a stop near the office building.

"The place hasn't changed, has it? I mean it's as if the

setting of the camp projects a mood that seems to steal you away from reality." Malachi mumbled as if to imply that as long as we're here in this quiet place - and being protected from the chaotic outside world, things make sense.

"You're right, things haven't changed much," I concurred. "It does seem lonelier though, more tranquil."

A few seconds later an elderly gentleman came out of the office smiling. "Hello, are you boys lost?"

"Hi," I responded, "Uhh, no not really," I explained, "we're supposed to meet some people here."

"The camp is officially closed but as long as you promise not to make any trouble I don't mind."

"Oh, no sir, we have no intentions of causing trouble. You see, we were here for the hurdle camp last year and we kind of missed the place."

"These people you're waitin' for – are they from the same camp too?"

"Yeah, we're kind of having a reunion."

"Well, okay, just let me know when you plan on leaving so that I know everything is all right. If I'm not here, I'll be at the old house over there," he pointed, "Okay?"

"Okay, thanks."

As he walked back into the office Malachi, and I got out of the car, and I sat on the hood as he began to fidget with his clothes. I could tell that he was unnerved so I attempted to calm him. "Relax Malachi, you look fine. Besides, you know it won't matter to Cammie." Shaking his head in agreement, he stopped messing around with his clothes and sat beside me on the hood.

Soon the sun began to set behind the high hillside. The sky was cloudless and not much wind to speak of. After a few minutes Malachi grew worriedly impatient.

"Are you sure we were supposed to be here at six o'clock? Do you realize that it's ten after?"

"Be patient, they'll be here." I reassured in an uneventful tone.

A few minutes later we heard their car coming towards us. Cammie was driving and Jane accompanied her riding in the passenger side. She pulled behind my car and got out. When I first laid eyes on Jane the first thing that came to mind was my mother's comment, 'She's cute!' She dressed the cute part perfectly; she wore hiking boots with faded jeans that lined the contours of her hip and thighs and a soft looking white cotton button-down blouse with the top two buttons tastefully undone exposing a moss green lace cami; to complete her outfit.

Cammie was wearing a light green western style button down shirt with dark blue, flare style jeans complete with a silver, oval belt buckle with gold letter "C" and her signature cowgirl boots. Her eyes partially absorbed the shade of the shirt making the hue of them appear to be floating the color of the Caribbean Ocean, transparent marine blue. She wore her hair feathered as the long ends draped over her shoulder.

Smiling; she delivered a warmth that rivaled the sun. Her beauty was unmatched and her magic real. I contemplated that somehow my friend was supposed to summon the courage to let her go.

"Hi," Cammie said in an uneasy manner as she approached Malachi.

"Hi," he responded in like manner as they embraced.

"It's so great to see you again," she welcomed him.

"It's nice to see you too."

As they took a step back from each other, he grazed his eyes over her appearance then back at her mischievously. She peered back at him while raising her eyes.

"What?" she asked, questioning his stare.

"Nothing," he replied, looking away still smiling.

"Come on, tell me." She said as she poked him gently on the side of his abdomen.

"I was just thinking of how you looked better than I remembered."

She looked at him shyly as her smile grew bigger exposing her irresistible dimples, "That's sweet."

"It's simply the truth," he replied then continued. "I'm relieved that I finally get to see you again; it's been such a long time."

"I'm sorry I had to wait so long but you did know that I wanted to see you... didn't you?"

"I was pretty sure, but I did have my moments of doubt."

"Yeah, I understand and I'm sorry that I couldn't talk to you on the phone, but it did make things easier for me."

"There's no reason to apologize, we're here together now... that's all that matters."

She stood looking at him nodding her head as she reached into her purse, pulling out her gloss. She showed it to him, waving it once near his face, teasing him. Then she opened it and put some on her lips.

"Still hooked on that stuff, huh?"

"Of course," she confessed playfully, "you know it's my life."

They were silent for a few moments as Malachi stared at her shiny lips with an eager look. His cheerful disposition slowly dissolved into one of concern as his smile dwindled. Reality must have set in to his cognitive reasoning as he realized that the time of their visit was limited.

"Well...we don't have long, and we are here for a reason," he solemnly sighed.

"Yes, we are," she answered as she lowered her head.

"We'll see you guys later." Malachi said as they began walking down the same path that they had the year before. At that time Jane turned towards me.

"Well," she questioned, grabbing hold of my arm as she brushed her body against me, "we have some time to burn… what kind of trouble you think we can get into?" she invited.

I looked at her smiling, figuring that I'd get one step ahead of her in an attempt to show off my new 'bad boy' image. I shrugged my shoulders saying, "Follow them as usual, what else?"

"Follow them?" she questioned, astonished. "I came to see you. We have our own catching up to do. Besides, don't you think that they may need their privacy? Things just might get a little too personal, 'Mr. Goody two-shoes'" she scolded.

"I came to see you too, but don't you realize how important this is? It'll be helpful for me to know what's going on." I explained while assuring, "We'll still have plenty of time to talk, but right now this is crucial. I can't explain the importance now; just please, try to understand."

"Do you promise that we'll have time to talk later?" she bargained.

"Scout's honor." I pledged, holding my two fingers up.

"Were you ever a scout?"

"No, but what's that got to do with it?"

"Nothing, I guess. Except that I'm not sure I can accept that as a true promise unless you were." she reasoned.

"Oh, come on." I said as I grabbed her hand in tow.

We walked down the trail continuing to hold hands. Since we were sure of where they were going, we followed them by a sizable distance. We still had to take care and watch closely to where the trail was leading and walk quietly because it was growing increasingly difficult to see the path – due to the setting of the sun. Jane continued to interrogate me as we made our way through the brush.

"Hey Zaylen," she whispered. "…did you miss me?"

"Huh?" I questioned not paying full attention. "Yes, of course I did."

"Good." She praised as she smacked my butt.

"What do you mean good...?" In mid-sentence I stopped talking because I realized that we had almost arrived at our destination. Jane hadn't yet realized how close we were and so she was still expecting to carry on a conversation.

"What?" she questioned. "I couldn't hear yo..."

"Shh," I cautioned. "We're here…they're right up ahead. We'll talk about this later, okay?" I turned to face her, "For now, we start to climb…"

She released my hand and grabbed my face on either side and leaned forward to kiss me. I instinctively grabbed hold of her shoulders and pulled her close as she sighed out a quiet satisfying moan; she had moistened my lips with her tongue and as a sensual gesture I licked my lips expressing approval of her taste then she pulled back looking square into my eyes as she explained.

"Now, we can start to climb. If you're going to take over command of our mission; you have to give your trooper, the proper motivation." She smiled pleasingly.

I conceded, nodding my head, "Point well made." I acknowledged. Then we began to scale the boulder. Because of nightfall it was a little more difficult to climb because we couldn't rely on our vision; rather, we had to anticipate where the bulges were on the rock. Although I could hear that the two were conversating I was barely able to make out what Malachi and Cammie were saying.

"Come on, tell me," I heard Cammie stating

commandingly as it sounded like she was playfully hitting him. "What makes you happy… besides being with me? I'm trying to get to know more about you… you didn't answer that question last time we were here, but you're going to this time."

"All right, I'll tell you. There's no reason to get vicious. The thing that makes me happy is being surprised."

"What kind of surprise?" she inquired for details.

"Pleasant surprises. Like when I got the news that I was going to see you. I like the kind of surprise that I can treasure for a lifetime… I'm still waiting for that miracle surprise."

"What might that be?"

"The one that says you'll stay…"

By that time, we had reached the top of the rock and had assumed the same positions that we had a year before, with Jane lying to my left. We had returned to the place where it had all begun and we were there for the same reason but because it was night, the scenery was much different.

As I turned to lie on my back, the dome shape of heaven immediately caught my attention. The trees appeared as black shadows against the bluish white western sunset. Directly overhead, the stars that were already visible continued to illuminate brighter as many others began to appear in the blackening eastern sky.

For an instant a silent spark traveled a short distance with its glittering tail disappearing in that same instant. I breathed in quickly which created a quiet sighing noise reacting in amazement of what I saw. I pointed upward to draw Jane's attention, but it was too late…the sparkling tail vanished instantaneously. There was no trace of a breeze; the cool air around my face was calm, yet the lake still had a voice as its waves with a soothing rhythm smacked against the bank.

"I can't get over how nice it is to finally see you again," I heard Malachi speaking in a soft voice. "I know for certain now that my feelings for you have not diminished – and yet, I'm still reluctant to show you just how grateful I am to see you - because you're going to be gone soon."

"I know … I feel the same way. I want to touch you but I'm afraid that if I do – it'll be the last time that I feel alive. When you touch me it's as if you're touching my heart. It's been a long time since my heart felt as if it had life.

Seeing you brings tranquility to my soul." She compelled. "I know I'll never be able to explain your impact on me, the important thing is that I've only felt that touch from you, and no other feelings have come close to making me that happy."

"You know, Cammie; you have a gift for capturing the moment."

There was silence for a few moments broken momentarily by a sigh as Malachi stumbled to say something. He would say a few words then stop seemingly deciding against speaking. He would start to speak, then stop, only to then start over again. I rolled over and crawled to the edge of the boulder, inching ever so slowly to remain as quiet as possible to see what was going on. At last, I could see them in the clearing below observing that they were facing each other as they stood apart.

"What is it Malachi?" Cammie asked. "Come on now, if you said it once, you've already said it a thousand times in your head. So, whatever it is - you might as well just tell me."

"Okay," he sighed profoundly. "I was just wondering… What do we do now? What happens to us?"

Cammie paused for a moment as she looked away from him and toward the ground, "You know how I feel. It's just that I can't take this. Don't you understand? Don't you know what my parents put me through?"

"Yeah…" Malachi moaned intensely as his words dragged out. "…I do." Cammie walked away from him and stood with her arms folded and her back towards him. Malachi stood close behind her as he spoke again. "What?" What did I do?"

"You're just saying that" she spoke pouting with a shaking voice. "You're patronizing me; you don't really understand what they're putting me through. They're ripping my heart out of my chest by forcing me to give you up…and I just don't know how to do this without their support. I wish to God I knew how to survive on my own, but I don't, I'm so afraid… I don't have your strong independent spirit."

"No, I'm not being patronizing," he reassured as he put his hand on her shoulder. "I really do understand. I didn't mean to sound sarcastic but the reason it sounded that way is because I do very much understand; I just don't want to believe that I have to lose you in order to make things right for you.

I know that you want to be with me, and I realize that you don't entirely understand why we can't stay together. And it's then I see you punishing yourself for hurting me. But what you need to understand is; I'm not hurting because of you…" he explained passionately. "I'm hurting without you."

"I'm sorry!" she whimpered. I could hear the cry in her voice as she turned, facing him. She put her arms around his neck as she pressed her forehead into his chest. "I want to be with you more than anything, but I have no choice… please forgive me."

"A lot of things have happened," he qualified definitely. "But nothing has changed. I still love you; and no matter what happens, I'll always be faithful to you."

"I really mean that much to you?" she asked.

"Saying how I feel isn't near enough for me to show you the genuine devotion I have for you; and yet of all the many ways I wish I had at my disposal; what I say and how I say it at this moment are all I have to rely on. Since the first time we kissed, my life has been laser focused about thoughts of you.

But I fear that after tonight my heart will be forever changed – and emptied of all hope.

Sadly, I realize that there is nothing I can do to stop it. I wanted lots of things in my life; but until now I never *needed* anything until you came into my life. Now my heart aches with so much despair that it would be a relief, and it would be more favorable and humane for me to perish than to be forced to live without you...."

"How can one thing keep us from having it all?" she protested. "This isn't fair!" she lamented with a downcast expression as she buried her face in her hands. "If my parents only knew how happy I am with you – if they only knew how you've touched my heart; things might be different."

A long hesitation followed as he stood arm's length away resting his hands on her shoulder. Then with his right hand he wiped a tear from underneath his eye. Cammie raised her head with her eyes widened like a child as she intently focused on his face. Malachi beckoned in dramatic fashion drawing her intense attention as he spoke in a lowered voice.

"Cammie," he instructed. "We can no longer focus on wondering how good things might have been or to speculate any longer as to what went wrong. We have to turn our attention to deal with where we are now and accept what we must do. The hardest thing for me to do is to let you go, but I have to, for your sake. I had to realize that the *act* of love is giving sometimes through magnificent loss ... but love is not taking; so ... in the spirit of an expression of my devotion to you – I volunteer to surrender our relationship and give you back to your parents by I'm taking myself away," he stated boldly with an obvious saddening pitch in his voice.

This intense statement was perhaps the best tangible exemplar of unselfishness. It was a powerful expression of true self-sacrifice in the interest of love. It was a fascinating moment to witness him orchestrating this well controlled and premeditated suicide to their future; the words on his tongue were a fatal weapon against optimism, acting to simulate the lethal effects of a cyanide pill that act to destroy any hope, and effectively etch the moment and manner of the demise to their relationship.

Cammie pulled Malachi into her embrace as they held onto each other as if nothing could come between them. I could hear her whimpering reflecting the uncertainty that swirled around them and I empathized dearly. It was an exceptionally heart wrenching tender moment to see such genuinely nice people be so devastatingly discouraged.

It didn't take long for the visual evidence to prove that I was emotionally compromised. I was swept up in the moment as I felt my face warming with my own tears surfacing to stream down my face. I peered in the direction of Jane as I tried in vain to wipe my face dry before she saw me, but her eyes looked directly into mine just as more tears developed. I was relieved, however, to find that she echoed similar sentiments as I witnessed tears trickling from her glossy eyes. When her eyelids closed, I noticed her body shaking, so I extended my left arm and grasped her soft warm hand tightly. Quickly she opened her eyes, and I bit my bottom lip as I nodded my head in a comforting manner.

Then I heard Cammie's soft and solemn voice attempting to revive some remnant of hope, "Someday," she declared, "I promise – I will be back. I don't care how long it takes… when the time is right, we will have each other again."

"I have something for you," Malachi said as he took a piece of paper from his pocket. "I prayed I would have the chance to give it to you in person.

"What is this?" she questioned as he handed her an envelope.

"It's a poem that I wrote for you." He explained.

"Would you mind reading it to me?" she asked in a loving style.

"I don't think so," He explained, denying her request. "I write better than I recite."

"I don't care… I want to hear the words from your voice. I want to be able to remember how it sounded coming from you."

"Okay," he conceded… "here goes nothing as he began, 'Promise of a Lifetime.'" He precluded as he prepared to recite.

Love…

That enchanting serenade –

The melody I longed to hear resonating within my ears

That coveted chorus you vowed never to sing

Until for you… it became ultimately true –

In an instant, your words became… my, "moment of a lifetime."

Never before were such sweet lyrics ever composed;

Then of that delightfully and heavenly declaration

of your soul devotion to me…

And I believed in you – In that one moment…

for an enduring lifetime.

Echoed from that pledge was a reciprocal commitment of all I am,

A dedication of all I would ever be -

A promise that was intended to harmonize our lives

from that very moment…

and intended to extend - into a lifetime.

Alas.

I failed to foresee life's tragic intervening influence …

I hadn't anticipated that meddling power that was to prey upon our love

I was blind to the force which would compel a ghastly
appeal from you;

of beseeching such a dreadful request for the abandonment of
our future.

And to dismiss our life of bliss -

Not for a single moment… not in this lifetime.

Now -

– Tormented forever by the Want of your charm,

I am remanded to a life of solitude -

Confined to suffer; secluded to contemplate the loss,

Every moment… for a lifetime.

And now…resigned with the hopelessness of craving to be in
your arms -

I would eagerly, and with willful contempt - forfeit…

for a single moment…

a lifetime.

In an instance a single thought raced through my head, as
I was impressed how the poem was able to capture the essence
of a tragic moment in such a profound, yet simple way. I
watched those words systematically break Cammie's spirit
causing her to weep. When he had finished, she crossed her
hands around the back of his neck as she pulled him toward
her, and they began to kiss. I turned to Jane who also had been
watching, as I whispered. "I've heard enough. I don't need to
hear anymore."

"I don't either," she whimpered as tears continued to roll
from her glossy golden hazel eyes.

We climbed down the boulder as quietly as possible
and headed for the cars. When we emerged from the forest a
few yards from the cars Jane stopped and kept her head down

trying to hide her eyes. I gently turned her body to face me as I felt a tear trickling down my cheek. I quickly wiped it away then raised her head with my hand underneath her chin so that I could look at her.

"What's wrong with this world?" she voiced her objection of how the world's philosophy can be hurtful. "Why does the world reject good things so often?" She questioned as we singularly struggled to make sense of what we had witnessed.

"I don't know," I answered as I pulled her close to my body, "This makes no sense."

We stood there motionless for a while longer not speaking. Her head was resting on my shoulder, and I could feel her warm tears roll down my arm. I tried to keep my tears from falling once they had built up in my eyes, but again my effort was futile. Finally, after a few minutes I was able to gather enough composure to talk to her.

"Are you alright?"

"Yes, I'm okay, it's just that this kind of stuff doesn't usually get to me." she spoke still struggling to gain her composure as more tears rolled quickly down her cheeks.

"I'm sorry that we didn't have a chance to talk."

"That's okay, I understand now; we can talk another time. But promise me that this isn't going to happen to us."

"I promise, and next time; it's just you and me." I reassured, and as we embraced to console one another, it started me thinking of how good it felt having her looking after my well-being.

We turned as we heard them coming out of the woods. A few seconds later we could see them. When they were a few feet from us they stopped.

"You guys, okay?" I asked.

"Yeah, we're all right." Malachi answered.

We all walked silently together as couples the rest of the way to the cars, with each perspective pair joined by the hands. Malachi and Cammie stood on the opposite side of the car while I assisted Jane with her door. In a swift unrehearsed motion, she spontaneously grabbed my jaw, turning my head towards her and clumsily pressed her lips against mine.

Still unsure of how I might react, she hastily pulled away and gazed into my eyes searching for approval as she declared in a sultry drawn-out tone, "Ah…I'm so-o gonna miss you." Then without waiting for a response from me, she stood on her tiptoes and tightly grasped the collar of my shirt to pull my head downward. In that same instance she thrust her body firmly into me, pressing her soft, warm, lips to mine. This time I responded favorably by reaching my arms around her hourglass figure and lifting her body into me with a firm masculine embrace.

At this point I took special notice of her voluptuous feminine contours as our bodies meshed together. Her soothing lips separated slightly allowing me to inhale her warm breath as we caressed. I realized at that moment that the perfectly blended fragrance she adorned would act as a robust olfactory imprint to my future memory. Momentarily she gently bit down on my bottom lip, as she released a sigh of satisfaction.

"Mmm…" she hummed with a pleasing satisfaction. "Now… I'm okay with 'us';" she cooed, flipping the collar of my shirt with her thumbs, "From now on, I want this to be my safe place from this crazy world."

I was amazed at how wonderfully comfortable and willing I was to accept this new role as *her* protector. This strong, independent, feminine personality chose to seek refuge in my arms. I felt very privileged to learn that I had earned the envious honor of shielding the infamous, Jugular Vein Jain from the pains of this world.

While we were still in each other's arms she leaned back

slightly and intently gazed at me with her shimmering hazel eyes. "Remember …" she whispered as I felt her sweet breath brush past my face, "you promised; next time… just you … and me."

"I promise," I replied smiling.

We embraced a while longer staring into each other's eyes, it was an awesome moment to experience the extension of our rapidly maturing emotional closeness in such a physical way.

"So… what are you thinking?" she questioned intuitively as she shifted her eyes from side-to-side gazing ominously into each of mine searching to read my thoughts.

"I was just thinking about my desire to savor this wonderfully expressive time that I have with you."

"Good boy! That's what I wanted to hear." She answered with a beaming, sensual grin. Then with a quick kiss she lowered herself into the car. I shut the car door then kissed her one last time through the opening in the window. "I'll be thinking about you sweetie." She assured me while stroking my cheek with her soft warm hand.

"Rest assured you're permanently etched on my mind." I responded. "See you soon." I began to walk to my car; it was then, I noticed that neither Malachi nor Cammie was smiling while they said goodbye to one another.

"You'll always be my first," I heard Cammie saying as she leaned forward on her tiptoes to kiss him one last time. She then got into the car and drove away while Malachi stood motionless watching. His frustration was elevated but he maintained his composure as he approached our car.

"This sucks!" he blatantly expressed his disbelief, shaking his head as the girls rolled out of sight. "How do you just accept something that is not right?" he inquired rhetorically.

"Hey man, you're tough." I encouraged. "I know that this is hard but remember where your hope rests. It's not that God won't give you more than You can handle – rather he'll never give you more than HE can handle. Just keep in mind that I know our friendship is not the relationship you want but for now, I am here for you. I have plans for us to do fun things together to keep you from dwelling on this. I know that all this is devastating but you don't have to go through this alone; and I don't intend to let you."

"Thanks," he acknowledged. "I know that I'm going to survive this; mainly… because I have no choice - but life has certainly lost its luster."

It was difficult for Malachi to accept but he understood the difficult dilemma that Cammie found herself. She desperately wanted to follow the desire of her heart to be with him, but she had a fear of abandonment that had been instilled in her from her childhood.

Her fear was that if she made the choice to ever discard her family's belief system and try to stand alone to rely on her own intellect that she ran the real risk of living her life in isolation. As a result, Cammie made the desperate attempt to honor her parents' wishes and move on. She pressed on trying to accept the belief that it was just their loving way of protecting her.

Eventually it became apparent that she was unable to dismiss the yearning of the committed relationship that she had for Malachi. Her parents were incapable of being a viable substitution for the kind of relationship Cammie yearned for. Additionally, it became obvious that she would be unable to foster a meaningful romantic relationship with someone else while comparing others to the high standard she had become accustomed to with Malachi. Malachi's genuine demeanor had become the towering benchmark for her expectations.

In realizing this, she finally decided to desert her family's influence and to commit herself fully to Malachi and to their relationship. She re-engaged their communication, and they made a plan to meet at the Ohio Capitol building with the renewed promise of the prospect for them to begin their life as a couple. Jane and I wanted to show support for their endeavor, so we included ourselves with their travel plans.

Malachi had arranged a rendezvous with Cammie to coincide with the arrival time of me and Jane who were coming into the airport from a trip. The coordinated arrangement was for Cammie to meet Malachi on the south side of the Statehouse in Columbus that same day. It was convenient because I was returning home from Kanas with Jane after I had finally met Jane's parents, and she was returning with me to meet mine. She was scheduled to stay overnight and fly back the next day.

It was late evening when Malachi picked us up. I recall thinking of how we were back in the slow-moving rainstorm that was responsible for the torrential downpour in the Midwest the previous day. When we arrived at the Statehouse, Jane and I sat waiting patiently in the car listening to the radio while Malachi went up the stairs to anxiously wait for Cammie's arrival in a visible position by the tall, majestic columns.

Surprisingly, Jane and I never discussed the matter of 'the kiss' that happened between Malachi and Jane at camp. I figured that since we were in a wait and see situation, I would decide to use this downtime as the opportunity to finally inquire about the pressing matter of "the kiss."

"Now that we're alone…" I prefaced. "I've been wondering about something for a while… but didn't know how to bring it up." I started in a nonchalant manner.

"O-kaayy?" Jane acknowledged, waiting inquisitively for me to continue.

"I just gotta ask once and for all…what's the real scoop on that kiss you gave to Malachi?"

"The kiss? …with… Mala…the…What?" she

questioned, astonished and confused as she was caught off guard and unaware of what I was asking - then suddenly her face lit up as it became apparent that she realized what it was that I was inquiring about. Then she chuckled dumbfounded as she besieged me with a barrage of questions. "Really?!! Are you serious? You're bringing that up now? That was months ago. Actually, over a year…what makes you want to bring that up now?"

"It's been burning in my brain, and I've been curious about the evolution of the conversation that materialized between the two of you girls. When I tried to reason the logistics of what transpired I get lost on trying to dissect and understand what could have prompted Cammie to think of coaxing you into allowing her to press her glossy lips onto yours so that effectively through your lips, a kiss would be directly delivered from her to Malachi.

I've also been wondering what resistance, if any, you put up regarding her audacious request. Did she give you stipulation on how and how long to kiss Malachi? Did you like kissing him? I'd like to know the whole premise of your mission."

"Boy, that sure is a lot of questions…" she observed. "…and the tone…oh, wow!" She announced defensively. "So… this is to be an interrogation huh?" she questioned defiantly. "If I'm gonna be ordered to answer under oath maybe I should just provide you with my name, my rank, and my serial number; maybe I should withhold crucial, 'need to know information' to see if you have the skill to coax the mission parameters out of me. Hump…" she rhetorically contemplated, "if I play my cards right… this just might turn out to be fun."

"Come on Jane; just tell me." I pleaded for an answer. "I've been wondering about this for a while." I admitted. But rather than simply complying to my reasonable request, Jane instead went into character to 'roleplay' as a super spy who was being interrogated.

"I know who you are!" She bobbed her head with an attitude as began her defiant monologue. "You're that famous hostile investigator alias, 'R. Maberi!' The 'R' stands for 'Ruthless.' You're known for extracting the most sensitive Intel from the best spies in the business. But you don't realize who you're dealing with this time… Ruthless Maberi! I'm the wildcat known as Juglar Vein Jane… super spy… Code name…Kenny Kid – 7, alias J.J.

Yes, I admit…that you have accomplished what many men and a few women have tried unsuccessfully to do," she playfully referred to the attempts that others have tried at dating her. "You have finally captured the infamous, master spy 'Jugular Vein Jane.' Wanted worldwide for being a slayer of both Men and Hurdles." She playfully declared continuing to divulge her nefarious resume. Born into an espionage agency that has been around since July 22, 1956.

My superior officer, "Killer Cammie" sent me on a suicide mission, code name, 'Double Tap Romance,' the mission parameters had two objectives, first to deliver a coded message to agent 11-11-11 code name Malach1…and second, to gain intel on the famed R. Maberi yes that's right you were a residual secondary target. But I was sworn to never divulge the details of the mission…" Jane declared while remaining in character as the defiant captured 'super spy.'

"I'm bound by the agency to the female code to secure the feminine secrets from the opposite sex to my death." She scripted; then she continued in dramatic style. "So, go ahead… and restrain me so that I can't protect myself; and do your naughty deed and torture the information out of me with extreme prejudice… that is…if you dare try…but I warn you, - I'm a highly trained special agent… an expert in withstanding the most hostile tactics. So… do what you will – but I warn you…you'll just be wasting your time because… I'll never tell!"

"Jane…" I said calmly with no expression on my face to downplay her theatrics and to emphasize that I had any interest in playing along in her charade. Then I gave her an exhausted, silent stare. I figured that those measures would be enough to get her to stop "acting" in her melodramatic fantasy, but my attempt to bring her back to reality was in vain as Jane continued to escalate her role play.

"Ahh, trying the calm subtle approach instead, huh? "She conceded sarcastically, "Seduction is going to be your method of choice to extract the sensitive, 'Need to know' Intel, eh? Well played, my sinister Nemesis! Well played! My intense training did not anticipate an ecstasy type of interrogation from such a hot guy.

I concede to you that - that tactic might very well work to your advantage and yield some favorable results. Of course, you'll still have to find the right buttons to push." She encouraged me. "So… go ahead I'm ready… start your dark deed – tie me to the steering wheel…and render me vulnerable," she submitted with a menacing smirk, then raising her backside toward me in a sensual manner she suggested, "…and be gentle… or *not!*"

"Jane!" I shouted in a scolding tone.

"Well, alright," she reluctantly relinquished her spy act expressing her discontentment of being dejected that I was not playing along, "You're no fun," she retorted, "You know this role playing could have benefited both of us. But if you want to be a boring 'tarty tart' I'll just tell you what you want to know. If you're really interested in what happened… like I said… there was a dual purpose. It was Cammie's idea for me to kiss Malachi to use it as a ploy to make you jealous."

"Say what?" I questioned, baffled. "To make me jealous? I don't understand. You're telling me that you two, came up with a plan… and the genius of that plan was for you to kiss Malachi, her boyfriend…in order to make me jealous? That seems a little overly ambitious don't you think? Where did that idea even come from?"

"Cammie had been writing a story and in the story the girl uses her friend as a maneuver to make the guy who she's interested in jealous. Then, once he gets jealous, he realizes that he wants to date her and so it prompts him to act. She was pretty sure that you liked me and thought that you were moving too slowly, and she wanted to see if her theory would work in real life."

"Are you serious? You two made an act of a romantic gesture for Malachi to use as a ploy to use me as a guinea pig to prove some theory? You kissed him? Just to prove a theory?"

"Well… not entirely, you're still looking at it too one dimensional." She explained. "You just happen to be the perfect candidate to test. Originally, she suggested that I use my fingers to put the gloss onto his lips. The "lip gloss kiss" became an innovative concept. Cammie was insistent about really wanting to do something sweet for Malachi, so she proposed having me spread some gloss onto his lips with my finger. I was to then give him the message that 'he couldn't put it on that way.' By the way…I still don't know what that statement means, it's some inside joke between the two of them.

But just after she gave me those instructions, I could tell that she got some kind of creative idea because she got this big smile on her face. I could tell that she was thinking of something cunning when she actually said out loud to herself that, 'he really isn't allowed to put it on that way.'

At that point she asked me if I wanted to kill two birds with one stone. When I asked her what she meant, she asked me if I liked you and whether I'd like to do something to speed up your approach. Then she proceeded to tell me about her plan to get you motivated, using a kiss.

At first, I was kind of reluctant about allowing her to put her lips on mine - but she was persistent with her request and adamant about the necessity of my role to deliver the perfect message to Malachi. That was the proverbial one bird; the second bird, she insisted, was that the plan would work to get you motivated to show that you're interested in me.

Since my style is being wild and unpredictable, I eventually reasoned that a little risqué action is actually right up my alley. Besides, I'm also a sucker for cool romantic things and she did a good job of dangling the right incentive, which was you. So eventually I conceded and volunteered my services. So… as you see, it was for all three things, it was for Cammie to send her message to Malachi, it was to benefit us, by getting you motivated, and finally to check a theory for her story."

"Wow," I said bewildered, "no wonder they say women are complicated."

"Well, since you brought it up, tell me for posterity… did it make you jealous? As I recall, you looked kind of uneasy and uncomfortable when I kissed Malachi. I was a little disappointed because I actually thought for a moment that the plan was going to make you burst out of your skin but then when you had a chance to let me know how you felt when you dropped me off at my cabin, you didn't' kiss me that night; but certainly the way you're acting now seems to confirm that our experiment was a total success."

"Well…" I hesitated and hung my head down. I waivered still trying to think of a way to deny that their strategy was an achievement. I was hesitant to admit that their cunning plan worked because I didn't want to give them credit for having been able to manipulate me the way she had done to Seth back at camp.

"Come on now, be honest …this is for research." She coaxed.

"Well, yes I was jealous," I declared shamelessly as I embraced recalling my thoughts at that moment. "I even noticed your lips sticking together after you pulled away."

"Wow! You really have been thinking about this; haven't you? So, why didn't you kiss me that night?" she questioned as she lightheartedly hit me with each word that she recalled. "I wanted so badly for you to take control… you had me lying awake all that night wondering if you liked me and then even the next day you made me make the first move!"

"Hey, watch it!" I retorted, throwing my hands in front of me attempting to defend myself from her onslaught. Then I began to explain. "I was left thinking about you too. I was miserable all that night after you went into your room - and believe me, Malachi wasn't much help of a consoling friend. He actually used your kiss to taunt me for not making a move on you! And besides, you gotta admit that your unpredictability can be a little intimidating; I was afraid that if I made a move on you and it turned out that you didn't like me that you might beat me up… like you're doing now."

"Ohh, you so-o-o owe me…" she warned, hugging and kissing me on the cheek. "I sent so many signals to you that night, almost begging for you to kiss me. I can't believe you made me wonder what I did wrong that whole night."

"Isn't it all that matters…" I attempted to trivialize my procrastination, "- is that we're together now?"

"Sure, that's what you want me to believe, but what also matters; is how we got together."

"Well, how about calling it, "The Night We Didn't Get Together?" That makes it cool because most people don't have that kind of story and think about how special it is that we were both thinking about each other."

"Really? Is that where we're going with? Is that what we're doing now?" She retorted. "You're condoning how much of a brat you were for making me wait and you want to make the excuse for your inaction as a romantic story that we, 'Didn't get to together?' That's creative and I'll give you points for that, but you still owe me for making me make the move!"

"Okay," I conceded, "I'll owe yo..." I stopped mid-sentence as something in the rearview mirror caught my attention. I noticed a lady crossing the street who appeared to look much like Cammie's mother. I was puzzled as to why she would be at the rendezvous point, and I turned to look behind me as I rolled down the window to clear my view of the raindrops. That enabled me to verify that it was in fact her mother.

She continued to walk directly towards Malachi who saw her approaching and was displaying a look of disbelief; possibly fear that he thought that the mother must be coming in place of Cammie. This occurrence had drawn my focus away from our conversation and as I began to fidget – Jane expressed curiosity about what had preoccupied my attention from her.

"What? What's going on?" she inquired about the reasoning of my abrupt distraction from our conversation.

"Uhh, I don't know...." I answered, opening the door. Then, while qualifying my suspicious reaction I explained, "... but it looks like Cammie's mom is here."

"What? Cammie's mom? What's she doing here?" she responded rhetorically as she turned to look for herself. "Where's Cammie; is she possibly here with her mom?"

"I don't know; wait here; I'm gonna go find out."

I rolled the window back up to protect the inside from the rain then I emerged from the car so that I could see everything that was happening. I shielded my body from the cold elements by zipping up my cycling rain jacket while raising the hood to cover my head. I stood near the trunk of the car and waited for traffic to pass so that I could cross to get a better vantage point to determine what was transpiring. Since I didn't see Cammie accompanying her mother, I began to prepare myself to lend support to Malachi. I suspected a devastating blow to Malachi's disappointment that we would probably be headed for home without the company of Cammie.

Within a few moments however, I noticed a car in the distance turning out of traffic and toward the curb coming to a parked position. The taxi – driver was honking the horn. To my surprise Cammie emerged popping out of the back seat before the car rolled slowly to a complete stop. It was apparent that her plan had not changed as I had feared after all. My elation for Malachi was quickly overshadowed by the loud yelling I heard coming from the statehouse steps.

My attention was drawn away from Cammie and towards the commotion being created on the stairs. I could see the white mist caused by the crisp damp air coming from Cammie's mother as she yelled sternly. Her words, like before, were intimidating and loud and her eyes were piercing and cold. Malachi displayed a wryly look of disgust and agitation in response to her irritating behavior.

"What's wrong with you?" she shouted with a familiar deep scratchy voice as veins showed on her strained neck. "What can you possibly be thinking?"

"You don't understand Mrs. Cannon…" he attempted to calm her with sound reason.

"Don't you say my name!" she abruptly interrupted as it became obvious that her intended question was meant to be rhetorical in nature. She did not want an answer to her question; rather she sought to degrade him while stripping all his hopes of being with Cammie. She continued as she displayed a half smile that sarcastically taunted him. "Did you really think that you could be happy…" she paused to accentuate "…with *my*… daughter? I warned you not to have any contact with her." she alerted as she began to pull something from her pocket, "… this cannot …and will not happen!" she categorically declared.

With her left hand she reached out and grabbed Malachi by the arm, pulling him closer to her. At that moment I could see what it was that she had pulled from her pocket, which she covertly shoved into his abdomen. Malachi, however responding to the commotion of Cammie's arrival of the frantically honking horn had turned his attention away from the mother's actions and thereby unable to notice what object emerged in her right hand. At that moment I heard Jane screaming from within the car – the decibel of her frantic warning was muffled by the closed windows.

"Oh, God, please! Malachi! No!" she exclaimed, and I could hear her begin to exit the car.

Reflecting light from the lit streetlamps that were illuminated due to the darkness of the overcast day, I could see the tiny object shining as it came into view. I took a running step to quickly move in the direction of Malachi.

At that moment the events appeared to suddenly unfold in a methodically, slow, and deliberate frame by frame motion as my consciousness felt as though it were moving in time-laps measured sequence. As I began to take my second step, I opened my mouth to holler out a warning to Malachi. My cry of caution, however, was eclipsed by a deafening sound that echoed throughout the entire area.

Even from a significant distance, the shockwave had the strength to reverberate throughout my body with a tremor, and a tingling sensation. I could only imagine what type of profound impact Malachi must have experienced as I observed the horrific vision being the sight of blood spraying from out of his back.

The force of the small foreign object penetrating through his body lifted his feet up off the ground as it violently ripped through his body. His head whiplashed aggressively forward toward Cammie's mom as he instinctively grappled onto her shoulders with both hands in a desperate effort to find support. He fell feeble down to his knees - due to the effects of the bullet that instantly stunned and weakened him.

Time was at a standstill as the appearance of the 'frame-by-frame' slow motion suddenly grinded to a halt. In that moment, my cognitive perception miraculously shifted into the dimension of the spirit. I was empowered with the omnipotent ability to acutely conceive everything that was transpiring around me.

A single snapshot of time represented both a second and a lifetime in the same instance. This intensely captured 'flash' occasion enunciated the single methodical grossly understated two word phrase, "Oh,…" followed by a pronounced cerebral pause, before expressing "No!" to rifle through my mind.

While I struggled to process this ghastly scene with its potentially unsatisfactory prognosis; that frozen block of time chaotically thawed instantly into a flurry of action. Precipitated by the sudden ringing out of the thunderous flash lightning as the gun forced yet another bullet to rip through his body. Malachi's face turned pale, his legs buckled, and the expression of agony intensified on his face and his strength disintegrated.

With one hand he clenched at the wound on his abdomen with the other he clung tightly to her shirt in effort to stabilize his stance on his knees – but instead he fell helplessly toward her, and his grip caused the shirt to rip exposing her shoulder as he slid down the length of her body to his knees. – In a deliberate act of callousness – she pried his hand away from the support of her body and pushed him to the ground.

By that time, I was running full stride up the stairs. Malachi was lying helplessly on the steps moaning in anguish still clutching one of the wounds where a bullet had entered. She continued her onslaught attack by pointing the gun at him again bracing herself with a broad stance as she spread her feet for a wide base. She was so ferociously focused on the demise of Malachi that she was unaware of how near I was and unaware of the intensity with which I approached to intercept her.

With fortitude, I made a last desperate gasp and leaped with fortitude, diving into her body just as the gun rang out a final time. Her head smacked violently against the pavement steps, and I compounded the impact of the fall by landing on top of her. That valiant act left her body lying in a state of apoplexy and effectively ceased any further assault instigated toward Malachi.

I pushed myself up from the horizontal position to a sitting posture. At that point I noticed a burning sensation shooting through my left arm. Instinctively I grabbed my shoulder and noticed that it felt numb. I noticed a wet, warm sensation on my fingers and soon realized that I had been struck by the last bullet. I looked at my hand and saw blood on the fingertips. The residual pain had not yet materialized as it had been masked by the high level of adrenaline surging through my veins. In a semi – dazed state I became acutely aware of the simplest actions of the surrounding area.

Cammie, having witnessed the event from a distance, was frantically weaving her way across the street as traffic came to a screeching halt. Bystanders began crowding around as they emerged from the safety of their hiding places that they had sought during the shooting. I noticed that the ivory handled gun had landed several steps above my head. There were noticeable traces of smoke rising from the hot barrel of the .380 caliber pistol.

I made one final visual assessment, to determine whether Cammie's mom was still a potential threat. After evaluating that she was unconscious and no longer a danger I turned to my side and focused my attention on Malachi. In that surreal moment, and as if it were an afterthought, I leaned on my elbow in an uneventful nonchalant manner and gazed down at Malachi whose body rested a few stairs below me.

I was astounded by the horrific scene that was laid before me. My subjective opinion was that his appearance was dreadful; I made a quick assessment of whether my involvement could do anything to improve this shattered scene. The conclusion of my evaluation however, exposed grave concerns for my friend's welfare– and any confidence of his survival waned. Selfishly I was hesitant to move towards him.

He lay face up near motionless. His only sign of life was the slow, unstable, and labored rise and fall of his bloody abdomen. As he attempted to breathe his aimlessly, shifting, glassy eyes searched to focus on the reasoning for what had just happened. The hand that I had previously noticed that he had used to cover one of his wounds was now uselessly off to the side. He apparently now lacked the strength to hold his arm in place to clutch where he felt pain.

His torn shirt was soaked more from his blood that seeped out of the gaping bullet holes that had been torn into his flesh than from the rain pouring down. I can recall thinking to myself of how there was, 'blood, too much blood…' from one body flowing down those stairs.

I slowly repositioned myself as I crouched to my knees to an upright position. But rather than approach and assist him during his agony I continued to allow the fear of his survival prognosis to influence my actions. Instead of moving closer I unintentionally distanced my proximity from the dreadful vision of his riddled body by rearing back onto my ankles. With emerging pain, I clenched my bleeding shoulder.

In her haste to rush to Malachi's side, Cammie had unknowingly bumped my shoulder with her hip which sent a massive wave of pain throughout my arm as she hurried past me. Upon approaching him she hesitated momentarily as she assessed the seriousness of his injuries.

She stepped gingerly over his body which placed her on the lower side of the steps. As she turned, facing upward towards the top of the steps and in my direction, she slowly knelt beside him. Pressing her knees up against the step to allow his body weight to be used as leverage to keep him from sliding, she rested him onto her legs.

It was then that I was bewildered by yet another revealing implausible surprise; Cammie's belly was protruding significantly; she was with child! My heart instantaneously descended to an unfathomable sorrow as I watched this miserable surreal scene continue to unfold with the addition of this previously unimagined "joyous" tragic twist. By that time Jane had arrived on the stairs and was frantic about assessing the wound on my shoulder and began asking me if I was alright.

"Oh, my goodness… you've been hit Zaylen! Are you okay?" she questioned sincerely as she immediately began nurturing and assessing the wound on my shoulder. All I could muster for a response as I gazed at her in my perplexed state was to widen my anxious eyes and to nod my head in a downward gesture to prompt her to look at Cammie. Confused about my attempt to redirect her attention away from me, her eyebrows scrunched down as she shook her head puzzled; peering at me with the 'Duh, you've been shot!' look.

While she continued mulling over what my intention could possibly be for directing her attention elsewhere - she reiterated her previous statement with a renewed alarm in her voice as if she were concerned that I may be disoriented from my injury, "Maybe you didn't hear me…" She stated clearly while looking me directly in the eyes. "…but… are you not aware that you've been shot." Without a word I motioned again with my eyebrow and nodded more prominently in the direction of Cammie. Then I broke the silence and voiced my instruction so as to prompt her to look.

"Jane…" I stressed calling her name to ensure that I had her full attention, "…Look!" I insisted.

Hesitant, Jane slowly turned her head to follow where my eyes were guiding for her to observe; to Cammie's belly; at last, she envisioned Cammie's "predicament" causing her eyes to widen, which translated to a physical impulse response that expressed her uninhibited bewilderment.

"Oh my God!...She's pregnant!" Jane spontaneously uttered, as she attempted to conceal her astonished incomprehension by covering her gaped mouth with her hand as her jaw literally dropped with surprise in that instance. Her animated reaction made it evident that the same troubling thoughts that were rifling through my mind of the concern that their child would be left without a father were rushing through her mind. She stood next to me paralyzed in the moment from being able to act. The best that either of us was able to do effectively, which was not at all helpful, was to gawk at the scene and be witness to the events as they unfurl.

This occasion was already exceeding in the strange department but it became somewhat more bizarre when a melody popped into my psyche that caused me to marvel at how I would record this infamous series of evolving tragedies into my memory. As that awful spectacle manifested itself and unfolded before me, as this story continued to evolve, with ever increasing in magnitude - I descended into intellectual thought.

The severity of this progressing story would transcend any other example of misery from this point on. That is to say that whenever someone wished to express a personal observation and opinion regarding any single event that could serve as a benchmark representation of a "terrible" situation; from hence forward in comparison of any other situation; I was bearing witness to an unfolding story that would forever be describe as a characterization of a 'worse" circumstance.

I was astonished at how acutely aware I became at just how well the country music song, "In Color" completely and simplistically captured the essence of that moment. I found myself living the meaning of the lyrics as it relates to the difficulty of painting this horrific picture with words to illustrate the full measure and epithet of this occurrence. The artist concluded that - 'If you think we looked scared...you should have seen it unfold in color.'

I took special notice in studying Cammie's nurturing actions as she approached Malachi; each of her movements became cautious and precise as she took meticulous care in touching him. She put her right hand underneath his head and cradled him into her lap bringing him close to her body. She leaned over to protect his body from the relentless, pouring rain.

She then wiped his face with her damp hand; and rocked him soothingly in her arm while covering the rest of his body with his coat. As she attempted to keep her emotions in check, to emulate a calm appearance for his sake, her chin quivered with tears trickling down her rain wet face.

"Malachi, darling… I'm here." Cammie spoke in a carefree loving, nurturing voice. He likewise responded in a laborious jovial tone.

"Hey, you," he responded, mitigating the seriousness of his condition with a taxing effort to smile. "It's good to see you." Then looking at her protruding belly he added with a strenuous grin, "Wow, it's good to see all of you."

"I was hoping to surprise you – what do you think?"

"It's a real nice surprise," he commented as he coughed - unable to conceal his increasing difficulty in breathing.

"Do you still love me?" she questioned with an earnest heart. Assuredly the right corner of his mouth stretched toward his ear as his signature mischievous smile made its appearance, "You're showing your daddy's ornery grin -" she cooed. "What are you thinking?"

"I was thinking about my own little surprise and how the timing is so much more pertinent." He said as he pulled a small box from his pocket and handed it to her. Tears spontaneously trickled down her cheek as she took the small box from him; opened it and ceremoniously removed the item from the box. It was a diamond stone mounted on a white gold engagement ring.

As she marveled over the enormous implication of this small item, he continued to deepen the magnitude of the moment; "I can honestly say that I've never loved you more, than at this very moment;" he then strategically placed his hand on her belly, "I want to make this right for this little one, and I want to be yours." He inquired asking, "Will you marry me?"

"Yes!" she stated emphatically. Her lips quivered with a nervous emotional show of relief and appreciation of the enormity of his adoring expression, "Yes, yes…you're so wonderful. I am so humbled that you think I'm worthy to be your wife; I'll be delighted to take your last name. I'm so relieved that you're happy about my being pregnant. My parents were pushing me to do something dreadful."

"No!" he stated with an emphatic disapproval.

"Don't worry Honey, I wasn't going to."

"How… Far… Along…" he asked, placing his hand on her belly as each exhausted word became its own sentence.

"Far enough along to know it's a girl," she paused surreptitiously, "as well as a boy, sweetie." She answered.

"Twins!" his eyes widened "ya…should-a… told me." he insisted as his condition noticeably deteriorated.

"I know." she concurred with him lowering her head shamefully acknowledging regret "…I'm so sorry."

"Okay… it's okay…" he excused forgivingly. "Got… names picked?"

"Yes…I'm thinking Clara Spring for the girl… I thought of life growing in your "Sommer" and figured Clara would work as a feminine form of chlorophyll which symbolizes life… and "Spring" will eventually grow into someone's "summer" like I did for you. – I know it's kind of a reach, but I want her to be special. Do you like it?"

"Very pretty…I like." He stated clearly then he choked

as a little blood sprayed out, he continued, "Ch-s-sh-she's goin'na be sweet ch-just like you." He marveled. "And the boy?"

"Malachi of course; after you." She explained. "Malachi Isaac, his initials would then be M.I.C., and his name would run together like yours when you drop the "I" and the "C", MalachIsaaChambers. He's going to grow up wanting to be just like his daddy."

"Good girl." He smirked approvingly.

He began to wheeze, and I wondered if it might be caused by a collapsing lung – so I instructed Cammie to encourage him to lie still. "Cammie… tell him to save his strength. The squad is coming."

She acknowledged my suggestion by nodding her head as she cautioned Malachi to stay calm, "Be quiet now babe," she nurtured. "Helps on the way."

Shaking his head negatively, he choked, which caused blood to spray as he struggled to speak. He whimpered as tears streamed from his eyes. "No…time," he conceded, conserving his words as he took the opportunity to articulate his thoughts, "…take care of our babies. Tell them that – daddy's sorry he can't be here…tell them…daddy loves them."

"I will sweetie but save your strength you're going to be alright just hang in there… ok?" she encouraged in an attempt to downplay the seriousness of his injuries. Then she continued whimpering in disbelief while surveying his wounds as she again wiped his face with her trembling nurturing hand, "Oh… my poor Malachi."

Within the multitude of 'by standing' witnesses was a collection of Mayors from around the state who were attending a conference at the statehouse. One of them approached and made a generous gesture; offered his services to perform an immediate 'on the spot,' marital ceremony.

"If you don't mind my interrupting," he interjected, "I'm Mayor Gadd. I've been watching what's been going on and I feel compelled to offer – that is, if you will accept my proposal, I have the authority to perform legal marital unions…- I would be honored if you would allow me to unite you two in marriage."

Cammie looked at Malachi who knotted his head in approval then she graciously accepted the mayor's offer, "Thank you. We would be extremely grateful and indebted to you."

"No, you will not be indebted to me for anything," he rationalized his motivation with an arousing plea. "I've officiated countless superficial so called 'storybook' weddings and out of the thousands of marriages I have performed; I had never seen anything that can rival the pure expression of emotion that I have just observed. This is by far the most genuine and passionate thing that I've ever witnessed in all of my 68 years. I am honored to participate with any small role to immortalize your relationship before God.

"My Gracie would be proud of me," he reminisced as he explained. "For those reasons, it is *me,* who is grateful for your compassion, and it is me who is indebted to you." After his poignant statement he then addressed me and Jane, "Will you two position yourselves near to them and act as witness to this ceremony?" Without a word we both immediately moved, positioning ourselves next to Cammie.

I kneeled down on her right side close to Malachi's head while Jane squatted down at her left side. Both of our arms wrapped around Cammie in a show of solidarity as she continued to hold Malachi in her lap. The small-town mayor wasted no time proceeding and began to commence with officiating the ceremony. "Your names are Cammie and Malachi?"

"Yes," Cammie answered.

"Thank you, let's proceed. Do you, Malachi, take Cammie, to be your lawfully wedded wife; to have and to hold; to love and cherish from this day forward till death do yo…?" he paused as it was evident that he recognized the gravity of the unintentional severity that the last five words of that question might present.

He stumbled over his words momentarily as he attempted to acknowledge and qualify his error. "I'm sorry I didn't mean to…" at that point Malachi interrupted him and instead elegantly embraced the reality of the moment by acknowledging the unspoken question by answering the question in full.

"I do…" he stressed faithfully then gazing affectionately at Cammie with tears streaming down the side of his face he added a more lasting tribute of his devotion in omnipotent fashion declaring, with three distinct whispering breaths, "… and… forever…and beyond!"

That simple statement deeply stirred my emotions; and I felt the sensation of pressure pushing on my eyes making them feel as if they would burst if they were not relieved of the tears building. I could feel Jane's arm shaking as I heard her begin to succumb to the emotionally compromising moment. The ability to be strong and supportive for Cammie and Malachi was becoming impossibly difficult as I became cognizant of my own strength quickly disintegrating.

The inescapable contrast of the moment; that being the confluence of the conflict between happiness and tragedy spilling into the river of sorrow was unmistakable. Effectively, we were participating in a joyous celebration of unconditional love while the dark cloud of an unsurpassable sorrow of their predicament loomed.

The lingering unanswered question that became prevalent with each unpredictable passing moment was to inquire, how much more unfathomable strain could we all withstand? The mayor tearfully inhaled deeply, summoning his resolve to accept the strength from Malachi's bold answer and continued with the ceremony.

"And do you Cammie, take Malachi to be your lawfully wedded husband to have and to hold, to love and to cherish…" he paused and swallowed noticeably as he made an obvious attempt to fight back tears before finishing his statement as his voice cracked, "…till death do you part?"

As she visibly broke down ever so more, she summoned her resolve to strongly respond, "I do…" then looking passionately at Malachi in a sultry voice she too audaciously declared, "…and… forever… and beyond!"

"Place the ring on her finger," he instructed. Cammie put the ring between Malachi's thumb and forefinger so that he could hold the ring and then she slipped her finger through the hole. "And now, repeat after me…" he instructed. "'With this ring, I thee wed.'"

Malachi repeated with labored breathing, "With… this rin…I wed."

The mayor then stepped forward and continued with his generosity to present tangible surprises with his seemingly unlimited selfless gestures. He took his wedding band off of his finger and stretched his hand out toward Cammie motioning for her to take it; but she shook her head stating simply, "No, I couldn't…"

The mayor then explained, "My Gracie died four months ago; we never had children. I know my Gracie would want you to have this; consider it a wedding gift. Here…" he insisted, stretching his hand toward Cammie. "…go ahead, take it and put it on his finger."

"Thank you," she whimpered as she took the ring from him.

"Now, you repeat after me… 'With this ring, I thee wed.'"

She looked at Malachi and slipped the ring onto his finger and declared, "With this ring, sweetie, I Thee wed."

The mayor then made an official declaration, "In the sight of God and in the presence of these witnesses: by the authority vested in me as Mayor of Byesville in the Great state of Ohio; I now lawfully pronounce you as husband and wife. You may kiss your bride." As the Mayor concluded Jane and I slowly moved in unison away from them and observed them from the side.

Cammie leaned down and kissed him. She then gave him a command as his new bride, "I'm your wife now, so you have to listen to me. Malachi," she lovingly ordered. "…you hold on now… help is on the way. Don't you leave me…you hear? You hold on now!…" She insisted as Malachi's condition deteriorated noticeably moment by moment.

She raised her head and glanced at me with a distressing, tearful, childlike demeanor as she continued rocking him in her lap. "Just look at him…" she instructed despondently, with her voice cracking as she forced the words past her accusatory tears, bending the corners of her mouth, frowning, and shaking her head. "Look what I did to my poor sweet Malachi."

I stood just gawking – still reluctant to move – even though I managed to reposition myself and be able to participate with the impromptu ceremony, I still tried mentally to distance myself from this miserable scene while endeavoring to control my grief-stricken emotions. Every muscle in my body was static as I stood like a statue in shock. Then that ever present suppressive anguish poured into my heart causing it to throb heavily and making my throat feel thick. At that terrible moment, I was powerless to repress exposing my emotion. It seemed that every terrible experience in my life had been heaped on me all at one time.

My eyes became warm, but it was an unwelcomed warmth because it would reveal an open and visible presentation of the emerging despair I felt. The ultimate visible message that would be conveyed to Cammie would express my belief that Malachi's condition was beyond conventional help and that his demise was imminent.

At the sight of the first tear streaming down my cheek Cammie sensed my despair. Her eyes darted around aimlessly, as she searched in vain to find hope from any source. Her chin quivered with more intensity as she bit down on her bottom lip then it appeared that after she abandoned looking at me for support, she instead sought support by looking toward Jane.

But Jane, whose emotions had long since abandoned her, had tears streaming down her cheeks. Unable to withstand the emotional strain Jane turned away from Cammie to hide her visible sorrow. – It must have appeared to Cammie as though she were abandoned by her closest confidants in her most vulnerable time of distress, this observation became evident as she cried out hysterically.

"Malachi, no!" she screamed in desperation. "Don't you leave me!" she wailed with vigor.

At that moment Malachi responded to her plea as his eyes shifted ever so slightly in her direction, responding in a conscious manner to her command as his breathing noticeably became slower. The raw, wet weather conditions contributed to producing a small cloud to form and quickly dissipate with each precious, shallow breath he took. Noticeably as his strength disintegrated that cloud appeared clearer with each passing moment.

Somehow, he had summoned the strength to move his arm, lifting it from his wound, drops of blood fell from his fingertips. Then reaching into the inner pocket of his country style trucker jacket he pulled out a folded sheet of paper… lethargically raised his hand to give her the paper.

His hand was shaky and unsteady as he methodically moved his hand up to her face and gently touched her cheek he slid his hand across her skin with an enduring touch. This action left three scarlet streaks streaming down her face causing ruby water droplets to collect underneath her chin, before falling to the ground.

She smiled lovingly and with her left hand she held and pressed his hand firmly against her cheek. At that solemn moment she reiterated her appeal for him to fight; pleading with him as she requested quietly, "Please don't leave me, Sweetie … you're my strength, I need you to be in control. I need you to tell me what to do…I'm at a loss at what to do." she sobbed. "Please baby, no…"

That somber moment continued with its pitiful trail of tears as the rain still found its way onto his face and his coat that had shifted from his movement – which once again exposed his wounds to the downpour. It was a surreal scene to see the raindrops splash into his open bloody wounded abdomen. His breathing became progressively more heavily labored. At that moment he offered his final, inevitable, cognitive thought in an effort to reassure her of his devotion beyond this life.

"Wha… hha…wherever you go…" he pledged lovingly as he struggled weezing intensely for each fading breath, "I…Ihh'll…hha… I'll be with yo-uo…" At that moment a deafening silent ambience descended as an overbearing ominous oppressive presence, and I felt sick as I began to experience that preverbal "tunnel vision."

Then – without warning the shallow cloud that had formed with each breath, ceased and the smile on Cammie's face dissolved as she gazed blankly into his aimlessly, staring, crystal, golden brown eyes. She placed his hand down gently on his body and softly rubbed the right side of his face as if she were trying to awaken him from a light sleep.

"Malachi!" she called to him in a whimper. "Please, God, no! Please don't take him," she pleaded while holding her belly in a nurturing manner. "We need him so desperately."

Then looking up at me she shook her head more prominently as if hoping to convince me that our eyes were deceiving us.

It was then I noticed the extent to which the rain had slowed from a downpour to a drizzle as a hint of auburn illumination gleamed from her teary eyes. A radiant glow had manifested on her face that was caused by the break in the clouds in the far west. This break marked an end to the storm and exposed the sun for the first time in days as the sunset cast its fading golden rays over my shoulders.

I found it ironic about the manner in which that miserable day was coming to a close. It was as if a revelation had been revealed, philosophically, that just as the day brought an end to the monsoon and subsequently produced an opportunity of a promise for a bright clear tomorrow to be ushered in… the ironical symbolism suggested that if Malachi could have perhaps held on for one more day that their troubles; along with the clouds in the sky - likewise, would have eventually passed over.

Cammie's breathing suddenly quickened, and it became quite noticeable that her response was becoming more panic stricken, "He can't be dead…" she cried openly in denial. Defiantly she was emotionally unwilling to accept what her senses revealed. "See… his eyes are still open." She insisted, and then looking back at Malachi she repeated, "He can't be dead!"

She began rocking in an effort to consol herself while holding him close to her body. She gently removed the paper from his hand and opened it. I repositioned myself so that I could see the paper from over her shoulder while still holding and nursing my wounded arm. The letter was titled,

"The splendor of HIS magnificent creation."

'As the season "falls" into the depths of winter;

These cool, clear, October days are reminiscent of the bittersweet thoughts that I have - as I'm missing you.

The brilliance of a bright day is rivaled only by your saintly aurora.

The sky jealousy emulates the depth and shade of the lucid windows to your soul…

And without consideration I would instantly trade the whole exhibition of autumn's flavors for the solitaire color that is so wonderfully flaunted by your smile.

I look at you and pause to wonder – what kind of creature could flawlessly display such vibrancy.

It is now that I long for the warmth embrace of my Sommer – but she is now so far away.

I still fight desperately for your attention; all the while believing that you'll never understand the reason why - as I contemplate these thoughts.

'Why would He create such angelic radiance to be so far from Him… yet, so close to me.' How could I, a mere mortal, resist the temptation to possess such elusive beauty?'

Then, as Malachi's finale he composed this poem as his final thought.

?

Yesterday…

I believed in you; and me.

I dared to believe in your eyes.

My innocent heart was pure when I touched you,

And pleasant thoughts filled my mind.

But… that was yesterday.

Remember me…"Us"

Yesterday

!

An eerie sensation crept through the members of my body…; the devastation of Cammie's psyche became visibly complete. It was an unlikely phenomenon that he would have prepared this letter as though he had expected for something tragic to happen. I immediately recalled the conversation that he and I had that first morning at camp, when he described 'the feeling of a cold whisper' warning him as regards to the likelihood of something sinister looming about pursuing their relationship. I couldn't help but wonder; if this was the future that was foretold by that 'cold whisper?'

The drizzling rain slowed to a mist as her tears quickened, streaming from her eyes. Malachi's body lay limp and motionless in Cammie's arms, and for a few – quiet moments she appeared to be in apogee. It seemed as though all the rage of opposing forces in the world simultaneously congregated in her heart. These ingredients of sorrow simmered in her like a pressure cooker for this single, wonderfully, miserable moment as all the contrasting basic emotions of love, hate, hope and despair would in unison collide to compose a chorus that would fashion a perfectly ferocious, unforgettable, hysterical, panic-stricken shriek.

"No-o…!" she shouted with a massively soul draining cry as Malachi's head slumped lifelessly away from her. "Please,

God...no! We need you so bad... I can't do this without you! Please... live for me!

In that instant my concern dramatically shifted from the hope of his survival to the immediate anxiety of contemplating how she might manage to survive from this emotional moment.

That familiar, distinctive, refined persona of a delicate flower that she had so elegantly emulated - was now in absolute disarray. Her typical flawless and majestic facade was now more reflective and reminiscent of a rare, vintage stained-glass window that had been shattered. She was like a fragile masterpiece destroyed – with the frazzled expression on her face resembling the sentiment of a combat soldier under siege.

Soaked by the torrential downpour, much of her curled hair now clung to her face, with his blood dripping from the ends. Her designer clothes sagged on her body due to the saturation of the heavy rain and were also stained crimson being soaked from the blood that had seeped out of wounds.

Scrutinizing these events, I pondered at the universal accepted platitude that; 'It is better to have once tasted the sweet purity of unconditional affection... only to then be subjected to suffer an emotional catastrophic loss. A loss that compels the unfortunate romantic a return to the sentence of being remanded, back into life's depressive lukewarm mediocrity. Than to have never been graced with the opportunity to engage in that wonderfully, uninhibited delight.'

The evidence, however, supports that those who hold to that simplistic customary belief that, 'it's better to have once loved and to have lost...than to have never experienced love at all,' have never truly been exposed to the irrepressible euphoria that is cultivated through the enlightenment of that absolute addictive affection, simply entitled, Love. Nor have they been witness to the suppressive sorrow that is fostered in the heart by the denial of that glorious touch – after having once been enlightened.

Finally, I gave consideration to the habitual lesson that is taught regarding the amount of endurance that is necessary for any hope of surviving such disastrous anguish. The desperate belief is that; simply the passage of a substantial amount of time is the universal remedy to mend all wounds. But instead, I've learned a prophetic message… the mortal wound - will never heal. From such a catastrophic injury, one's heart could never be restored to health stemming from such a profound; - perfect sadness.

My solitude contemplation was interrupted by the sound of the emergency hi-lo sirens that had been echoing from a distance but now had finally arrived on the scene. The rush of the first responders to render aid, unfortunately, was in vain as my friend's body lay lifeless. Three medics who arrived in a squad and a fire captain who arrived in a sedan labeled "Supervisor" approached to assess those who had been wounded and to set up triage for the need of on scene primary care.

Other than myself, Malachi, and the mother I noticed one woman screaming hysterically holding her leg. By protocol the medics quickly identified Malachi as the priority and began working on him. The third first responder approached the lady with the injured leg. The captain surveyed the perimeter to determine how many injuries needed to be addressed. She approached to inspect Cammie's mom for injuries then she took a quick visual assessment of my injury and then dispatched for additional backup.

"Fire Rescue, this is SR7 to County…over."

"Dispatch…go ahead Supervisor-Rescue 7." A feminine voice echoed back in a robotic sounding voice.

"Dispatch…this is SR7 … Rescue Command Alert!" she began in an authoritative tone. "We are on location at the Ohio State House – I have a Code 6; repeat we are operating on an unsecure scene. We have made initial assessments to prioritize treatment of multiple victims on site. Prep for assessment details...

We have multiple victims! Stand-by for assessments: 'Vic one: possible Code Blue – multiple abdominal wounds due to firearm injury, 'Vic' two: unconscious head trauma, - possible blunt force trauma object. 'Vic' three... medial shoulder laceration from firearm projectile, 'Vic four: unknown... stand-by. Repeat...police do not have area secure!

Please advise law enforcement that on my call - Medic 7 is on scene to treat critical victims in unsecure scene; request immediate response from law enforcement. Send additional Rescue squads... recall Engine 9...Code 6... Time out 20:11 over."

"Roger, Rescue 7; Copy. Scene on location is Code 6 unsecure at State House; will advise law enforcement that first responders are active on unsecured scene. Repeat Code 6 acknowledged; Squad 9 in route...over."

The supervisor then addressed me directly as she made a more thorough examination of my wound, "Are you alright son," she inquired in a nurturing tone, "I saw that you've been injured... is your injury painful?"

"Yes, I've been hit but I'm okay; go ahead and take care of my friend."

"We will." She said as she tore open a gauze packet and pressed it against my injury while instructing, "Keep this pressed against your wound. You hang in there... I'll be right back." She reassured as she headed to examine the status of Cammie's mom.

She opened one of her eyelids, flipped a flashlight from side to side and took her pulse at her neck; then she proceeded to the lady further up the steps. It was necessary for the medics to have room to safely provide treatment to Malachi, so it was necessary to remove Cammie away from him. The first paramedic decisively moved Cammie.

"Please, we need space to work on him." He asserted his request respectfully of Cammie as he gingerly helped her up to her feet backing her away from Malachi. "Don't worry;" he assured, "we'll take good care of him."

While the medic pulled Cammie back, Jane walked over and put her arm around her shoulders for moral support. Cammie's frail shaking body exhibited a demeanor that she was experiencing the early stages of going into shock. As she sobbed, her face appeared frozen with no emotion. It was surreal that since her meltdown she looked as calm as a schoolgirl waiting for the bus.

As she was drawn back the other two medics immediately began to perform CPR on Malachi. One placed a portable Oxygen mask over his nose and mouth while the other ripped open his shirt to begin pushing on his chest. "Wow," one of the medics noticed. "He's really fit. That may prove beneficial to give him a good chance."

The first medic then left Cammie in the care of me and Jane and then proceeded to get the defibrillator charged as it laid next to Malachi. After a few moments it beeped, "Clear!" he commanded - warning the other two medics to stop touching him as the paddles were placed strategically on Malachi's chest and side.

Then, the medic discharged the electrical impulse into Malachi's body. The delivery of the electric current caused the muscles in his lifeless body to violently contract while arching his back off the ground. That distinct mechanical sound created by the transfer of electricity proved to be an emotionally compromising, loud, sharp, and harsh noise to sensitive ears.

Cammie was noticeably disturbed by the pugnacious reverberating resonance of the device. The convulsion of the machine startled a physical response from her causing her body to jerk as if it were she that was delivered the shock. My immediate concern as they worked to revive him was that all of this was simply pomp and stance and would only serve to manufacture a false hope to Cammie of his chances of survival. I reasoned that the result of this false hope would only serve to display an unnecessary resurgence of Cammie's excruciating suffering.

"Still have no pulse!" the second medic reported. "Hit him again!" As they prepared the machine to recharge to apply another treatment, the dispatch beckoned again medic 7.

"Dispatch to Medic 7?" the robotic female voice hailed on the radio.

"Medic 7… go ahead, Dispatch."

"Medic 7, stand - by for County transport orders to Lincoln Memorial."

"Medic 7…standing by for orders."

The defibrillator beeped after being recharged and at this point the first medic once again warned, "Clear!" as he applied the paddles again sending another electrical discharge with that deafening double clunck-clunck sound. After several seconds of finding no heart beat the second medic slowly shook his head to signify the lack of positive response… at that moment the hospital was heard hailing the medics over the radio making a request for an update.

"Lincoln 1-1-8-6-5…Medic 7 please respond." She summoned, authenticating the hospital's call signal.

"Medic 7, go ahead Lincoln."

"Please advise as to the patient status and treatment administered."

"Finalizing those reading now, Stand-by for patient 'E-vale…'"

"Lincoln standing by…over."

After a few more seconds of reviewing the data the first medic responded to that request by relaying a number of medical terminologies that detailed their efforts. A chronicle of the lack of progress that the treatment was yielding prompted the medic to make the heart wrenching request.

The importance of the medics to clearly relay the raw and unfiltered medical reality relating to the medical opinion of Malachi's prognosis took precedence. The concern for discreteness to protect loved ones from overhearing dismal observation was secondary to the professionalism of providing medical care. The medics opinion was ubiquitous and highlighted the professional protocol as he relayed the specifications to the hospital.

"Lincoln?" He beckoned "- Medic 7… we have the vitals… prep for 'Patient E-vale'" He paused for a moment, "… we have a male approximately 20 years old: 6 foot 200 pounds athletic build. Initially there was an arrhythmic faint pulse.

Patient is now in full cardiac arrest with two… anterior abdominal wounds caused by a medium caliber firearm projectile! One medial and one lateral. With explosive secondary dorsal exit wound in the lumbar region measuring approximately 5 centimeters in diameter.

The artificial respirator is engaged… "I.V." has been administered… we are actively performing Cardiac Resuscitation. Vitals remain negative; blood pressure has bottomed out! EKG is flatline. Patient has been unresponsive to advance medical treatment. There's no pulse despite two cycles of the defibrillator. Status: Code Blue - running time approximate 1 minute 30 second. Requesting permission to cease resuscitation…please provide instructions… over."

"Cease resuscitation…" I mumbled to myself, "That's it."

"Lincoln reference #1-1-8-6-5…Negative! Repeat… request denied… do not discontinue the administration of medical treatment…stand by for Physician instruction!"

She paused for a brief moment holding the receiver before continuing. "Please reference Physician number 6-8-6-8 - in log… designate: medical order number 7-8-6-8 in report … permission to administer 10 cc's injection of adrenaline into cardiac cavity… continue cardiac massage resuscitation. Repeat! Instructions…provide 10 cc's induction of adrenaline into cardiac cavity…continue chest massage and transport patient as quickly as possible… please confirm… over."

The two medics looked at each other with a strange look as he responded. "Copy that…Lincoln 1-1-8-6-5! Medical order number 7-8-6-8; administer 10 cc's injection of adrenaline into cardiac cavity and continue cardiac resuscitation…transport patient a-sap… Roger that. Be advised; E.T.A. three minutes. Status: Code Blue running time 2 minutes and 40 seconds… copy?"

"Copy Medic 7; Code Blue, R.T. 220…E.T.A. three minutes.

"Ella! Go get that adrenaline shot ready, I want to give it to him as soon as we get to the squad." The first medic ordered to the third medic. "Then get into the driver seat…we've got to move."

"I'm on it… I'm on my way," Medic Ella acknowledged. Then she turned to reassure me as she dashed off, "…don't lose hope we're gonna take good care of your friend."

The scene became more chaotic as the second squad arrived with noise of the "Hi – Lo" siren. Multiple echoes from other sirens also joined the raucous concert as several police units had also arrived from varying directions and were setting up a perimeter around the crime scene. The new medics were directed to provide treatment for the hysterical lady who had been struck by a ricocheting bullet with a flesh wound to the thigh.

Three of the police officers tended to Cammie's mom first handcuffing her while she still lay unconscious then rendering first aid and an ice pack to her head. The first squad quickly prepped Malachi and then lifted him onto the gurney. Heavy gauze was placed on his abdomen to plug up his wounds, "I.V." tubes were taped to his arm to secure the needle from pulling out. A blood pressure gauge was strapped tightly to his upper arm as the Oxygen mask was secured onto his head.

The medics were in hurried motion trying to stabilize Malachi for transport. The blue surgical gloves were covered in bright red blood while stethoscopes were dangling from one's ears and from around another's neck. Once they had all of the medical devices secured, he was hastily strapped to the gurney. The monitors had to be placed all around him to free their hands to push the gurney as they rushed him to the ambulance.

"I want to go with him." Cammie requested of them as they began to carry him down the steps to the ambulance.

"What is your relationship to him, ma'am?" the medic asked.

"It's his wife," Jane announced, answering for her. "They're newlywed's as of five minutes ago." She explained.

The second medic looked at me and explained, "There are things we're going to need to do to him during transport, trust me… she does not need to see." He explained his concern of Cammie's request to be in the ambulance. "Stay with her," he advised, "…and bring her to the hospital." At those instructions I halted Cammie's advance toward the ambulance. They hurriedly shoved the gurney into the back of the ambulance, jumped in, closed the door and sped off.

In my heart I still had a smidgen of hope lingering that as long as they work on him there just might be a room for a miracle. That morsel of optimism hinged on the expectation that Cammie's short prayer might be answered, and that God might grant mercy for his new wife and unborn children. In my intellect, I knew that based on what I saw, and from what I knew to be certain that the outcome was all but final. Therefore, I forced myself to embrace the reality that I had seen my friend for the last time.

"Come on, we'll all go to the hospital together." I comforted Cammie. It was then that I realized two distinct things about my condition. My arm felt unnaturally warm and heavy, and I began to feel my head swirling to a faint.

"I don't feel very well," I mumbled incoherently to Jane in a whisper. Jane would later recount to me. "My heart's throbbing like crazy." My head began to swirl more pronounced, and I leaned heavily slumping onto Jane. She had to reinforce her body against mine to lower my body gently to the ground as my legs buckled as I began to lose consciousness.

"Hey, what's wrong with you?" she inquired - but I did not respond at least not coherently. "Somebody please," she called out frantically, "…help me! There's something wrong with him." The two new medics who were attending to the lady left her with the captain and rushed to my aid.

"What's wrong with him?" The first medic inquired of Jane as he began putting a blood pressure monitor on me and feeling my forehead for a temperature while the second medic began immediately to evaluate my swollen arm. "Where's his injury?"

"His upper arm," she directed.

"Did you notice anything abnormal about his behavior?"

"He was hit but he said that he was fine. He just complained of a burning sensation. He's been walking around and everything;" she justified, "…then all of a sudden he said that he felt faint and fell into me."

"His hand and arm are swollen," the second medic reported. "I'm starting an "I.V." Better call Lincoln and inform them to prep for another critical!"

"Critical?!" Jane asked. "What do you mean critical? He just got hit in the arm. He said that he was fine."

"He's showing signs of going into shock." The medic explained to her. "He has a hemorrhage somewhere; we just have to find it. With the blood filling up in his arm it's a sure sign of internal bleeding. That much blood in this short amount of time is a clue that his brachial artery was hit. If we don't stabilize him; he'll quickly bleed out." He explained.

The medics continued to quickly administer the first aid by tightly wrapping gauze around my arm to slow the blood building up in my arm. "Lincoln…" he hailed into the intercom as he began relaying my deteriorating condition without hesitation… "Lincoln… Squad 9 reporting. We have a new priority 'vic'…our patient is male 6 foot 200 pounds athletic build semi – conscience, with possible hemorrhage of the brachial artery. Respiration is shallow; heart rate is 178; blood pressure 90/60, pupils are dilating. He is going into shock."

"Lincoln 1-1-8-6-5… squad 9 we read you. Standby for treatment order… Physician 0-7-2-2; medical order number 1-5… administer 500 ml bolus, stabilize and prep for transport.

I recall seeing them start to work on me. I watched in a fog as the medic prepped the dosage by shooting some of the solution of the syringe in the air before poking a hole and injecting the fluid into the" I.V." that had been secured into my arm. Then they strapped me to a gurney.

At that point I made a request for Jane to stay with me. "Please don't leave me." I pleaded with an exhaustive whisper.

"We need to travel with him;" she insisted. "…he doesn't want me to leave him."

"We only have enough room for one." The medic stated.

"Well, her husband was just taken by the first ambulance!" Jane hysterically explained. "I can't leave either one of them." she reasoned "She's in no condition to be left alone and he needs me to be with him." She insisted.

"Okay, you can both come but it's going to be a tight squeeze. Here you can help," he said as he handed the I.V. to Jane, "…hold this up and stay close."

"Can you make out what he is saying?" Jane asked the Medics. "Sounds like he's saying something about the cemetery."

"He's hallucinating, that's not good! Come on, we gotta go…we gotta go now… let's move." The second medic ordered as the two medics got to each end of the gurney, "One, two, three…lift."

I recall that as I looked up in my hazed state, I saw Jane holding a clear bag near her head as she looked forward, rushing me to the ambulance as my conscience faded. My next recollection was awakening in the back seat of a car between my mom and dad being in a confused state. Looking out of a cloudy window. The background scenery was gloomy, there was a fog that was smokey grey in color and I had no recollection as to how we got there or how it was that we were heading to Malachi's burial plot so soon.

"How'd I get here? Where are we going? What happened to Jane and the ambulance?" I asked a barrage of questions trying to make sense of my surroundings.

"It's alright dear," my mother consoled in a nurturing tone, "We're on our way to the cemetery for the ceremony; Jane is in the Limousine with Cammie just ahead of us… remember?" my mother answered as she explained. "The doctor said that you might have some temporary memory loss during your recovery due to the extreme shock you've suffered - so we thought it would be best to keep you with us. It's been several days since Malachi has passed. Try to remember."

"So… Malachi? …Is dead?" I confirmed reluctantly.

"Yes, I'm afraid so dear. Do you remember now?" I was unable to answer instead I just slumped into my mother's arms and sobbed.

"Poor dear," my mother consoled as she pulled me close to her bosom. "You keep slipping into an amnesiac condition which makes you forget everything and then you suffer rediscovering the sad news about your friend."

When we arrived at the cemetery, I noticed my movement became involuntary as there was no instruction from my mind relating to the function of my body's movement. My body just seemed to respond moving without any cognitive thought - instead my acute awareness was trained on the surreal scene that was now forced upon me to witness.

Exiting the cars, we all moved to stand around the casket at the grave site. Jane put her right arm around my waist and held my left hand with her left as I leaned into her for strength. Then suddenly there was a change in the scenery... the cloudy - grey turned into a bright foggy amber glow as of a twilight sunset.

Then my thoughts seemed to drift with the fog and I appeared to be hovering above everyone as I gazed down on all that was happening. I became overwhelmed with an insuppressible feeling that I was alone amidst the crowd at the site. The bright illumination of the day gradually drifted into darkness, I became dazed and confused and unable to see anything. Suddenly I began to plead solemnly to Jane; 'Please don't leave me.'

"Zaylen...babe. You're dreaming" she said softly, "wake up; you've been hallucinating. Hey babe... It's gonna be alright," I heard her reassuring me through the darkness as I noticed that her voice sounded as though it was coming from a far distance.

"Please don't leave me," I repeated as I coughed.

"Don't worry, I'm not going anywhere." She reiterated lovingly.

"My throat hurts. Where are you? I can't see you," I stated confused as I heard a third voice join in on the conversation.

"Nurse's station. Do you need something?"

"He's waking up…" Jane replied.

"Okay, we'll be right there." The voice informed.

I repeated, "My throat is sore … don't leave me."

"Hey, babe… I'm right here…" Jane soothed, "I'm not going anywhere." she consoled as she put a straw just inside my lips. "I just pushed the button to the nurses' station. She'll be here soon to help with your discomfort," She explained. "Here, sip this, it will help you to feel better."

I sucked in from the straw as instructed and as a result I felt an immediate cool, sweet, quenching sensation in my mouth that drained to the back and down my throat. It did not relieve the soreness I was feeling but the refreshing liquid did seem to revitalize my senses. The sweet taste was so invigorating that I instinctively drew in a second time more deeply, perhaps a little too much as I choked and coughed. "Aww, that hurts." I moaned, referring to how the cough agitated the pain throughout my body.

I became more aware of my surroundings as I stirred conscientiously still in a mental fog with a throbbing headache. I could hear a low rhythm beep and slowly opened my eyes allowing for an adjustment to the light. It was too bright and so I reconsidered and closed my eyes again. I struggled to hold my head still as it bobbled from the lack of muscle control. Then I heard a voice over an intercom that sounded as though it was from a distance. "Dr. Kyenna… please report to room 4460 for observation."

I began to moan as I tried to move but my body felt as though it was weighted down. Jane called out to me again as she tried to get me to respond coherently. "Zaylen…sweetie, can you see me? I'm over here." She directed. "Can you open your eyes for me please?" she requested. I slowly turned my head to the left to find what I was looking for. My eyesight was still blurry and unfocused but once I located her, I knew in an instant that it was Jane. "Hey, you… are you in there, are you awake, do you know who I am?" she questioned.

"Jane." I answered.

"Yes, I'm here." She whispered reassuringly.

"I'm thirsty." I whimpered with a scratchy voice.

"Here sweetie, drink some more of this 7-up… slowly," She instructed as she held the cup with a straw to my lips. It was that familiar, sweet, cold, refreshing liquid. I sipped a few continuous times before she stopped me by pulling the straw away from my lips. "Careful sweetie, don't take too much at a time." She nurtured. "How do you feel?"

"I feel tired and sore; it hurts to breathe, and I can't move my arms too well."

"That'll get better," she explained. "…they said it'll take you a while for the meds to wane for you to get your strength back. Just relax; I'll get you whatever you need."

"What happened? Where am I?" I questioned, baffled.

"What happened was that you gave us a big scare." She answered as she kissed me on the forehead.

"What happened?" I questioned again trying to recall the events wondering if I had passed out at the grave site.

"You passed out, babe. A major artery in your arm was hit and it was bleeding, but we didn't know until you fainted. Once you got to the hospital they found and sewed up the tear in your artery and gave you a blood transfusion. But you were not responding as they had expected so they had to medically induce you into a coma because you stopped breathing. It took them a few hours and a CAT scan to discover that the bullet lodged in your chest underneath your arm and punctured your lung. For a few days we thought that you were not going to pull through."

"Did you say a few days?" I questioned, puzzled.

"Yes, you've been in here for five days."

"I've been out for five days?" Before I had a chance to get further details a nurse walked in.

"Oh, look who's finally awake, that's good to see, and how are 'we' doing?" she inquired as she prepped the thermometer and checked my 'I.V.'

"Not too bad." I responded.

"Are you having any pain?" she inquired as she made her way to my wounds.

"Mainly my side… It hurts to breathe."

"Yea, that's not surprising, they had to do some work in there once they discovered that the bullet was lodged in your side. Here, let's roll you over so that I can check your bandages. You have some good meds in you that will keep the main pain in check; you're due for some more in another couple of hours but if things get worse let me know and we'll ask the doctor if you can have more. Well, all your bandages are secure;" she reassured, "…the night nurse will change them. Other than that, how are you feeling?"

"I guess ok." I responded.

"The doctor will be glad to hear that. She'll be in to see you within the hour. I'll let her know about your labored breathing. Okay put this under your tongue." She instructed as she grabbed my wrist to take my pulse. After a few seconds the thermometer beeped, and she took it out and recorded the readings. "Things are looking much better," she acknowledged, "Do you need anything, extra covers, more pillows…"

"Well, I am hungry…" I informed her.

"Well the doctor has to clear you before you can eat; when she does, we'll make a special order for the hero…okay? You are encouraged to get as much fluid in you as possible, the more you're able to drink and keep it down the sooner you'll be cleared for solid food. Do you prefer soda or juice?"

"Do you have cranberry?" I asked.

"Sure do, I'll bring some in. My name is Nurse Jadyn just let me know if you need anything else, if you do, just push this button. I'll be right back with a warmed cozy blanket."

As Nurse Jadyn exited the room, I inquired from Jane as to what the nurse was referring to, "What's this 'Hero' reference she's talking about?"

"Don't you remember? You got shot while volunteering to run into a bullet while trying to help Malachi. If you had died, I would have killed you for leaving me alone." Jane began to explain with comic relief. "It was a local story that got picked up nationally when the video of the shooting was released. It was all caught on video. A videographer was in the process of videotaping the State House for a public access history program and incidentally caught everything on tape.

It's been all over the news about how brave you were at what is being dubbed, 'The Tragedy at the State House.' You have a lot of fan mail and cards from people praying for your recovery. Even people from Hollywood are offering compensation for the 'Rights to the Story.' Outside this room it's been absolutely crazy.

"Humph! Yea, some 'hero' I turned out to be…" I chastised my actions. "My friend is dead. I should have gone and stood with him while he waited on the steps."

"Sweetie," she consoled. "You did everything you could, to prevent that from happening. You've been with him every step of the way. What happened was not your fault, it was the actions of a spiteful irrational person.

Malachi's parents expressed many times during interviews about how grateful they are that you were with him, and they acknowledged that you sacrificed your life to save him.

You have nothing to be ashamed of…" she scolded with a nurturing tone. "You acted very heroically and I'm very proud of you. And so are your parents who are here too," Jane informed me. "They just went down to the cafeteria to get something to eat."

"Oh, yeah," I was recalling the reason that she came home with me. "I guess you would have met them by now, huh? I'm sorry that you had to meet them by yourself. How did that go?"

"It went really well. You're gonna make me cry thinking about how wonderful they are. It was so emotional because we didn't know if you were going to pull through. Your mom kept insisting that I come to your home and rest, but I told her that I couldn't leave because you asked me to stay with you.

Your mom hugged me like she knew me forever and kept thanking me for staying with you. Your dad said that he had taught you to never settle for things less than the best and that he was very proud of your choice of selecting me." She said as she "teared" up. Then she made a joke for comic relief recalling, "I didn't have the heart to tell your dad that I had to force you to choose me."

"Oh, is that so…," my dad interrupted, walking into the room behind my mom. "Now we get the whole story. That would make more sense." he reasoned. "It would have had to be the girl who has to coax you into a relationship with your procrastination personality. I'm getting to like this girl even better."

"Hi son," my mom said, rushing to my side, and kissing me on the cheek, "…it's good to see you awake. We were listening outside in the hall and thought that we'd let you two have a few moments alone. It's been such a trying time for Jane. It would seem that this girl is way too humble about telling you how much she has actually done for you." My mother expounded.

"The true story is that just before you had passed out you had apparently asked Jane not to leave you; and believe me, she didn't. As a matter of fact, to start off she insisted that the medics allow both her and Cammie to ride along in the ambulance with you because she couldn't leave either of you alone. She insisted and was determined that she was going to be by your side and Cammie was too distraught to be left on her own.

Then when you got to the hospital, they initially kept her out of the emergency room but while she and Cammie were being consoled by the Chaplin outside of the emergency room you apparently took a turn for the worse, and she heard them calling over the intercom for additional assistance.

Several nurses then rushed past her entering the room, so she ran in with them and began talking to you in your ear. While she was with you - your vital signs stabilized. Then one of the doctors told a nurse to escort her out of the emergency room. As they began to usher her away from you - your condition subsequently worsened.

At that point the surgeon said that it was okay for them to let her stay… and stay she did. She spoke into your ear and once again you responded. It was noted that your vital signs miraculously rebounded. The surgeon confided to us that she's heard of "faith healing" but had never witnessed it until now. She actually documented her professional opinion on your medical chart as Jane's influence on your improvement as being: 'inspirational' to your recovery.

The doctor further affirmed that the medical staff cannot take credit for saving nyou but rather conceded that it was Jane's presence that kept you alive, and that all they did was to, "plug up the holes." Jane has essentially nursed you back to health and has not left your side. She has pretty much held a vigil at your bedside. The medical staff nicknamed her "Nightingale." The truth is that when I thanked her for staying with you, I was really thanking her for keeping you alive."

"Yeah," my dad chimed in. "We talked to her parents

over the phone, and they explained that she has always been tenacious and that whenever she gets her claws sunk into something that she; just like a wild cat; doesn't let go. So we went ahead and unofficially welcomed her into our family."

As I looked at Jane, I felt the urge to express my feelings; and having been comatose for several days I playfully and lovingly asked Jane a rhetorical question, "Hey you," I questioned with a smirk, "…have I told you in the last few days that I love you?"

"Yes, babe. You have. With every breath and with each heartbeat." She affirmed as she leaned over to kiss me.

"That's my girl," I complimented. "She always has a good answer."

"I thought I saw Cammie before we came in this morning, has she been on to see that you're awake?" my mother asked.

"No," Jane responded, answering for me.

"Well if it were her, she probably would have been in here by now, don't you think?" my mother reasoned. Then she inquired inquisitively, "So, if she hadn't been here yet then Zaylen hasn't been told about Malachi yet?"

All of a sudden there it was… "The avoidable topic." Although I wasn't purposely avoiding talking about what happened to Malachi, I was also in no hurry to accept erasing the nugget of hope that remained of the possibility that he may have survived. But as fortune would have it – it would not be my choosing of when and how I was to confront the reality of the tragic fate of my friend.

It was apparent to me that their plan was to surround me with as much support from loved ones as possible. That supposition became more evident to me when there was a quiet knock at the door as Cammie peaked her head in whispering, "Nurse Jadyn told me that someone was finally awake. Is he ready for visitors?"

"Yes, he is..." Jane acknowledged. "...come on in."

She pushed the door open and slowly walked in and then walked to the back side of the door while continuing to hold the door open. I braced myself for the somber mood that would materialize with her arrival as the newly minted widow but then surprisingly from directly behind her emerged the most improbable image.

"Hey 2-Pac..." Malachi jested as he was ushered into my room riding in a wheelchair pushed by my brother who was doubling as a photographer to video record my response upon entering the room "...there's my hero!"

At the first sight of his appearance my heart throbbed as my intellect had problems processing what was actually transpiring. 'He's dead,' I reasoned, 'there's no way I can be seeing what I'm seeing.' I stared at him or perhaps it would be a better illustration to say that I gawked at him.

My logic of what I think I saw hinged on two assumptions: First, that the medicine had possibly impaired my judgment, and the second assumption that crossed my mind was that a terrible misguided joke was being played on me by my brother in an effort to cheer me up. My next oral response was in the form of a question that was based on the wisdom of those who live by a simple code of not being gullible; that philosophy of, "not to believe everything you see."

"What are you doing alive?" I questioned, astonished and confused about how to word my question and not sure of how to react as I measured my emotions.

"Look at him," my brother stated, amused, "He doesn't know what to make of it."

"What are you up to Matt," I chastised him, "I know that you mean to do well...but that's not funny." I stated, still in disbelief.

"Babe," Jane consoled, "...it is Malachi."

"But I know what I saw," I reasoned with mixed emotions, "he's dead…" I concluded by recalling the events of my twilight vision as I began tearing up. "I rode with mom and dad to the graveyard: You were in the lead car with Cammie. He was in a casket, and we were standing at his grave site. That's when I passed out, remember? That wasn't a dream… right?" I rationalized in a confused state. "I was there…I saw it." My emotion became very strong with unresolved feelings as I thought about the traumatic events that had transpired several days earlier. My mom chimed in to help reason my recollection.

"No, son, you've been in the hospital since the shooting… you must have been dreaming about being at the cemetery while in your coma."

The belief in my sad, alternate recollection only began to wane with their continued reassurance as I cautiously dared to allow myself to start believing that Malachi was in fact sitting before me. I studied him as my brother and dad helped Malachi to stand to his feet and then gingerly escorted him over to my bed.

"Hey buddy, snap out of it…it's me..." he reassured as he displayed his wounds. "…it's really me. You remember our 'high sign' don't you?" he reminded as he first motioned with his thumb and index finger as if to measure an inch and then making a circle with his index finger and thumb, "Little to nothing." He explained.

"Yeah," I responded with familiarity, "Little to nothing."

"I wanted to surprise you and to thank you in person for backing me up by putting your life on the line to save mine. Jesus said, 'No greater love… than to lay your life down for a friend.'" Malachi expressed his gratitude "One more bullet and I'd been a goner for sure. So how are you doing, buddy?"

Tears rolled down my cheeks as I finally accepted the good news that my friend was indeed alive as my doubt faded into an exhilarating reality, "Hey man, I thought it was going to be the last time I saw you. I don't have the words…I can't tell you how good it is to see you up and around."

"You know, you're the one who gave all of us a scare. You were unconscious for days. We didn't know whether you were coming or going." He qualified as I noticed beads of sweat rolling down his forehead from the strain of standing.

"Hey, you better sit down," I cautioned.

"Yeah, I'm still trying to get around on my own." He explained breathing heavily as my family helped him back into his chair.

"So, what happened, how'd they bring you back? The last time I saw you the medics were asking to cease resuscitation attempts."

"Well, that was interesting. The simple answer was that Cammie's prayer was answered. In the spiritual realm I was very aware of her praying for me and I was aware of God's gracious response to her prayer. At first, I had no choice about living or dying and my body was completely spent. Without divine intervention I had no power to remain but then I felt the urgency of angelic intervention. I heard a voice talking but not speaking to me saying, 'Not since Jesus wept at Lazarus' tomb has heaven witnessed such a heart wrenching plea for mercy.'"

"Say what?" I inquired bewildered.

"What I'm trying to tell you," He explained definitively – "…is that not only was I dead I was well aware that I was dead; my spirit was out of my body, and I was gone. I was actually able to interact with my unborn children and felt remorseful compassion about leaving them and then Cammie made such an emotional and inspirational plea that it reverberated throughout heaven.

I then requested permission to return and was granted mercy on behalf of my family. I was told by a voice with authority that now was not my time. By that time my body had been transported to the hospital. Looking down I saw the surgeon working on me, I was told by the voice to wait until the right time before returning. When the medical staff hit my body once again with the defibrillator my spirit felt that jolt and knew that it was time for me to return.

The next thing I heard was a nurse with red hair yelling, 'We got a pulse.' Then I went into a peaceful sleep. After twelve hours of being in the "ICU" I regained consciousness. I know it sounds strange," he rationalized, "but my account matches the medical records. I was medically dead for approximately seventeen minutes and had no ill effects from a lack of oxygen and my account of what happened in "ICU" was also recorded. They noticed my body convulsing several seconds after the electrical impulse was applied with the defibrillator just before my pulse returned."

"That's not only cool, but inspirational. I'm just so glad that you're still here. Like I said, I don't have the words to describe how I feel. I love you man. It's really good to see you." I expressed. "Oh, and by the way, I didn't have the opportunity to congratulate you and Cammie. How does it feel to be an old married couple?" I joked.

"We are very happy; so many people have reached out to us to lend their prayers and support. The shooting of course was in the news and our marriage has been celebrated as, "The Shot-Gun Wedding That Transcends Time." The newspaper coined that title for our wedding based on our vows as being, 'And forever and beyond.' We are very grateful because we have each other and two wonderful children on the way; our future is very bright. Life is so much better than fairy tales." Malachi said as Cammie put her left hand on his right shoulder which caused her new ring to sparkle.

"Yes," I acknowledged, "near death experiences can be an inspiring motivator that refine your focus of appreciating the importance of people – rather than taking them for granted and prioritizing the stuff in your life. As a matter of fact... I have unfinished business of my own," I declared as I turned my attention to Jane addressing her.

"What I have learned from you since that first time that we were on the dock is that romance is not about trying to create the perfect moment. Romance is about making the most out of each moment, while creating unforgettable memories with your one true love. Thinking back now, I believe that's when I realized that you were what I wanted. I regret forcing you to make the first move due to my lack of action; but I don't plan to duplicate that mistake."

"Oh, my...he's going to ask her..." I overheard my mother whisper to my dad.

"I must concede," I continued. "...that I would have loved to have had the opportunity to plan for a more worthy and appropriate venue that could yield the discreteness necessary to promote the magnitude of this moment. I would have favored to create a memorable *romantic* setting for you.

I would also have preferred to be standing to enhance more prominence and splendor to this moment to show you just how important you are to me. Not to mention, I also don't have a ring to give you - that is just not yet. But nonetheless, despite the lack of pomp and stance... I want this moment to belong to us."

I noticed tears rolling down her cheek with anticipation of my next words, and so I didn't hesitate any further to express my intentions, "Jane, I want you to be the last thing I touch before I go to sleep and the first thing I see when I wake up in the morning. My desire is to enjoy that for a lifetime. I would be more than humbled if you would settle to marry me?"

"Absolutely!" she declared as she hugged me. "I don't care about all of the theatrics; it's you that I want. As long as you make my last name become Camble; you'll make me one happy girl."

Everyone in the room sporadically in unison congratulated us as my mother interjected, "I don't mean to interrupt this beautiful occasion, but if you will indulge me for a brief moment, I have something for the two of you." She explained leading up to her reasoning for taking off her engagement ring and handing it to me.

Then as she addressed Jane directly, she happily described the magnitude of her ceremonious announcement, "I gave Zaylen life, but you gave him his purpose for his life. What you two have is a stunning love story." She expounded as she handed me the 24 -Karat white gold 1-karat princess cut diamond engagement ring. "This is a Camble family heirloom that was given to me by Isaac's mother on our wedding day.

When she gave it to me, his mother explained that this ring symbolized the importance of the Camble heritage that was being entrusted and passed onto me. This ring is to always remain in the family and represents the hopefulness that I too would always remain in the family. This ring now welcomes you;" she concluded ceremoniously, "…the future matriarch of the next generation of, 'The Camble,' family."

Jane put her hand towards me, and I feebly held her hand so that I could place the ring on Jane's finger. It was a slightly loose fit to her petite finger, but it would suffice as wearable until it could be properly sized. As I slipped the ring onto her finger, I noticed that her hands were actually trembling.

It was cool to discover how much Jane was genuinely affected by the 'pomp and stance' of this significant monumental occasion. It was evident that this ring brought with it an unmistakable reverence of christening Jane with this momentous ritual.

"Wow!" Jane marveled. "I'm not the kind of girl that cares about a lot of glitz and glitter but I've gotta admit that I'm overwhelmed. For some reason this ring seems to complete the mood and makes it all feel so much more special. Thank you, Mrs. Camble, this was very generous, and this ring is really pretty."

"You are most welcome," my mother responded cordially then interjected. "But there's two things you're going to have to get used to, young lady. You're part of our family so first off call us Krysta and Isaac, and second you're gonna have to get used to that "nice" ring because it's now been entrusted to you."

"See, what I mean," she said justifying her earlier statement, "your parents have been just wonderful."

We would be married on July 22. As it would happen, it was the same date that my parents had been wed 36 years earlier. We asked that same small-town mayor who married Malachi and Cammie to conduct our ceremony because of his endearing generous style.

We would go on to have five terrific children, three "mother hen" girls and two ornery boys all who contributed to an extension of our gleeful love and devotion to one another. It would be an error for me to state that my life became "complete" when I met Jane because that gives a false pretense that my previous existence came to an end. Rather truly it was the start of a pleasing duty for the two of us to complement each other with reaching our full potential to create the kind of nurturing home environment that I grew up in.

People often declare that the 'best things' that have ever happened to them in their lives have been single isolated and 'independent events.' I have found instead that the grandest events that can happen in one's life - those, 'biggest and best things ever,' are not any single event.

The best things in one's life are achieved over a series of lifetime events that are spent with loved ones. Together, Jane and I have been able to create a world in which the pursuit of "the good life" recognizes that the only true and valuable currency is time, and that currency is best spent building memories with family and where a successful career is measured in love.

We have been blessed to live the quintessential dream nearly every boy and girl grows up desiring. To live the "Joy of life," rather than to just survi…

"Wake up!" I called out disturbing his slumber.

"Huh? What?" my friend questioned as he stirred awake.

"Hey, hey, Colin wake up…" I called out again to awaken Colin, who had been asleep and dreaming in English class. I had pushed on his elbow with a nudge to dislodge him from the comfort of his relaxed sleeping position. The act of my awakening Colin from a much-needed rest and perhaps a good dream would be all that Colin would have been able to recollect about the end of the first period.

He had taken the advantage of a lengthy nap during the extended English Class period. He would not have been cognizant of the subtle event that compelled me to take directions from the teacher to awaken him from the slumbering solitude moments that he stole while in Creative Writing Class. It was his snore that drew the attention of the English teacher.

"Okay, let's get our creative thoughts going," the teacher encouraged during a lecture as Colin slept. "'If a picture paints a thousand words… then,'… what?" she instructed, "Fill in the blank." As the teacher waited in that moment for a volunteer to participate, there was a silent pause from her instruction which illuminated a slight snoring noise that redirected her attention from teaching the class about creative writing to Colin's inattentiveness. "Colin…Colin?" she called out, attempting to stir Colin awake. Unsuccessful in her endeavor she requested my assistance with awakening him. "Mr. Tenaj, (Ta- na -ja)" the teacher instructed, addressing me, "would you mind too terribly if I asked you to please wake up your friend, Mr. Maberi so that he doesn't miss out on the assignment?"

We were in Ms. Conaway's Writing Advanced Class

(WAC). It was a rigorous college prep course with an extended double period of time. It was the type of class in which students could earn college credit. The class was designed for people who planned to attend college as English Majors and possibly become aspiring authors.

There were only three boys in a class with fifteen students. The male representation consists of myself, my friend Colin, whose seat was to the left and behind me. He in turn sat directly behind the third named Hoss, our 6 foot 6, 320-pound football center lineman. Hoss was relatively intelligent and learned quickly but this course was above his writing abilities, and he was admitted into the class only to fulfill the curricular credit requirements necessary for him to participate in sports.

Colin and I were charged with tutoring him with completing the assignments to ensure his success in the class. Since Colin sat right behind Hoss, "The Human Building," he had reasonably good cover to remain undetected to rest his eyes during the class lectures, or to engage in other playful covert activities he may wish to take part in.

One time the teacher didn't even notice that he was absent until he arrived with a tardy pass. But this time he would be discovered by a snort caused by a deep relaxing REM mode sleep from the pain medication Percocet. He used pain medication to find relief as he continued to recover from his injury. Just before the teacher noticed him sleeping, I thought that I heard Colin snort out a quiet snore as he slept. This ultimately drew unwarranted attention to him from Ms. Conaway. After the teacher gave me instructions to awaken him, I responded submissively.

"Yes ma'am." I acknowledged to obey her request as instructed while making an excuse for Colin's indiscretion, "We got in late last night from the mini invitational track meet from Wheeling Park and it was Colin's first road trip with the team since his injury. I think that he's still not used to being up that long."

"I understand," Ms. Conway stated compassionately, "Go ahead and wake him up please."

"Hey, hey, Colin, wake up…" I called out as I reached my hand back and pushed on his elbow.

"Yeah, huh? What… what's wrong?" he inquired, coming out of his slumber.

"Wake up…" I instructed. "Ms. Conway heard you snore." She's going over our new assignment." I explained.

"Sorry, Ms. Conaway." He sincerely acknowledged stretching his arms toward the ceiling as he became cognizant of his surroundings, "I think that the meds are still making me groggy, and it was a long night." He conceded as some of the girls giggled shyly at his antics.

"I understand. Are you okay? Would you like a pass to the nurse?" she redirected.

"No thank you. I'm okay now." He reassured, still stretching as he yawned.

"Then may we continue now?" she asked sarcastically.

"Yes," he continued with their playful banter. "Please continue. I'm with you now."

"Good," Ms. Conaway acknowledged as she continued with instruction by readdressing the rest of the class. "Now that we have Mr. Maberi among the living, let's try it again." She suggested. "As I was saying, as writers you have to find ever new creative ways to capture the reader's imagination. Often the writer seeks to discover a way to convey a thought that may have already been communicated many times by other writers but express that familiar sentiment in a memorable way that highlights a fresh creative skill and ability of artistic originality.

As a writer you have to find an interesting way to make the reader imagine what *you* want them to see, and to express how *you* want them to feel, and for the reader to want what it is *you* have them to covet. For example, the popular saying, 'If a picture paints a thousand words…' how would you try to fill in the blank to be different?"

Hoss raised his hand, "Yes, Hoss you have an answer?"

"I know the answer…If a picture paints a thousand words, then why can't I paint you?"

"Yes, Hoss, that's the line from a song. That is something that's already been said," she explained. "Do you have an original idea to share? Something that is saying the same thing but in a different way?"

"I bet Colin does." Chloe volunteered in a flirtatious manner. "He has such a beautiful mind… along with other big things." She offered her insight coquettishly as other girlish giggles emerged in agreement. Chloe was the outspoken, opinionated, sexy, blonde who was the captain of the cheerleading squad. She had pursued Colin for years but to no avail.

"Okay Chloe," Ms. Conaway admonished, "take a deep breath and kick it down a notch, I don't want to have to send you to take a cold shower to cool down. However…" Ms. Conaway conceded, "On the other hand Chloe is right about the mind thing. So, Colin, do you care to share something with that brilliant mind of yours now that you're well rested?"

Colin shook his head and stretched his arms up yawing once again as he contemplated his thoughts for a moment and mumbled. "You guys brought me out of the best dream I've ever had for this?" Then he began to talk out loud to himself. "Let's see…" he took a minute to assess the purpose of thought. "You're tryin' to explain to someone how difficult it is to say in a few words just how special they are."

Then he looked up and definitively declared, "'If a picture paints a thousand words, then you are an epic motion picture with blockbuster sequels.' Or maybe, 'Rembrandt painted priceless masterpieces, but he was just a man. It was certainly the hand of God that painted you.'"

"That's my star pupil." Ms. Conaway praised. "Sorry to disturb you while you're having the dream of your life but it's nice to have you back with us. That was poetry."

"Wow!" Chloe observed wooing over Colin's intelligence. "Like I said, 'That beautiful mind of his.' And then there's all the rest of him…"

"Ok, now for today's assignment:" Ms. Conaway prepared the class to receive instruction. "Explore an emotional concept of your choice that you will later contrast in a story. This will help you to refine the direction for your final manuscript. I'll give you the first period to develop your main idea about your chosen concept and then you will present your thoughts during the second period."

We had about a half hour to develop and write out our contrast before the bell rang to end the first period and then the class exited into the hall for our break. Mainly our break was used to get a much-needed change of scenery from sitting in one classroom for two periods as we watched other students pass by moving to their next class. When our second period was about to begin for WAC, we all returned to face the gauntlet of sharing our precious work.

"Alright, let's all quiet down. Let's get started so we can get through all of these contrasts." Ms. Conaway instructed us as she started the second period. "Onicha, do you want to get us started? Give us your contrast and a brief antidote that explains your thoughts."

As the teacher finished Onicha stood up and cleared her throat to prepare to share her work. "Uh, hum," she began, "'Fear *of death is what makes you feel alive.'* It's often said that people never feel more alive than when they're almost dead. I was kind of thinking of like when people have near death experience or old people start thinking about missed opportunities or someone who's been given 6 months to live comes up with a 'bucket list' of things that they always thought about doing but were afraid of getting hurt or dying, but then realizing that they may die before they've had a chance to really start enjoying life they finally start to do fun things. The thought of dying makes people think about living."

"Okay good, Onicha has us off to a decent start, who would like to go next?"

"I'll go!" Colleen raised her hand to eagerly volunteer.

"Okay, Colleen go ahead then, you're up."

"Alright," Colleen began proudly. "Mine is a little bit of a brain teaser, *'Don't lose Tomorrow, Today, because of Yesterday.'* – If you keep looking at mistakes from the past in a negative way instead of using the experiences as a 'lesson learned,' then that time is counterproductive and wasted. As a result, the opportunities that might present themselves today may be overlooked because of what happened the day before. This then can also cost you losing the opportunity that could be beneficial for the future. You can only control the moment that you are actually living in; and it's your decision of whether to dwell hopelessly in the past and thereby fail to act in the present thereby costing you the ability to build a better future."

"Okay, Colleen, I like this one." Ms. Conaway praised. "Nice catchy phrase. Very good being able to take a complicated topic and appropriately overly simplified. Secondly, it's not just a contrast of two things, it's a 'con-*tri*-ast'. That's right people, I just coined a new term. Very creative to be able to counter three things in the same thought. I think that this could be in the running. Alright, I'm looking forward to hearing the rest. Next up, Leah."

"Mine is a little on the prophetic side," Leah introduces. *'Experiencing living or lie down dying,'* Don't be afraid to try different things. Plan and enjoy doing fun things in life. If you sit around thinking of all of the things that can go wrong, all you're doing is waiting to die."

"Alright, short but thorough. Very thoughtful. Okay, how about you Opal, it looks like you're chomping at the bit to do yours. I like that you look excited."

"Love hates Hate, and Hate loves… to hate love."

"Ooo-oo, nice… a brain teasing tongue twister," Ms. Conaway expressed. "Two opposite words that use the other to express discontentment of the other's existence. They are being used as both a noun and a verb. That's a good one! The phrase speaks for itself but go ahead and educate us."

"Well, it's kind of weird how much Love and Hate each totally relies on the other. To truly love you can't hate anything except for Hate itself and so the act of love hates the idea and the existence of Hate. Then Hate doesn't want anything good and so Hate, hates Love just because it's something good. Hate itself is evil but hating hate is Love."

"I'm so confused…" Hoss said, burying his face in his hands. "Please make her stop."

Opal continued her explanation as if Hoss hadn't said anything, "Love and Hate want to be separate from each other because they have two totally different agendas, but they cannot stand alone because they are really simply a flip side of the same coin. One side tries to never see the other side. It takes two to make one. Without Love you have no concept of hate."

"Okay, Opal I see why you were so excited to share. That's a good one. We have a lot of impressive competition going on here. Okay, Hoss, how about you next then?"

"Yes ma'am, mine is simple," he qualified, "Not some nightmare brain tease like Opal's. Mine is actually scientific," he explained. *"'**Night and Day are not opposite… together they make up one day.**' I figure that people think of them as being a contrast but actually they are exactly the same."

"Okay nice Hoss that is true and it's a nice look at contrast." Ms. Conway supported as she moved on to the next student. "Chloe let's keep it rolling. They have all been pretty good so far."

"'Bravery can only exist in the presence of experiencing fear.' Chloe announced proudly, "Only when someone has the willingness to confront that which they fear does bravery become in existence. "People often perceive that a brave person is someone who is not afraid of what will happen to them but only a stupid person is not afraid of danger. A brave person is acutely aware of the imminent danger and would prefer to avoid facing the danger but the character of the individual to do the right thing drives them to do it anyway.

This sacrificial act is performed despite the fact that it may cost a person something of great value, possibly even their own life. The strength of a brave person is having the full knowledge of what the high cost may be and still moving forward…toward the danger. The consequences are weighed but the cause takes precedence. If there is no risk involved or if the act is done without a noble cause, then it is not bravery."

"I don't get it," Hoss interjected, "What's her contrast? Do good or do bad?"

"No silly," Chloe explained. "Bravery and Fear. In order to be brave you have to fear something first. You can't get one without first having the other."

"Yes, nice, Chloe, that was brilliant." Ms. Conaway reinforced. "You have to have the one before you can get the other. And Hoss points out that you may even be able to interject a second contrast with yours. Alright," Ms. Conaway addressed me, "Ryland, are you ready?"

"Sure, teach. Mine takes care of everything that we're discussing: money, power, fame, love, even the bravery topic. ***'To get everything you must be willing to have nothing.'*** The more you try to accumulate owning things the less control you have." I elaborated, "Until you are willing to give up everything you won't have anything. People are often able to achieve possessing something that they *think* is desirable only to later find out that it's not enough to satisfy their increasing craving and want the next best thing. So then, when you actually get something that you wanted only to turn around to want something else instead… 'If so, fact so,' you really don't have anything.

You have to realize that truly having something is to be satisfied with having only what is necessary. If you happen to be blessed with more than the necessities, then consider it a plus. No one actually has everything until they have the freedom to live in peace and harmony.

Often, having something is not as desirable as wanting it. As the Bible questions the logic of getting everything you want only to lose that which is most important. 'What shall it profit a man if he should gain the whole world and lose his own soul?' You must be willing to sacrifice everything, only then can you truly have anything."

Even Egar Allen Poe suggested that the tighter you try to hold on to something it still seeps out of your hand. "I hold within my hand…grains of the golden sand. How few yet how they creep, through my fingers to the deep…Can I not grasp them with a tighter clasp, can I not save but one from the pit less waves?...."

"Okay, Ryland, an appropriately thorough explanation from you. A quote from both the Bible and Poe. Now we're getting really deep. Good job. Malissa, what do you have for us?"

'The presence of Evil is what highlights the Good.' In the Garden of Eden, the tree itself was not evil, it was the *choice to disobey* that presented the evil. Without choice there is no free will, without free will there is no opportunity to do "Good" which is the decision to do something right, and no chance to do bad which is the choice to act by doing something wrong."

"Okay good Malissa, first I like the reference you used to explain your point. Secondly, very short but still spot on!" Ms. Conaway applauded, "Alright, Dasie, tell us your thoughts."

'It's better to experience good even if it's taken away from you, which is bad.' Bad things happening to you means that you had it "good" at one time. Even in the worst conditions as long as you have been able to live you had to have it good enough to be able to survive.

Hard work is the only way to earn a well-deserved rest. You have to work hard to rest well."

"Good principal to live by... nice job, Dasie. Okay, Sebastian, you're next."

"My contrast is, ***'Believing in Heaven when Hell is near.'*** People often say that they believe in God and act like they are good Christians but only act appropriately when they believe that people are watching. In effect they are really "prostituting" the gospel for their own gain. These people prey on the innocent and act like Saints when actually they are the worst offenders, "wolves in sheep's clothing."

They offer no compassion and often cause great pain. They will experience the worst punishment in the end. They are enjoying the only Heaven they will ever know now while on earth, but Hell is just around the corner waiting for them. "Vengeance is mine, says the Lord."

"Okay. Looks like we have a sermon coming from you, huh? Pretty deep thought, and thorough. Very nice. Colette? Are you ready?"

"Alright, my dad is a Marine and a real 'Bad Ass'... whoops, sorry that slipped. That's what happens when you grow up in a real soldier's home. Anyway, I had to honor him so mine is, ***'Peace is only understood with the realization of war. Peace is not derived from peace itself. Peace cannot bring about war, but War can bring about peace.'***"

"Okay good Collett…" As Ms. Conaway was about to call another name Collett interrupted…

"Do you want me to explain?" Collette inquired, wanting to finish her thought.

"I'm sorry. I'm moving too fast. I thought you were finished. Sure, go ahead and finish."

"Well, I've asked my dad why he doesn't just quit being a soldier and stay home with us and he explained that he doesn't choose to be away from us and that he does not want to go to war but that our country needs to always be strongly prepared as a deterrent from people wanting to do us harm. He says that's true for both foreign and domestic.

He had me remember a quote from one of our founding fathers, that, '*We should never trade freedom for the perception of safety because if we do, we will lose both and don't deserve either.*' So even though our soldiers are trained to kill it is only done to protect the innocent and to preserve peace. Without a strong deterrent you are bound to find war."

"Alright, I'll be looking forward to reading your complete thesis. Okay, Sara, tell us about yours."

"Well, I think since we are doing contrast, that I would express our observations about all of our concepts put together, **'What we're saying is that it's complicated to be simple.'** You often hear that acronym KISS because people are always trying to simplify things but instead things become more difficult. It seems that our contrast assignment highlights that nothing really stands on its own, to understand good, you have to experience bad, to love you have to reject hate, light is understood by experiencing the dark and it goes on, and on.

No matter how simple something appears to be there are always complications. Computers are supposed to make things easier, but something always goes wrong. Convenience makes it easier too, but then convenience is more expensive, and may cause health issues. We become lazy which ends up complicating matters."

Beauty and pleasure are what exposes the ugly of sin. Sin is bad as it uses covetousness to make something that is wrong appear to feel right and good. The experience of bad helps with the appreciation of good.

"Okay, go ahead Kerry."

"Mine is the obvious, *'Pleasure is Pain, and Pain is Pleasure.'* "Sometimes pain can be perceived as pleasurable…"

"Boy, I'll say so…" Chloe chimed in, interrupting with playful sexually charged banter. "Make it hurt so good…" she expounded with a playfully sensual tone. As some of the girls giggled and began to express their approval of her clandestine jovial sensual referenced observation. Ignoring Chloe's statement Ms. Conaway gave a unilateral instruction to quiet the class and to keep the banter down to a minimum and then redirected the attention back to Kerry.

"Alright class… let's keep it clean now, let Kerry finish."

"That's what *she* said…" Chloe blurted out with another zinger making the whole class laugh out loud."

Even Ms. Conaway was caught by surprise. She closed her lips very tightly as a spontaneous smirk appeared on her face. She sighed heavily as she sought to conceal her amusement while choking back an inadvertent chuckle. She then lowered her head to reestablish a stoic demeanor. Once her composure was restored, she rolled her eyes and announced in a professional tone. "Ms. Hart!" She addressed Chloe harshly. "Stop it! Kerry…" she redirected calmly, "…please continue."

"Thank you, Ms. Conaway." She acknowledged with a professional tone. "Well although it is documented scientifically that some sensual pleasure can be attributed to pain, I was trying to keep it clean by using examples such as exercise, the slogan, 'NO PAIN, NO GAIN.' The pain you suffer leads to a healthy life which is pleasurable. Acupuncture and squeezing pressure points like the ear lobe can relax stress away. The body is weird. Also, things like discipline may be perceived as being painful but it can produce pleasurable benefits that may not have happened without the experience of the painful event."

"As we witnessed, that can be a very delicate topic," Ms. Conaway observed. "But you presented your observation with dignity and class." She praised. "You may include the example of the sensual topic in your writing provided that it is done as tastefully as you presented this. Very good job. Alright Emily let's wind it down."

'Is love, Love? Love may actually be hating that feels like love.' "It's a question that can be explained that Love is not love just because someone wants to call their experience love, for the sake of love." Emily explained, confident that her topic was an inquisitive masterpiece.

"Oh, no, here we go again…" Hoss complained. "I can't take it anymore… my head is going to explode."

Emily continued, "Many abusive relationships hinge on the premise that the abused person remains because they believe that they *Love* the person and remarkably believe that the abuser loves them back for some special unexplained reason. But the reality is that instead the perceived devotion being called love is actually an unhealthy dependency, and delusion of caring. Also, there are many situations that 'feel' right and good but there is a hidden destructive force. The Bible details what love is and with whom acts of love are appropriately shared. Anything contrary to that acceptance is not Love but a counterfeit."

"Okay, powerful, strong conviction. Impressive." She said as she prefaced introducing Colin. "Okay Colin, since nobody ever wants to go right after you, we saved you for last. So enlighten us with what Chloe keeps referring to as… 'Your beautiful brain.'"

"Well," he began to explain, "I titled my contrast, "Blue Island" because that's where lonely hearts go. I envision a place where every single heart has its own isolated island. Each heart can be pierced with one of cupid's arrows. Although the heart is red, it bleeds blue symbolizing the lonely color. The contrast that I came up with is the phrase, ***"Love our Enemy"*** but the word love is a noun not a verb. So, it should not read like we should love our enemies rather it should read like, 'Love, as a living being… *is* our Enemy.' The phrase means that Love, as a noun *IS* our enemy and not to read the word, love, as an action verb suggesting that one is instructed to, '*love* our enemies.'"

"Wow!" Malissa turned in his direction amazed. Then she looked back at Chloe awaiting a comment from her. Chloe did not disappoint, taking the opportunity to offer her observation once again by restating her earlier observation.

"Like I keep saying, that Beautiful mind of his, and he's just getting started." She continued, unable to restrain her lustful observation, "I wonder what his body is like when he gets it started."

"Okay, ladies," Ms. Conaway interjected. "Let him finish."

"That's what *she* said…" Chloe whispered without looking up to conceal that it was she who made the statement.

"Really?" Ms. Conaway chastised. "That's what you're going with? That's enough Chloe. Let's try to be a little more grown up. We only have a few minutes left before the bell rings. Go ahead Colin."

"Blue Island" Colin narrated.

Love is our enemy! Because of that, we are doomed for eternity. Everyone searches for love but even if there were some who did not search, Love would find them. Love's presence and effect is more addictive than any drug or habit, more elusive than trying to contain the air, or the sea, and more powerful than the strongest storm or any other force of nature. Even the most logical cognitive thought can be swirled into confusion. Experiencing Love's punishment is worse than any consequence of all sins combined.

Love's influence is so severe that it makes you forget your fear of death. Love is greedier than the grave. One cannot escape Love's imprisonment because it incarcerates the soul. Love mercilessly consumes everything in its path. You can't hide from Love, and you can't escape life unscathed from its effects because love seeps into every crevasse and every fiber of one's being. Therefore, even exposure through the 'butterfly effect' Love will confine and imprison Life itself. Life is not worth living without the hope of experiencing love. Rather it is Love that creates the moments for which we live.

Love rejects the concept of sympathy and therefore, man's faithful companion… Death is the only viable solution for any hope of escape from Love's oppressive effects. But even that potential escape is burdensome and leaves substantial, residual, collateral damage. The rich cannot barter, or bribe Love and the poor receive no charity or empathy from Love's devastating effects.

Love claims only tears and broken hearts for payment of admission. Even the potential relief of Mercy and Grace are inferior and subservient to Love. The concept of the elusive, 'true love' hinges on an unattainable jubilation that is fostered from another's selfless commitment. The bible declares that 'Love never fails!' As such it is truest of statements reinforcing that the reason for which Love is undefeated is because Love never fails, *itself,* because *it*…being Love, is all powerful."

"Very, very nice." Ms. Conaway expounded. "You certainly did not disappoint."

"I bet he never disappoints!" Chloe interrupted offering her flirtatious opinion.

"Chloe! "I'm warning you." The teacher threatened her with disciplinary action. Then Ms. Conaway continued to address Colin. "I can hardly wait to see your final product."

The teacher interjected before finalizing her instruction for the assignment. Since the bell was due to ring shortly, she wrapped up her instruction, "Okay people, listen up so that I can give you your assignment. We've been building your portfolio all year so that you will have a completed manuscript to submit so that you can utilize it to show potential publishers your writing style.

You also have to get used to making deadlines with quality work so this assignment will be very difficult." She cautioned as she laid the groundwork for our assignment. You will take what you've been writing in class and create a final product. There is a coveted prize for the best literature work… The first prize winner will get to meet the CEO of the Publishing Company to discuss a contract for having your manuscript put in print and an initial payment of $1000.

This could possibly springboard one of you into being an immediate American Author. Pretty exciting, huh? Second place will receive a $500 prize, and third place $100. The stakes are high, so I want to encourage you to be prepared to put in your best effort.

I want you to take the weekend to work on it, have it ready to be proofread by your partner. We'll use most of next week to refine your work to have your final product to be ready for print on Friday. Connecting all of your work into one complete project is going to be tricky. That's all. The rest of the period is yours."

"Hey, Colin," Lance called in a strained whisper. "Are you going to go to the dance tomorrow night?"

"I don't know, I hope to," Colin replied. "It all depends on whether or not I can get my homework done. What about you, Ryland? Are you going?"

"Yeah," I said. "I'll have to see if my parents will let me use the car."

"All right," Lance started while addressing Colin, "Call me…"

Just then, the bell rang. Lance's mouth was still moving, but neither Colin nor I could hear him.

"What did you say?" Colin asked Lance when the bell stopped.

"Whew-y!" Lance exclaimed as he rushed out the door. "The weekend is here. Call me tonight, all right? See you guys later!" he yelled while dashing out of the classroom.

"All right, Lance. Maybe around 7," I called out as he exited then turning my attention, I recounted Colin's slumber. "Gee, Colin. You sure were sleeping soundly in English class."

"Yeah, I had a long-detailed dream. The kind you're sorry to come out of. I'm hopeful that it'll make for a good story to win that competition. My contrast about Love as a verb and noun came out of what I had dreamed about. Towards the end of class when everyone else was giving their antidote I started to jot down some of the main points so that I can start to editorialize a story."

"That sounds cool, I'm looking forward to seeing how it turns out. What'ya have so far?"

"I have the theme in mind, the title and the main characters."

"Okay, I'm intrigued, enlighten me."

"The theme will hinge on the method of how strangers ultimately meld into a couple. It's kind of cool to dissect how individuals encounter relationships… spontaneously flourishing in a flash from being total strangers to becoming closer than anyone else.

Everyone enjoys the initial addictive euphoric infatuation that is cultivated by the exposure of new intimacy. Those same people confidently vow that the preliminary excitement will only increase and strengthen as the relationship progresses.

Often, however, the relationship is doomed to fizzle as the unselfish nature gives way to self-interest above the partners. I'm gonna challenge my ability with creating more than just a story to take the reader on a romance journey. I plan to create a mood that will immerse a reader to embrace their own euphoria to happen repeatedly. I'm hoping that when someone reads this story their own unique encounter with love will be reinvigorated.

The main characters will incorporate me with my tenacious, caring personality. Janet the aspiring picture of strong femininity…and You… the intuitive, faithful friend but I need one more…."

"Oh! I'm in your story?" I interrupted excitedly. "That's cool. Maybe I'll become famous through your work."

"Yes, you're in the story…" he downplayed my importance. "I need a narrator for the story and you're the man for the job. Don't get a big head about it yet." He commented as he continued to highlight his outline. "My dream had the scene being cast in the country. I'm trying to figure out how to have you tell the story which means that I gotta create the right girl for you. Something fiery but, yet adorable."

"Really? Is that what you see me with? A fiery adorable girl?"

"Yeah, I'm thinking someone who can keep you in check but at the same time she's vulnerable only to you."

"And why do I, as the narrator role, need a girl companion at all?" I questioned. "The narrator typically knows all as a bystander."

"Yes, but your actual role in the story is acting as a character who has an interest *in* the story. You're gonna be someone who is experiencing the moments as a participant. You're not just the 'storyteller'" He explained.

"Okay, I guess I'm feelin' it. The girl for me…are you thinking like Chloe the cheerleader? She's pretty spicy."

"No, she wouldn't fit as a good companion for you.

She has a one-track mind and is too sex crazed. No, you need someone with more depth. Someone who can challenge your intellect." He reasoned.

"Well, thank you…I'm glad to see that you consider me worthy of someone tailored made for me." I joked. "Now, you said that you had a title in mind. Wha'ta ya thinkin about?"

"*'Private Lake,'*" he pronounced confidently.

"That's pretty definitive." I questioned. "Why 'Private Lake'?

"I have a scene in mind that will elaborate the purpose of this being the perfect title." He shook his head proudly.

"So that's how you geniuses come up with good ideas, huh? Success just comes to you in a dream while sleeping. It must be nice." I jealously remarked. "The rest of us have to work for every little morsel." I can't believe that you have that much figured out already just from a dream. Why don't you be a friend and throw some of your creative crumbs my way will ya?" I begged. "Well, we better be getting to practice. I'll meet you on the patio, okay?"

"All right, I'll be there in about twenty minutes. And Ryland… this time don't start the workout with me please."

"Well, I waited a long time for you the last time and I was left just hanging out by myself. You know I don't mind waiting, but after so long, it does get boring."

"I know," Colin acknowledged while hastily backing away. He was in a rush for his routine rendezvous. "I'm sorry, but what do you expect me to do?"

"Maybe you should work on finding that real-life perfect companion for me. Just go-ahead Colin, I'll wait."

Within a few moments he was out of sight, on his way to meet up with Janet Lake. Janet was a junior, who had a terrific personality, and it was ambiguous of people's opinion that she was the prettiest girl in school. She was five feet, ten inches tall and weighed about 150 pounds. Her physique was literally celebrated as a picture of health as she was hailed in a national teen magazine that modeled her as the perfect feminine athletic specimen.

She was in perfect condition; it was a common event for her to place first when she ran in track meet events. Her eyes portrayed a mesmerizing calmness, which in concert with her warm smile she could figuratively melt a cold winter day into the delightful welcoming warmth of summer. Her feathery, brunette hair accentuated her brilliant, lucid emerald, green eyes.

She had always dressed stylishly, but Colin had expressed it to me numerous times when he believed that she looked her best. Those were days that her hair would drape midway down her back in loose curls as it surrounded her slender face. She would dress in feminine laced camis that hugged the contours of her shapely body.

Her flirtatious ensemble was completed with a cute camo mini skirt that covered three quarters over her silky feminine athletic thighs with white heeled pumps that heighten the dimples in her defined calf. She adorned an intoxicating gentle sweet-smelling fragrance called 'Wind Song' that assisted in amplifying her angelic aurora.

It seemed obvious to everyone except Colin and Janet that they belonged with each other. They openly showed that they cared for each other as very close friends; however, nothing further had ever been pursued about the two of them becoming a romantic couple. Every so often, Colin or Janet would go out with someone else, but that relationship was strained and ultimately doomed because it was a mere distraction to their own relationship. It was apparent, they valued time with each other more than anyone else.

On several occasions I offered to be the mediator and tell Janet how Colin felt, but he refused to let me. He would observe that, she seems content with how things are,' he'd reason. 'I don't know if she would be open to having a relationship with me. I love just being around her and I don't want to jeopardize our friendship.'

"But you two are always hanging out together. Haven't either of you thought that you two might be happier as a couple?" I'd reply.

"Maybe," he'd respond, "But I'm afraid to take the chance of making her feel uncomfortable by showing her my true feelings and drive her away. She hasn't made a move forward, and I really don't want to jeopardize our friendship."

"Did you ever think that she may be waiting for the man to make the move so as not to be perceived as being too presumptuous?"

"You may be right, but I just don't know how to advance to the next level."

This is the extent to how far those types of conversations would progress; every so often I would try to convince him to allow me to talk to her, but he refused my request. That was the routine until one eventful day, while sitting in study hall, one of our friends, Brent, convinced Colin into letting him tell Janet that Colin liked her.

"Come on Colin," Brent coaxed. "Let me find out if Janet likes you."

"Don't you guys start. Okay…" Colin begged. "I'm not in the mood for this conversation."

"I'm serious Colin," Brent continued. "Don't you think that this has gone on long enough? Everyone knows that she likes you, and deep down inside you believe it too. Why not just tell her or at least let someone intercede for you?"

"No, man, I don't know," Colin mumbled, seeming to break down a little, but as mentioned this was to no real surprise, as we could often get him to dialogue about the possibility. "I can't afford to lose her when she isn't even mine. Our relationship may not be much – but for right now, at least our platonic relationship offers something that keeps me close to her." He justified.

"Look, Colin," Brent confronted. "If you're worried about Janet feeling awkward and ending your friendship, I can talk to her in a way so that it won't raise any suspicion. It'll just sound like a curious inquiry from a bystander…she doesn't know that we sit together in study hall. And the purpose of the recon will be just to confirm if she has a favorable opinion of you. I'm not going to tell her that you want to date her.

Other than that, as I see it, you don't have anything to lose." He urged. "Look at it this way," he challenged, "If you don't make any effort then she may reason that it is *you* who prefers not to pursue having a relationship. She'll never discover that you ever liked her, and you'll never know for sure whether the two of you could have gotten together. You'll always wonder about whether things could have worked out knowing that you had a good opportunity to do something.

Come on man," he coaxed. "You two belong together. You know it, and she knows it, heck, everybody knows it," he insisted. "That's why you two never date other people for too long." He then closed his argument with a nurturing sentiment. "Colin, All I'm trying to do is to help." I was impressed that his argument was reasonably compelling; perhaps the boldest I've heard to date.

Colin shook his head negatively and muttered, "I don't know. You make a compelling argument." He conceded while qualifying. "I just don't want to mess things up." Then he turned toward me and inquired of my opinion asking… "Well, what do you think?"

"Me? You want to know what I think?" I was caught by surprise by the change in the direction of this conversation. Usually by this point in a discussion he was already definitely dismissive of the topic but this time he appeared to be seriously considering allowing Brent to tell her.

Regaining my composure, I began to share my coherent thoughts on the matter. "Well, the decision is up to you." I downplayed the importance of my opinion. "Personally, though, my observation is that I don't anticipate you encountering any problems with entertaining the opportunity to finding out what she thinks. Although cautiously you still need to prepare yourself to come to terms that you can deal with any potential unfavorable intel. I mean if it is determined that she isn't interested in pursuing an exclusive relationship you'll be okay with knowing.

Actually, either way it may have the benefit of making your friendship stronger since you won't have the strain of wandering any longer. Personally, if it were me, I would want to know. In this life sometimes the best thing you can do is to try. I would go for it." I reasoned, "If you don't play…you can't win."

"I would like to know, - you make both valid points about strengthening the friendship regardless, but…can I take it?" he pondered for a moment and hung his head toward the floor in deep thought. Then looking back up, he declared, "Well… Dag-on-it, maybe you're right…perhaps it is time for me to roll my dice and take my chance." He affirmed with a confident swagger in his voice.

"You mean you're going to let him do it?" I asked excitedly and louder than expected. My outburst caused unwarranted attention to our table. Mr. Lyons, the study hall teacher, looked up from his desk over the top rim of his glasses and sequenced his lips in a discontented manner.

I bent the corners of my mouth and covered it with my hand as if to signal my apology for the disruption and hoping that the acknowledgement of my indiscretion was sufficient to keep from being assigned a detention. He responded with a raised eyebrow to signify his silent disapproval and as a warning and then continued his work.

"Don't tell the whole school," Colin warned.

"Sorry, I couldn't help it." I whispered, still unsure of his willingness to pursue going through with it. "So, you're really going to let him do it?"

"Well, I'd rather you did it, Ryland. Maybe it's time for me to grow up and prepare to deal with the consequences," Colin rationalized.

As I was about to agree that I would, Brent defended his position spurting out, "No, come on Colin – Let me do it, it was my idea. Besides…" he argued, "think of it this way, she knows that you two are close friends, so she'll reason that whatever Ryland is aware of, you also are certain to know.

She may even assume that you put him up to it and wonder why you didn't 'just grow a pair' and ask her yourself." He reasoned, "So If you don't want her to be suspicious of what we're doing and retain your autonomy, then it has to be done by someone like me who does not have a specific link to you."

Colin looked at me and I wondered if he was reconsidering his decision as I disappointingly acknowledged Brent's reasoning, "He's right you know."

"Yeah, I know," Colin heaved out a sigh as he bit down on his bottom lip and shifted his eyes as he reexamined his decision. He had already committed himself within his mind to rationalizing that the time had come to get his nerves up and to face whatever may lay in his fate. The question now being waged – 'Does he now dare to shy away; yet again and risk losing this moment of resolution forever?' Finally, he exhaled deeply rendering his verdict. "Okay, Brent," he said, physically straightening his back symbolizing a stiffened resolve to his character. "The job's yours. Just be careful about how you go about it."

"Don't worry," he reassured. "I'll be very discreet. Besides, I'm confident she feels the same about you."

Although I was sure that she liked him, deep down I did have some lingering faint reservations and was somewhat nervous for him. I realized the magnitude of how much this meant to him, and I was uncertain just how he might cope with it if things didn't work out how we all had anticipated. For those reasons, I was relieved that I was spared from the job of talking to her and spared from perhaps being the cause of messing things up.

For the remainder of the period, we worked on contingency plans and rehearsed to prepare Brent for possible scenarios of her responses. We called the covert plan "Operation: Wind Song" referring to Janet's choice of fragrance and the hope that the news would be music to Colin's ears.

Brent was given a deadline to accomplish the mission of reckoning Janet's disposition toward Colin. He was to speak to her within the next couple of days and a second parameter that was put in place was for him to do it before lunch period so that he could give his report to Colin in study hall.

On the fourth day, I saw Brent down by Janet's locker talking to her before study hall. The fact that he came into study hall a few seconds after the bell led us to believe with yearning anticipation that he was late because he was finding out what Janet thought.

As Brent approached the table, I eagerly inquired of him, "Well... did you talk to her?"

"I was just about to do it, but I got scared." He claimed shamefully as he declared, "I didn't do it."

"You what?!" I exclaimed in a low harsh whisper while sending a barrage of questions. "You got scared? What does that even mean? You're not the one asking her out." I explained. "What do you have to be afraid of?"

"I don't know exactly what I'm afraid of … talking to her is… well, it's kind of intimidating. She's smart, pretty, and popular… I just don't know what to say to her to keep up a conversation and then I got to thinking about possibly messing it up and I got scared."

"Well, I just saw you talking to her, what did you even say to her then?"

"I told her that my girlfriend likes her outfits."

"Well? That's actually a good start." I commended. "It was a good way to break into a conversation."

"I was trying to introduce small talk to catch her off guard. I figured that if she knew that I had a girlfriend right away that she would not suspect that I was trying to 'hit on her.'"

"Okay, that makes sense. We're with you."

"Then I planned on telling her that I see her with Colin a lot. Then I would continue to ask her if she liked going out with Colin or if she were interested in someone else. That way it would sound like I never talk to Colin and make it appear that a stranger thought that they were already dating. I figured that if I asked that way that if she did not answer affirmatively, I could get the scoop if it was because someone else was the issue.

"Okay, it sounds like you put some tangible thought into this, Brent. I'm impressed, all that sounds really good, so why didn't you continue the conversation?"

"I just got confused." He continued to explain. "I planned so well on what I wanted to say so that I could guide the conversation, that I didn't prepare for how she might respond. I expected for her to stay with my agenda and focus on the interest of the relationship but instead she turned the conversation back to me telling me that my girlfriend was cute and asked where Renea shops."

"Well, that was okay, that means that you succeeded with engaging her in the 'misdirected' small talk you were hoping for. You had the conversation going exactly the way you wanted. What'd you say next?"

"I tried to rush the conversation to beat the tardy bell and blurted out, 'I think I heard Colin talking about you…' but stopped because I realized that in my anxiousness, I messed up by putting me with Colin."

"And so …what?" I asked, displeased. "You just stopped and walked away?"

"I didn't know what else to do. I didn't want her asking me about Colin."

"Yes, that's exactly what you *did* want to happen." I argued. "That's what we rehearsed. Remember, you're saying that you heard Colin talking about her as a third person bystander and that you were curious. You wanted her to volunteer her thoughts. You can't get her to talk about him… if you don't talk about him!" I emphatically concluded.

Colin put his head down, shaking his head in disbelief. I could see his disappointment, so I tried to rally to his rescue.

"Forget about it…I'll do it then," I proclaimed boldly, while staring Brent down. "You coward; I'll show you how it's done!" I scolded with a competitive spirit.

"No," Colin solemnly surrendered, "Just forget it."

"Nah, come on, Colin," I pleaded. "Let me do it."

I wasn't certain if I was so bold because I wanted to help Colin or whether it was to satisfy my own insatiable curiosity to find out what would happen if she were confronted, regardless, my pleading was in vain.

"No," Colin replied decisively.

"Why not?" I challenged.

"Because…" he reminded, "don't you remember? If you talk to her, she'll know what's going on, and that's not part of the plan so just forget it."

"But don't you want to know?" I said, illuminating my selfish intentions.

He looked at me plainly, and then said in a poignant, quiet voice, "Don't you understand? This isn't a game that I'm prepared to lose. It's not that I don't want to know; I want terribly to be with her… it's just that at this point, it isn't imperative for me to be able to hold her and tell her how I feel. In my heart I already have her as being mine through the time we're spending together. I'm not preparing to jeopardize losing our friendship.

If it should turn out that she doesn't feel the same way that I feel for her I'd be crushed. Perhaps it is a cowardly approach that prevents me from expressing my feelings to her; but it would devastate me to lose her without truly having had her. I guess I perceive it as, 'False hope is better than no hope at all.'"

When he finished, his eyes were gleaming. He shifted his eyes from the deep stare of aimless reflection he exhibited while he was talking. I noticed his troubled eyes. I could understand what I heard, and I could see the sincerity on his face from the words he had explained about his predicament.

His heart was honest, his integrity was found without defect, and his motive sincere and authentic; for those reasons more than ever, made me want to talk to Janet for him. It was heartbreaking for them not to get together because of one silly thing – that being ambiguity.

Being his best friend, I truly did want to help. I secretly contemplated doing a solo, covert, recon mission and speaking to her on his behalf, but that swirling doubt of the possibility that things could go wrong prevented me from doing so. The reality remained that Colin was right on one assumption – 'What if her response was unfavorable?' So instead, I honored his wishes and did nothing.

From that day, no one bothered bringing up the discussion.

Then several days later something bizarre happened. The day Ms. Conaway, the English teacher, assigned the class to complete our last manuscript. I was waiting on the patio for him when he came out to meet me after seeing Janet. He seemed to be acting a little strange, so I inquired about his agitation.

"Are you all right?" I asked.

"Yeah," he answered, in a dismissive - somewhat perplexed manner. "I mean… well… I don't know."

"Come on… what's up man?" I inquired further.

"Well," he explained, "I've been having dreams lately…," as he paused to collect his thoughts. I waited patiently for him to continue, then after several moments of a lengthy pause, I probed further.

"Yeah," I inquired impatiently. "What about them?"

"Well, I don't know how else to explain it – except to say straight up…they're real!" he decided to blurt out the unlikely explanation in a confused tone as if he did not know any better way to say what he meant.

"What are you saying? What do you mean by – 'the dreams are real?'"

He took my questioning as if I were patronizing him and not taking his observation seriously. He was deciding to dismiss the conversation; "Nothing," he expressed, frustrated, "just forget I said anything." As he began to walk away.

I expressed interest with my sincerity about his disposition because he appeared to be dwelling on something. I felt the need to pursue what he was talking about. So, I inquired from him again. "No, Colin. I wasn't trying to be condescending. I'm just trying to understand what exactly it is that you are trying to communicate. Come on, man. You can talk to me." I politely reassured.

He peered at me while looking directly into my eyes as if

searching for the sincerity of a friend to which he could confide. He then walked over to a bench and sat down. I sat across from him on a wall and waited patiently for him to share.

"All right, all I can say is that I seem to be having dreams that come true," he explained. "You know… when it feels like you've been somewhere before? Like you've already lived in that moment?"

"Yeah, you're talking about Deja vu."

"Well, yeah it's something like that, but I mean I really believe that I'm actually experiencing that phenomenon," he explained. "One moment everything seems normal and uneventful and then the moment starts to get surreal, and then I ease into a fuzzy feeling like a forcefield is surrounding my whole body.

At that point I feel paralyzed and frozen. I'm just a spectator watching life happen until time catches up with me. It's then that I can anticipate moment by moment what is going to happen because it is exactly what I've dreamed…because in my mind I've already seen this moment." He stopped and shook his head as if even he still couldn't believe the experiences that he was trying to convey. I encouraged him to continue.

"Go on, what then." I urged.

"Well, it's kind of difficult to explain. "The dreams are very vivid and very life – like. In a very impressionable and memorable fashion my interest is peaked throughout the night as if I'm going to be in control of my every desire that only dreams can promise.

All the dreams lately take place in different scenes and time genres. For instance, sometimes my dreams take place in familiar places like the school or the park and other times the scenes take place in strange unfamiliar places but oddly the places still seem familiar to me as though I have had exposure that I may have been there before…for instance like I've been in a previous life or something.

Last night's dream was poignantly descriptive… and it felt intensely more realistic. I was dressed up in clothes from the thirties decade and it was dark and foggy like in those vintage black and white 'film noir' movies.

I couldn't see myself but somehow, I knew it was me all the same. In the dream I was desperately searching for someone, but I didn't know who I was looking for or why I was searching for them.

Finally, I noticed a shadow of someone emerging through the murky, grey, fog colored haze as if I was watching a movie. I quickly began to chase down this person and was able to catch up with them from behind. At that point the only thing I was able to identify about the person as I drew nearer was long dark hair draped down to the shoulder, and I noticed that he was dressed in exceptionally sinister attire.

It was strange because the person was walking very quickly in an elusive manner, as if he were trying to avoid me. Instead of wanting to distance myself from the sinister looking person who was obviously trying to avoid me…I felt peculiarly drawn to the dark strange figure in an especially personal way. I tried ever so more desperately to catch up to this seemingly veracious specter.

Before long, I was able to overtake the pace of the apparition and catch up to him. But instead of attempting to engage the person to find out who he was, I decided just to keep pace, step for step right behind him. I thought it strange that he continued to walk ignoring my presence, so I just continued to follow, pacing behind him waiting, expecting that at some point he would turn around to confront me.

Instead, the person persistently appeared to even more, endeavor to evade me which heightened my curiosity. I was very intrigued as to why I was drawn to someone who was trying to avoid me.

Finally, I reached out with my right hand to touch the

shoulder of the shadowy figure to inevitably force him to confront me. With my hand resting on his shoulder I noticeably realized that I couldn't feel the body of the ghostly aberration; regardless, the figure finally did turn around to face me as if he'd felt that I had touched him even though I couldn't feel his body.

Surprisingly in an instant the figure magically changed forms and suddenly adorned a dark hooded cloak facing me. Although I was confronted face to face, the robe acted to conceal the identity, and the hood prevented me from seeing the face.

Instead, a murky shadow was cast from *inside* of the hood and exhibited the same grey fog-like mist that surrounded us. So, as it turns out, it was the glowing vapor surrounding us in the atmosphere that represented the face of the bizarre form. Even after that significant change, yet still another strange thing happened." Colin continued to explain.

"Emanating from within the mist that was contained within the hood, two dim faintly glowing green lights where the eyes should have been gradually illuminated the haze, but the clarity of the image was protected with a black laced veil.

From within the hood there was a nurturing warmth that encompassed the vision with a restoring familiar and inquisitive eye. As this entire manifestation transpired, I instantly became acutely aware of an unlikely disparity to this entire menacing scene.

Rather than displaying a scary, unpleasant atmosphere, a relaxing feeling was composed. A calming, sweet, and comforting aroma was emitted as the menacing haze dissipated while fading into establishing a realistic solid vision. Finally, revealing to me a human shape. It was that familiar scent that aroused my awareness and finally exposed the identity of the figure.

The clarity of the individual's face was a welcomed and

unexpected surprise – it was *her* eyes that illuminated from within the hood. My eyes were mesmerized, and I was charmed into gazing hypnotically deep into hers – it was Janet! In an instant, her face appeared unpredictably just as the hood once again disappeared.

For a fleeting moment, I smiled - pleased at finding that the mysterious figure was the object of my desire as I understood now why I originally was drawn to this person, the joy however quickly diminished when I noticed that she was weeping; mournfully.

I became acutely aware of each seemingly mundane act. A lone tear streamed out of her left eye and trickled down her cheek and clung to the bottom of her chin. It twinkled for a moment shimmering like a flawless gem, then in slow motion it melodramatically dropped from her chin. Forming a perfect translucent circle as it fell; it then disappeared as it dissolved into the ground.

The emphasis of this occurrence from the dream appeared to be significant as it caused an instantaneous reciprocal response from me. An impulse tear appeared from my right eye and proceeded to descend on my face in the same manner in which hers occurred. This seemed to symbolize our compatibility and illustrate the influence that we each impose on each other.

She raised her left hand to my face. Gingerly, she pressed her thumb in a nurturing manner, to my cheek swiping away the next tear. Her phantom touch resembled the sense of a cool gentle breeze that brushed against my skin. I could feel the wetness of the tear being smeared from my cheek, but noticeably absent was the soft warm touch of her fingers.

Instead, I got goosebumps and a chilly impression about her as she portrayed the strange, mysterious figure - that she empowered the cold bitter loneliness of Death.

Subsequently I became omnipotent to the awareness

that her previous evasive tactics were employed as the means to protect me. I realized too late that the very moment that I touched her, that it would be the moment that will turn out to be the sole act in which I will succumb to my demise.

Then the last thing that happened before I woke up is that a mirror appeared in front of me, and I recognized that after she touched me that she was 'Death' and the reflection that I saw in my mirror was your image."

"Whoa, okay… that's interesting!" I uttered in amazement. "What the heck is that supposed to mean?"

"I don't know, but there's more." He continued. "Remember that fuzzy wall I told you about that suspends me as time continues and how that makes me feel like I had experienced being somewhere before?"

"Yes," I acknowledged.

"Well, just now, when I was talking to Janet; our eyes met just like in the dream. It was as if I was on autopilot as the memory of my nightly delusion was superimposed over my conscience which locked my vision into that paralyzed deep stare. I was mesmerized by gazing long into her life-giving, chlorophyll poignant eyes. The sunbeam drifted a ray of light perfectly into her iris offering a translucent bright jade glint. Instantaneously, I was dazed into a trance, and my mind went into autopilot.

When she asked me what was wrong, her voice faded as if it were drifting from a distance by the wind. I felt paralyzed, momentarily unable to respond to her inquiry. I got locked into that hallucination spell with that elusive warm electrical forcefield surrounding me as my thoughts retracted back to the scene in the dream. The only acknowledgement I was able to express in response to her question was an instantaneous solitary tear just like in the dream.

Then just like in the dream, with a nurturing touch, she used her thumb and wiped my tear away. Unlike the dream however, her hands were distinctly soft and warm, instead it was me who was cold as I began to tremble, while my skin turned ice cold with goosebumps. She asked me again what was wrong this time with more prominence, but I remained unmoving and unable to answer.

At last, I regained my cognitive senses and apologized. I explained away my bizarre actions that I had just a moment of deep thought. She responded, telling me that she had been thinking about wanting us to have a talk. She mentioned that she was curious about what Brent had overheard me talking about.

With anticipation I inquired for her to elaborate as to what she had been thinking about, and downplaying that I had any knowledge about Brent. She was about to elaborate further but it was at that moment her mom arrived to pick her up.

She barely had time to say good-bye because she had to leave in a hurry to babysit for her little brother while her mom went to work. As she was leaving, she asked if I could meet at the city park duck pond so that we could have some private time to talk about "us."

"Are you serious?" I asked, astonished.

"Yep, it's strange how things turn out. She said it's about time that we have a serious talk and smiled flirtingly while caressing my cheek with her warm hands before scampering off."

"Wow, that sounds like pretty great news, I'm happy for you," I said. He, however, didn't appear as thrilled about it as I thought he might be, so I inquired about his demeanor. "That - is good news – isn't it?" I questioned sarcastically.

"Yes, of course it is." He replied unenthused. "At least it sounds good."

"Colin," I questioned facetiously, "I might be wrong… but isn't this - what you've been waiting for? And she's the one who brought it up…it looks like the plan was a success after all." I concluded with a confused question. "Why are you being so stoic? Why are we not celebrating?"

"It's that dream…" he uttered with a troubled voice. "I don't quite know what to make of it. It seems like I was being warned about something. In the dream Janet is embodied as my personal Grim Reaper and so during the dream she is trying to protect me by avoiding my effort to catch up to her, that's why in the dream she was being elusive.

It's like some force is cautioning me that I should leave her alone because if I ever make it to her somehow it won't end well. When she finally touches me in the dream, I feel her touch as being ice cold because it's the touch of my death. Somehow, I believe that the dream has unveiled some unfavorable, and inevitable fate. It's haunting me."

"Think about it Colin," I reasoned to dismiss any concern from his mind. "First…in real life…how could *I* ever just suddenly become *you*? Your dream is just your mind working on problems. Your mind is telling you to go for it. Maybe the part of the dream about me is telling you to listen to what I've been advising you to do, just in a weird way. The opposite tears must symbolize your relationship compatibility. It's your basic chemistry, 'Opposites attract' Dreams are always weird."

"Well, maybe you're right," he said as he slowly began to grin.

"Of course, I am." I reassured and got up heading down the stairs. "Come on, let's go."

I convinced him that the good news was worth celebrating so we skipped track practice and instead went home. I was at his house late that night. We worked on our journals for English class and then enjoyed some fun playing bumper pool.

The next day, since I knew that Colin had planned to work on his manuscript and was to meet Janet later that afternoon, I didn't bother to call him throughout the day. Instead, I went to his house that evening to pick him up to go to the dance. The temperature was moderate throughout that spring day but was expected to dip significantly throughout the night.

"Hello, Mrs. Maberi," I said cheerfully, while entering the door.

"My, my…don't' 'we' look nice?" She complemented, "And smell good too."

I was wearing a black T- shirt with a cow skull. My signature cowboy hat with dress python snip-toed cowboy boots with flare jeans that were fastened with an oval belt buckle. All of this was topped off by a brown suede motorcycle type jacket. I was cleanly shaven with a touch of softly scented polo sport cologne.

"Well thank you kindly, ma'am," I replied cordially. "… is Colin back?"

"Back?" she questioned, baffled. "Why, yes, he's been here most of the day," she said, looking surprised as if I should have known. "He's upstairs." She informed me and then she called out. "Colin! Rylan's here to see you!" Oddly there was no response. "Go on upstairs," she invited me. "He's likely in his room with the door shut. You know how focused he gets when he's working on a project."

I started upstairs calling his name to announce my approach, "Hey, Colin!"

"Yeah!" he answered back. "Come on up…I'm in my room!"

When I walked into his room, he was sitting at his desk.

"What are you doing?" I asked.

"Oh, nothing… just working on my manuscript."

"Well, are you gonna give me the details of what happened?" I asked. "How did it go with Janet?"

He finished writing the line he was on, then he slowly put

his pen down while exhaling exasperated. Then he swiveled his chair around to turn towards me. "She didn't show," he said in a plain voice.

"She what?" I asked, flabbergasted.

"She didn't show." He repeated. "I was supposed to meet her at noon, and I waited till one o'clock; but she never showed."

"Well, you know there must be an explanation." I declared attempting to encourage his hope.

"I don't know," Colin groaned out of frustration shaking his head in a dejected manner. "She asked me to meet her…" he reasoned. "I don't see how she could forget or at least call to say that she changed her mind."

"Maybe something came up," I suggested a plausible explanation.

"Possibly, but also maybe my dream was foreshadowing that we'll never get together." He reasoned. "I told you that I could feel there was something more to that dream.

"Maybe she'll go to the dance; you can talk to her there." I said, in an effort to get him to think positive.

"Maybe," he thought as he mulled over his decision.

I really don't feel like going."

"Come on," I encouraged. "What's it going to change if you sulk here alone wondering about things instead of hanging out with your good friend and trying to have a good time. At least at the dance the time will go faster." I reasoned.

"Yeah, I guess you got a point. I may as well." He reluctantly conceded. "Maybe it'll get my mind off things."

"On the way you can tell me about the progress of your masterpiece. That kind of stuff always invigorates you." I suggested. "You get passionate talking about your ideas. That kind of stuff always invigorates you."

"That's because I can control how things progress." He justified.

After he changed, we left for the dance. In the car I started the conversation about his manuscript to engage his mind into positive thinking. I asked him specifically to tell me what he was able to come up with.

"Well, is your story coming together?" I inquired.

"Yes, I had a breakthrough," he said excitedly. "You'll be happy to know that I discovered the kind of girl you need."

"Is she pretty?" I jested as if he found a real girl for me.

"I'm in the process of developing her character now." He proceeded as he explained the complexity of her character development. "It became apparent that the creation of the perfect character to engage in a relationship with your character's ego was not as simple as previously perceived."

"Okay, what's wrong with my ego?"

"Nothing…you know that you're perfect." He qualified as he smiled. "I realized that I couldn't just create a perfect character," he rationalized. "…rather for the story line to progress naturally, it had to be a girl that's a believable and perfect *fit* for you. Perfect, and 'perfect fit', well that's not the same thing. But I think that I have finally got it."

"Well, please enlighten me." I joked, compelling for him to elaborate. "I need to know what kind of girl to look out for."

"She's an independent strong woman." he declared self-satisfied with his achievement. "But that's not the designation that she promotes. Instead, she is confident with a non-declaration of her autonomy.

Her interests are not self-seeking. She is unapologetic about being her man's woman. She proudly promotes her allegiance to loving her God; loving her man, as she loves herself. She understands that the secret of her feminine strength rests with her confidence in submitting her faith to God.

In addition, she is alluring with natural physical beauty as she exhibits sensuality. Her practical nature strengthens her romantic appeal. She is self-sufficiently caring but comfortable with being vulnerable. She's an introvert while mastering the art of being infectiously charismatic.

Her signature quality is being predictably - unpredictable. She's everything that many real women seek to emulate but fail to accomplish because they are incapable of realizing the courage to submit themselves to being vulnerable to God's will. She possesses the wisdom to understand the magnitude of her true Godly value. I'm really looking forward to wrapping dialog around this characteristic." He finished as we arrived at the high school.

"Well, thank you for your thoughtfulness about finding my right girl…" I praised his efforts. "I agree with your choice of words…she's very alluring. I'm impressed."

With the help of our other friends, I managed to keep him entertained throughout the night. We even took a chair for him to sit and participate with us on the dance floor a few times.

Although he didn't join in with as much enthusiasm, we got him to laugh. He spent most of the night looking toward the door hoping to find Janet's athletic frame coming through the door. As the night weaned, his hopes of seeing her diminished. Eventually, the dance came to an end and with its conclusion, so also ended the hope of Janet miraculously appearing.

Usually, we all as a group would go to a restaurant after the dance to just hang out with others and to see who else might happen to show up. Colin wasn't in the mood to socialize because his leg was feeling sore and opted to just go home. So, instead of trying to prompt him to stay out, I did as he requested and dropped him off at home before heading back out to the restaurant.

"Get some sleep…I'll see you tomorrow," I bid farewell.

"Sure," Colin replied. "I'm sorry to spoil the night, but my leg is throbbing from all that standing. I'm goin' take some pain killers and go to sleep. Call me in time for church."

"Ok, I will, see you then," I reassured as he closed the door.

The next morning my mom came to my room shouting in a panic, as she called out to awaken me, "Rylan! Rylan! Get up!" She flung my bedroom door open so hard that it banged against the wall. She proceeded without hesitation to walk across the room and pulled the curtains open in an excessively animated fashion.

The sunlight beamed through the window and reflected off the mirror of my chest of drawers and directly into my eyes. For a few moments all I could see were spots before my eyes as I began to protest the abrupt awakening.

"Ahh, mom!" I shrieked. "Close the curtains! The sun is too bright!"

"Hurry and get up!" she persisted. "Mr. Maberi just called; they're headed to the hospital! Colin was involved in some kind of an accident! They'd like for us to come down!"

"What?" I questioned anxiously. "What's wrong with him?"

"I don't know, Rylan! All I was told is that he is being treated in intensive care. Just get up and get ready!" She ordered.

I immediately thought that he may have been having complications with his leg overnight. I thought about his last comment to me when I dropped him off - of him complaining about his leg being sore.

I began to feel guilty for insisting on him to go out but even more I felt that I had been insensitive to his need by not taking the time to ensure that he was okay before heading back to the restaurant. If it hadn't been for the bright morning sunlight, I would have contemplated whether I was still sleeping, perhaps just having a nightmare.

Quickly, I stumbled out of bed and headed for the bathroom to take a shower. I was in such a hurry that I mistakenly turned on the cold faucet before I jumped into the shower. The water felt like ice beating on my skin. "Yikes!" I screeched, instinctively, jumping out - then set a more desirable setting. After making sure that I used the hot water I checked the water temperature before entering the shower.

After a quick rinse I toweled off and then dressed in the same clothes as I had worn the night before, but instead of cowboy boots I opted for flip – flops. My mom had given me the keys to her car and told me to inform Colin's family that they'd be following soon.

My feet and ankles got wet from the dew drops that glistened on the grass in the morning sun as I darted across the lawn to my car. I rushed to the hospital quickly yet cautiously as I dared to bend a few suggestive laws along away. After being directed to the ICU I was greeted by Colin's dad who came out of the security doors to escort me to where the family was waiting. Colin's mom remained seated being comforted by other family members in the waiting room.

"How is he?" I inquired quietly.

"Well..." he began and then paused abruptly as he looked toward his wife, "come get some coffee with me, will ya?"

I could tell instantaneously that he didn't want to discuss anything in front of his wife and that he could really use some kind of mundane act to calm his own nerves, so I downplayed the urgency of the moment responding in a calm normal manner as we exited the room together.

"Sure, I didn't get anything on my way out this morning."

Upon arriving in the cafeteria, we walked over to the vending machines where he purchased a cup of coffee for himself and a hot chocolate for me. As he handed me a cup we walked over to a table and sat down.

Steam was rising from both drinks. I took a quick sip of my hot chocolate and burned the top of my lip. The drink was very hot, but it countered with a savory sweet relief as I felt it going down the length of my throat. This created a soothing warmth throughout my entire body as it entered my stomach.

I noticed the coffee having the same effect on Mr. Maberi, as he clinched his eyes shut from the initial shock of the hot drink followed by an irrepressible sigh of brief satisfaction. "M-m-m that feels good." He remarked. Then without warning he blurted out the news. "It doesn't look good, Rylan." He said with a flat tone as if to prepare me for the worst.

My heart throbbed heavily and at once it felt as though the drink that had nurtured a satisfying feeling had now sabotaged my stomach to feeling sick. I again inquired as to the nature of the situation.

"What happened?" I asked puzzled, "Is he having complications with his leg injury? He complained about it being sore when I dropped him off a little before two o'clock."

"Well," he began. "We really don't know. We were awakened by a knock at the door this morning about a half hour after you would have dropped him off. We were uneasily alarmed to find that it was a police officer who was asking if we knew where our son was, or about the possibility if perhaps our car had been stolen while we were sleeping.

At that point Tracy hurriedly went to his room to check for him while the officer explained to me that Colin's car had been involved in a terrible accident and was discovered down a fifty-foot ravine partially submerged underwater.

Looking in the officer's troubled eyes made me wonder about the fact that he gave no indication of the condition of the driver… that he was purposely withholding some crucial information. I feared that if it was in fact Rylan then he must be incapacitated to the point that he is not able to say who he is since the officer is asking of his whereabouts. My spirit sank and in the next moment I knew without a doubt that we were in trouble…because Tracy was frantically calling for me.

The only coherent thought I had rifling through my head was, 'Oh… no!' I knew in an instant that she hadn't found him there, but I instinctively ran up the stairs to his room calling out his name as if to elicit a response. We both stood at the threshold of his vacant room needing to hold each other in that dreadful empty moment."

Mr. Maberi paused in a conscious less dazed state for an instant, and it appeared as though he was transposed to reliving the ordeal of that moment. He was looking at me, but his eyes were sighted, fixed, passed and through me in a deep trance.

Then he continued with his recollection, "Eventually, me and Tracy descended the stairs together where the officer was still waiting at the open front door. He addressed us in a calming professional manner, 'Sir, ma'am, I can escort you to the hospital if you'd like.'"

"Can you tell us what happened?" I asked the officer to explain.

"We've found heavy skid marks at the scene which may suggest the suspicion that another car may have been involved. He may have been side swiped by that other vehicle and forced into the ravine. Substantial injuries were sustained in the accident. The investigation is ongoing as to the nature of what actually transpired to cause the crash."

It was then that I finally got the nerve to ask the unfathomable question… 'Is he alive? Please tell me he's alive.'

The response took the weight from my chest. 'Yes sir, when I left the occupant to come here, they were transporting him to 'JR. Clifford Memorial Hospital.'"

"You said that he *may* have been sideswiped. Is there another vehicle involved?"

"As I mentioned, sir, ma'am," he declared respectfully, "the investigation is ongoing all I can say is that we are exploring that possibility."

In a sudden shift, Mr. Maberi regained his composure and shook off his distant stare.

"Any idea where he was going?" I inquired as I recalled. "I dropped him off after the dance because he didn't want to go anywhere."

"It's possible that he maybe went to see a girl. I had left a message for him on the table before we went to bed that Janet had called to talk to him. She had asked him to have him call her back as soon as he arrived and that the time was inconsequential. She seemed anxious to contact him.

"Oh no," I said with a guilty conscience. "I talked him into going to the dance. Had he been home he would have been able to talk to her."

"Now don't start that," he cautioned. "Don't go blaming yourself…you got him home safely. And I want you to make sure that the girl doesn't go blaming herself either." He reasoned. "Neither of you forced that car off of the road."

"But he wanted to stay home…" I argued with remorse.

"You're a good friend; you did what you're supposed to do. "Come on, I don't want to be away from Tracy too long."

We got up from the table and headed back for the waiting room. He left his white Styrofoam cup half full on the table. I, however, took my cup of hot chocolate in hopes of trying to restore the feeling it initially provided to me.

As we returned, I noticed several officers standing near his room. The Department had put Colin under 'guarded' supervision. Several minutes after we returned to the waiting room the doctor came out. We waited with anticipation to hear of Colin's progress in anxious silence. The only disturbance came from a soft robotic sounding nurse's voice repeatedly calling out, "Code Blue… in the ICU" on the intercom.

The doctor first spoke to the officers, a short distance from the family. I was standing on the outside of the room where the family was, so I was able to overhear one of the policemen say, "possible negligence homicide." Oh, how my soul separated from my body in that moment.

Then the doctor approached and entered the room where the family was holding vigil and began delivering the horrible news. I was the only one who knew what was coming but it would have been improper for me to warn as to what was to come so I prepared to be a spectator of what was to come.

"I'm sorry," the doctor announced calmly, as he stood before us sweating. Colin's mother was immediately distraught and wailed openly without any need to wait to hear any more of his explanation. She had lost her son and that is all that mattered at that moment.

"We tried everything humanly possible." The doctor continued focusing his explanation on Colin's dad. "There's nothing more we could do. He passed away only a few moments ago. We were unable to stop the hemorrhage. There were several factors working against his survival. The toxicology report found an elevated amount of narcotics in his blood.

"Yes, he may have taken his dose of Percocet last night so that he could sleep." His father explained.

The doctor continued to rationalize his prognosis, "We also believe he may have had some predisposed congenital condition that complicated his ability to clot properly."

"But wouldn't that condition have been discovered during his leg surgery?" Mr. Beari asked, searching to understand.

The doctor answered, "Under a controlled surgery with minor wounds that condition may not have presented a problem but with the massive and multiple injuries sustained from a car accident, compounded with internal hemorrhages.

Well, I believe this contributed to his erratic condition that prevented us from being able to stabilize him. That ultimately led to his cardiac arrest." He confidently justified Colin's medical diagnosis. "We have a Chaplin available to speak to you if you'd like." He offered.

"No, thank you." Mr. Maberi declined. "That won't be necessary."

"Oh, incidentally there is one more thing," the doctor redirected. "I figured that you may appreciate hearing what his last words were."

"Yes," Colin's dad showed interest. "Please, that would be much appreciated."

"Well, I was reluctant to say anything," the doctor explained. "...because it was somewhat incoherent. But I figured that just because we were unable to discern what he meant it may be a family memory or something special."

"Well, whatever it is… we'd like to hear it."

"While I was working on him, he repeatedly tapped on my hand to get my attention. I noticed him blinking his eyes in rhythm as if he wanted to speak as he removed his breathing mask." The surgeon paused and dropped his head as he recounted the incident.

It was evident the doctor was concentrating on how to verbalize what he heard. "...it sounded like he was saying something about Santa Clause …" he reasoned with his logic to clarify what he thought he heard. '…through the snow or though he sleighs…" he struggled to make sense out of three incoherent words as he continued to convey what was spoken. Then he offered another possible translation. "The nurse on the opposite side of him thought that she heard, 'through the sleigh.'

"Whatever it was… he said it twice and attempted to repeat it again then his gaze shifted toward the ceiling as if he saw something just before his eyes froze into a fixed position …and then he was gone. We all acknowledged that we felt a sensation of calming warmth at that moment even to the point of asking each other if the experience was sensed by all. But I assure you that his last moments were peaceful…I hope knowing that helps."

"Yes, as a matter of fact it does…tremendously." Colin's dad explained as he consoled his wife in his arms. "We know exactly what message he was relaying. He was calling for his savior, 'Though He slay me…yet will I still hope in him.' His favorite bible verse Job 13:15. We know that Colin died with peace and is no longer suffering. Thank you doctor…this brings much comfort to our grief. He surrendered his life to his faith in God."

"Our baby went to see Jesus." Colin's mother moaned confidently.

Then the officers approached to request a brief interview, "Mr…Mrs Maberi." The lead officer introduced, "I'm detective Luke Calloway. These two officers are patrolman Sanchez and Sargent Lithopolis. Please accept our sincerest condolences." He asserted with a sincere tone. "We're conducting the investigation of the crash. I'm sorry to intrude on you at this solemn time but if you don't mind, we have a few questions so that we may complete the investigation."

"Yes, of course…" Mr. Maberi agreed. "Anything to catch that hit and run punk." He inadvertently exposed his knowledge about their investigation leading to the possibility of a second car.

The detective looked annoyed at the patrolman who quantified Colin's dad's statement. "I told them that potential skid marks were found at the scene but that no definitive conclusion had been made about any importance because the investigation is ongoing.

Without addressing the patrolman directly, the detective proceeded to begin his inquiry. "The investigation is preliminary." He explained as he questioned. "Has your car been exposed to an accident recently?

"No," Mr. Maberi answered, "Why?"

"You're sure that the car has not been involved in any accident?" The detective redirected.

"Yes, I'm sure." Mr. Maberi insisted as he inquired once again for the purpose of asking the question. "Why, what did you find?"

The detective then proceeded to explain their introductory report. "We found a wide streak of orange paint that had been transferred at some point to the driver-side."

"No, the car was pristine." Mr Maberi interrupted to clarify his recollection and to offer his observation. "It must have happened tonight." He declared.

"Yes sir, I understand, it is an integral part of our investigation. We are looking at multiple potential heavy skid marks found at the scene that may prove crucial. Before your son lost consciousness, he mentioned that he may have been forced off the road by another car.

His mother silently sobbed requesting to see Colin. "I want to go to my baby! He needs me!" she demanded hysterically. But because of the condition of his broken body from the accident it was recommended to Terry that she not see him yet – and it was further advised that she be taken home to get some rest. The doctor prescribed a mild sedative for her then Terry escorted her out to the car.

I followed with the rest of the family holding on to her purse. I got into my car and followed them home. When I got to the house Colin's mom and dad had already gone inside. I walked in with a few of the family members. I carried the purse to Colin's mom who was now sitting on the sofa in the living room.

"Is there anything I can do?" I asked, handing the purse to her. I was hoping to be helpful and to keep busy. I don't think anyone from Colin's family was emotionally prepared to go into his empty room, so she asked for me to take on that duty.

"Yes," she said, lethargically whimpering. "If you wouldn't mind, please pack Colin's things in a box and then make sure that the door is shut. I'm sure you'd know better what was important."

"Yes ma'am, I'll take care of it." I went directly into the kitchen and retrieved a crate, a couple of folded boxes and a broom and walked upstairs to his room. I twisted the knob pushing the door open slowly in the same motion. This caused the hinges to wrench and the door to crackle as it opened.

Then, as I walked into the room, I was acutely aware of the surreal ambiance, which was an overwhelming vacuum of silence that magnified the obvious permanence of the absence of Colin's presence. I mentally pushed myself to ignore that sad reality and instead focused on cleaning the room and packing his personal items away to keep his family from having to endure this task.

As I packed the things from his desk, I came across a key to a private box underneath his desk. Uncertain of what I might find I ceremoniously grasped the key tightly as I considered hesitantly whether to unlock the box to discover its contents or to leave it closed perhaps as a time capsule. I reasoned that the care of Colin's things was the task that had been bestowed on me, so I reluctantly opened the drawer to examine its contents.

Upon inspection I found three items; one was a photo of Colin and Janet with their arms around each other while they were hanging out together at the beach. On the back of the picture, he had inscribed with a smiley face: "My Best Moment!!" The other item was an envelope that was addressed to Janet. The third was the handwritten outline to the manuscript that he had spoken to me about.

'The work of a genius from only one day's labor,' I thought to myself, as I scanned the notes. Then recalling what Colin had disclosed to me, I could tell that he had the framework for a good story. Using his notes I was confident that I had the ability to finish his story as a masterpiece. Rather than packing these three items away in a box I decided to bring them to the attention of his mother. After finishing my work of straightening up the room I took the personal effects down to his mother.

"Mrs. Maberi…" I approached somberly, "I found these in Colin's locked drawer. It's a picture of him and his friend Janet and a letter addressed to her."

She took them from my hand and looked at them for a moment and after studying the picture, tears trickled down her cheek, "Take them to her please," she instructed handing them back to me, "… they belong to her."

"I also found a copy of his manuscript outline for a new story he planned to pen." I explained. "He had reviewed with me what he had in mind so with your permission I'd like to write his story for him. I think that it has the potential to be quite good."

"Yes, that'd be fine…I think we'd like that." She affirmed as she handed me the other items.

I took the items from her hands with the picture on top. Studying the image more closely I could see how they looked at each other with enduring sentiment; they just looked like the perfect couple. I couldn't help but notice how the two looked so innocently timeless in that moment in the picture.

Both exhibited the perfection of youth, beauty, athleticism, and exceptional intelligence. It was interesting to contemplate what their children might have been like. It saddened me to contemplate how such a waste that someone with so much promise and ability to contribute making the world a more pleasant place was now gone.

It didn't make sense… my friend shouldn't be dead… the two of them should have been together… they are what you would call a power couple. But now… the only question left to ponder about was their relationship. I was left wondering what force kept them from being together?

The next day at school I found Janet kneeling to get books from her locker. I approached her from behind with the letter in my hand.

"Janet," I summoned quietly. She stood up quickly and mistakenly responded favorably to a similar familiar voice.

"Yes, Col - n--…" she began to answer as she stood up gleefully until she realized that it was not Colin, who was beckoning her. I noticed that her eyes emulated a mourning translucent ruby color. She was dejected by my presence instead of finding Colin calling for her as she explained, "Oh my, I never realized how much the two of you sound just like each other."

Sadly, she lowered her teary eyes slowly back down toward the earth as her hope visibly diminished. She appeared to be in a dazed and surreal state as she qualified her demeanor as she shook her head in disbelief. "I'm still hoping that it's not true…I'm still expecting to feel his touch." She sobbed hopelessly.

I was curious about how she had discovered the news. I was hoping to be the one to break the terrible news to her so as to ensure that she heard from a caring loved one rather than just through speculating rumors. So, in a sentimental manner I took precautions as I approached her.

"Are you okay?"

"I think so," she responded, "…well under the circumstances I supposed I am," she qualified.

"…I have something for you." I explained while extending the picture and envelope. "I found this in Colin's room. His mother figured that I should give it to you." Janet reached out feebly and took the items from my hand. She looked at the picture; and apparently while gazing she reminisced about that past moment in the picture, the depiction of those two together.

It caused an instinctive reaction as she instantaneously managed to choke out a pleasing half smile. Then, she flipped the photo over and read the caption on the back side; her face became flush as a tear straight away rolled down her cheek. It was becoming obvious that her emotions were establishing control over her involuntary responses.

She looked toward the ground, breathed in deeply and let out a huge sigh in an attempt to summon all of her resolve. Then meticulously she opened the envelope and began reading. I wrestled over the decision of whether to step away to provide her with a solitude moment as she mulled over the contents but soon realized that it was a welcome benefit to her that I had decided to remain nearby.

Suddenly her emotions exploded with an expression of grief – as she fell back against the lockers for support. Her strength then entirely disintegrated. Her legs buckled under the intense emotional strain, and she slid down the lockers to the floor sobbing hysterically, squatting into a fetal position.

"Are you okay?" I inquired sincerely, kneeling to her. I couldn't help but notice the sensual tickling of my palm by her soft hair as I placed one hand on the side of her head in a nurturing manner. Despite her earnest effort to respond, being grief stricken, she was unable to muster a single word.

With the letter crumpled and clenched tightly in her hand – the only communication she was able to manage was to shake her head as she wailed hopelessly. Eventually, she released the letter from the clutches of her grip, and it dropped to the floor.

"I'm sorry Colin…" she wailed, crying out to her beloved; bawling into her chest, "… I really miss you."

I wondered what could have caused such an intense and sudden meltdown. Curiously I retrieved and then unrumpled the paper and began to read what turned out to be a poem dated ominously the day they were to meet; it was entitled:

"My Wind Song."

Reminiscing the joy of this timeless frozen amiable image –
This picture of 'US'…this is where the hope of my dawn still gleams.
My heart silently aches wishing to repeat that moment of you
– of 'US'
And stirs my desire to give way to be lost in my dreams.
It is then that I crave for a moment-
A chance to at last inhale your sweet breath in a kiss.
I fantasize of that sensational act…
that anticipated moment of my perpetual retreat -
I'm tormented as my spirit contemplates,
'Will this waiting ever cease?'
But alas.
This delightful passion, of you, that sustains my life –
This adoring affection, of wanting you, that encompasses of all my imaginings -
This dreadful obsession, of having you –
where at last I can ultimately find my escape…
I reluctantly… sorrowfully concede –
'You'…never to embrace.
Regrettably I've found this truth to be steadfast;
with regard to holding you.

And now, one closing deliberation lingers
as my illusion fades to dusk:
An occasion for sorrow
should not endure through tomorrow,
But... at long last,
I surrender our fate – and consign to that which I lust.

The words sent an emotional chill down my spine. The theme captured the melancholy hopelessness, and the excruciating pain he felt at the prospect of never having her. The reason why she was so overwhelmed became apparent. Colin's poem artistically prophesied the importance of their relationship as of being tied to his actual existence.

The sentiment of the poem accurately predicted the cost that will be owed and subsequently paid to Fate. It is Fate that will forever prevent them from ever getting together. I realized, unfortunately too late, that his strange dream about the phantom effectively and accurately had in fact foreshadowed these events. It was unlikely but just as in the dream when the two finally get to a point of getting together…fate stepped in to prevent it.

A teacher came over with a box of tissues and gave us both a pass to see the counselor who in turn recommended that we go home. We were both excused from school for the rest of the week.

The next few days were tough to get through. Each day I spent my time between the funeral home and Colin's house offering my support. Janet also spent a lot of time alongside me. The day of the funeral proved to be increasingly difficult.

School was canceled that day because so many students had been overcome with grief and wanted to pay their respects and offer their condolences. The funeral home's capacity was limited so only members of the family and closest friends were permitted to attend the funeral inside while most of the people formed the line of the motorcade waiting in their cars.

When the funeral services were finished, we all joined the motorcade to the graveyard. It turned out that 124 cars made up the parade. I was asked and accepted the privilege to act as one of Colin's pallbearers; my position being on the left in the rear.

The preacher held a brief sermon at the grave site mainly for the purpose of all those who were unable to attend inside. After the ceremony concluded people slowly filtered away, heading towards the Maberi's house. Janet and I, however, waited for about thirty minutes as the two workers quietly lowered and then buried Colin's coffin.

During that time, I struggled to fight back my emotions as I watched over Janet who would routinely succumb and quietly sob. When the workers had finished, one of the men picked a daisy from nearby and placed it respectfully on the grave. He nodded consolingly and then walked away. Janet then stepped towards the grave and stood gazing at the mound of fresh soil that lay before us.

As we navigated the experience of suppressive grief, I couldn't help but notice how graciously she exhibited a composed, enduring, timeless and radiant aura. Her hands were covered with vintage, white laced gloves, and she modishly displayed morning clothes with a black pleated skirt that fell just below the knees. This ensemble was topped with a sleeveless, button blouse covered by a black tweed blazer and black high heel shoes.

Her face, slightly pale, was lightly made up and flaunted a smooth, soft, stoic appearance, and her pouty lips glistened with a hint of pink shimmer. Square-rimmed designer sunglasses were fashionably used to cover her poignant luminous green eyes.

Her nostalgic epoch appearance was flawless, reminiscent of scenes from an old classic movie. Remaining in staunch character, she stood over Colin's grave for several moments before interrupting the silence with a simple request.

"May I have a few moments alone with him please?" she whispered in a soft controlled voice.

"Sure," I replied quietly as I backed away. I stood under a pin oak tree a short distance from the grave site. This provided her with a sense of privacy as I continued to watch while maintaining a supportive, concerned, nurturing interest.

She descended, kneeling gracefully resting her knees on the fresh soil of the grave. I monitored her meticulous movement as I observed her absorbedly watching as she leaned forward. In a unified motion she removed her sunglasses with her left hand as she reached out with her right, white gloved hand. She grabbed the fresh soil, squeezing it tightly into her fist with a firm grasp.

It was at that moment that I witnessed something strangely familiar. I was witnessing what Colin had described in his dream. Her green eyes seemingly absorbed the sun rays and noticeably appeared to exhibit a lighted kryptonite glow.

Then her eyes watered up and released a single drop that streamed down her left cheek. The translucent tear glimmered like a jewel and reflected the light from the sun as it continued to roll down, clinging to her chin. At last, the tear dropped from her chin, descended to the grave and disappeared as it dissolved into the soil.

At that moment a warm electrical feeling, much like Colin had articulated that he had experienced, of a frozen "Deja Vue" moment crept soothingly through the members of my body and I could feel a transformation taking place in me.

It was then that I realized the improbable significant twist of Colin's dream. I realized that we had misinterpreted a significant part of the dream. The part where he transformed into being me was indeed an unlikely event that now seemed to be a plausible accurate foreshadow.

It wasn't a literal conversion of him physically turning into me, instead his dream had predicted a *symbolic* transformation. With his absence now resolute, it was *me* who would be taking his place.

Already with his vacancy, it became my privileged duty to write *his* masterpiece story and also perhaps I had discovered that his difficulty with creating the perfect girl to be my companion in his story was because - as fate would intervene - that my perfect girl was Janet. The very girl who is alone and who is now the one who needs to be consoled by me in his absence.

I was greatly disturbed by this revelation and stood steadfastly in denial that his dream successfully foreshadowed these events of my assuming his role in life. I tried in vain to dismiss the reality of what was transpiring. My thought was interrupted when I overheard Janet speaking again to the grave… as if she were speaking directly to Colin. Her hushed voice had the pitch of a song… as the gentle wind carried her quiet words to my ears.

"You should have told me that you loved me." she whispered with her voice slightly cracking. "Because… I love you…still…ohh… so terribly. I always have, Colin." she recounted, sadly reminiscing. "I was so afraid of risking ruining our friendship," she confessed. "…because I didn't know how you felt about me until someone mentioned one day that you were overheard talking about *us*. After several days I finally got the nerve and was going to tell you how I felt that day we were to meet, but my family had an out-of-town emergency at the last minute.

I felt so guilty," she confessed remorsely, "about leaving town without getting a hold of you first, but I knew that once I was able to explain to you why I wasn't able to meet with you that you'd understand and forgive me. You're so good that way…" she said with a loving smile that quickly dissolved back into a somber mood. "I called and left a message for you as soon as I got back, and I was so excited when you called to say that you were on your way to see me.

While I waited anxiously for your arrival, I fantasized about your touch and was distraught when you didn't show." She lowered her head sobbing as she struggled to force out her anguish, "Why did this have to happen to us just when things were going right?" she questioned exasperated, "Why were you taken away to leave me all alone?"

She then stood up trembling as she turned away from the grave. Sensing her need for support I instinctively returned promptly to her, uncertain of what to convey to comfort her.

Instead of using words of comfort, I acted physically by grabbing her on either shoulder from behind and squeezed tightly to let her know that she had me to rely on for support. Her impulse was to turn around and embrace me as she wept inconsolable.

Sensing her feeble legs giving way I felt her arms cling tightly to me. In response, I stood steadfastly holding her strongly with a masculine clutch allowing her to cry all of her sorrow into my chest. For a few moments, we stood motionless, near the foot of the grave.

I struggled to articulate encouraging words on her behalf but was reluctant to speak because of fear of crying. I labored intensely to be her champion at this critical junction but found it increasingly difficult with tears filling my eyes. It was all I could do to keep from succumbing to my own despair.

Finally, after several minutes of attempting to fight back my anguish, I forced myself to maintain control and deliberately spoke boldly to mask the silent tears that streamed down my face as I offered the solution that would resolve both of our needs.

"We both loved him," I consoled, "Now we can both support each other through our grief." I offered confidently, "Anything - anything you need …" I declared. "I'll see to it that you have it."

I tried to resist this irrepressible sense of duty that came over me in that instance; but I was compelled in the absence of my friend Colin to now be responsible for the well-being of this wonderfully beautiful yet fragile spirit.

It entered my mind that if I could stop one part of that dreadful dream from coming true that I might be able to bring Colin back. It was then that I inhaled deeply breathing in a heavenly delectable scent. I became acutely aware that the swirling, sweet, feminine aroma, from the fragrance, Wind Song,' which emanated from Janet, was a reflective symbol allowing for the ability to blend our spirits into one.

As I breathed, I inhaled her soul into my lungs. At that moment, that last part of the dream - where I became Colin; was the symbolism of me now taking *his* place. The sensation became noticeably and eerily comfortable. It was evident that as she was hopelessly vulnerable, the responsibility to act as her protector now rested with me.

Despite my apprehension, I couldn't shake feeling Colin's presence urging me to assume his role. I fell back on the two philosophies that have sustained me: 'Work the problem' rather than being 'worked' by the problem and rely on the principle that 'if you eliminate the obvious, despite how implausible, you must accept the improbable.' I discovered that the further I examined my concerns the more the 'inevitable' kept recurring.

I had been chosen for Janet, and she was for me. I arrived at the revelation that being with any other girl I would be found…still 'wanting.' While it seemed implausible that both the girl who Colin had described for me and Janet were one in the same. But then I recognized an encryption emerging through a series of events. All three of us had been steered into a tragic intersection that would solidify Janet's future after Colin's demise.

First, it was not a real person but rather a mystery personality that Colin had conjured up as the girl to fit my character. No specific person was identified. That left the three of us as the characters for his masterpiece story. Colin's role, Janet's physical role, me, and then an unknown entity.

He revealed his plans for the master thesis of his work that prepared me to later write his story. This eliminated the need for him to survive writing the story. Then I encouraged him to attend the dance, he effectively missed her phone call… and once again they missed their connection. Later he would take his medication to relieve his pain and then drive impaired in a rush to his love.

Colin highlighted the importance of the scene of the tears falling from opposite sides of their eyes and interpreted it as compatibility. But it didn't reveal *their* compatibility as previously thought, instead it represented backwards and opposite, a palindrome.

In the dream the falling tears from the opposite side of each of them reflected her first and my last name as I transitioned into him. It is *our*, me and Janet's, inescapable complementary DNA compatibility. I recalled how restriction enzymes in the form of palindromes are used to create unique DNA profiles. In fingerprinting our relationship profile, Janet and I are 'cut from the same cloth'…complementary and made for each other.

The cold phantom touch of Janet wiping away Colin's tear foreshadowed that once there was nothing between the two of them, it would be fate that would be forced to remove him from the equation.

Then of course, in the most revealing part of his dream, Colin witnessed his reflection transitioning into my image. This symbolized an unmistakable and revealing component. The taking of his place. The implausible factor is *me*. It had been me the whole time who was standing between the two of them.

Private Lake Sound Track

1. Second Chances (Heart needs a Second Chance) - 38 Special Pg. 35

2. We Can't go wrong – Cover Girls Pg. 42

3. (Kissed You) It's a Good night – Gloriana Pg.70

4. Inn Too Deep – Phil Collins Pg. 81

5. Makin Love Out of Nothing At All – Air Supply Pg. 82

6. If Wishes Came True – Sweet Sensation Pg. 84

7. In Color – Jamey Johnson – Pg. 101

8. Flame – Cheap Trick Pg. 107

9. When I'm With You – Sherriff Pg110

10. Love Of A Lifetime – Firehouse Pg. 116

11. I'll Be There – Escape Club

12. Livin' On Love – Alan Jackson

www.ingramcontent.com/pod-product-compliance
Lightning Source LLC
Chambersburg PA
CBHW020755310726
48969CB00002B/552